About the Author

Amanda Given spent a peripatetic childhood people watching in South West England and Northern Ireland before her family emigrated to Tasmania when she was a teenager.

She studied English, Speech and Drama at university, working as a teacher and social worker. Business management roles in large organsations led to posts in universities, property development and counselling organisations.

Early short stories were published in magazines and anthologies.

Making Old Bones is Amanda's first novel, written in Suffolk where she lives by the sea and is an active member of the Felixstowe Art Group.

Dedication

For Sophie and Jemima

Amanda Given

MAKING OLD BONES

AUSTIN MACAULEY PUBLISHERS™
LONDON • CAMBRIDGE • NEW YORK • SHARJAH

A CIP catalogue record for this title is available from the British Library.

ISBN 9781528994323 (Paperback)
ISBN 9781528994330 (Hardback)
ISBN 9781528994347 (Audiobook)
ISBN 9781528994354 (ePub e-book)

www.austinmacauley.com

First Published (2020)
Austin Macauley Publishers Ltd
25 Canada Square
Canary Wharf
London
E14 5LQ

Chapter One

THE MORNING RUSH

Dullness circled the autumnal gardens of Gramwell Glade, that mansion where so many had come to deposit their elderly together with their inheritances over the four years since it had been built around a seventeenth-century turreted wall at the end of the Senerwell Golf Links in Essex. Pauline Graves edged her black BMW into the car port designated for the Home Manager at the end of the guest car park. She turned off the engine, silencing the Bee Gees who had been screaming 'Staying Alive', and reached over to the back seat for her briefcase, checking her lipstick cursorily in the rear vision mirror before sashaying through the autumn leaves on the driveway and into the light and warmth of the lobby to punch in her security code at the first set of double glass doors.

The inner doors swung open, filling the reception area with a rush of cold air and stray leaves to follow the intruder.

"Good morning, Mrs Graves. You ' right?" rattled Tayla Miles, quickly righting herself from a semi-supine pose of reception desk hibernation. "Menu's almost done," she added to offer a tinge of productivity.

"Good Morning, Tayla," gave back Pauline absentmindedly as she conducted her obligatory check of all stations in view. Her smiling photo was properly in place beside the antibacterial dispenser to announce Manager of the Day. *When wasn't she that very thing?* she wondered. This job had hijacked most of her waking hours, she reminded herself. Today's menus had yet to displayed on the noticeboard beside Ye Olde Tea Shoppe. Last week's flowers, lilies and greenery were slightly failing on the Reception Desk. A faint smell of urine tinged the swell of heat pumping through the main hallway. It was muted with the more dominant aroma of lavender from puffing air freshener distributors secreted above doorways.

Some crumbs lay across the wide entrance of Ye OldeTea Shoppe to the right. Tayla looked on sheepishly, ascertaining what her score sheet would indicate from this first inspection of the morning.

The corridors down to Daffodil Community were still in darkness. It was time that the Team should be waking their precious guests. No. It's their home, Pauline reminded herself. They are residents. She had to continually rehearse the vocabulary stipulated by the Empire Group of 'homes away from home' which differed dramatically from her training and experience in hotel management, where the emphasis was on an experience out of the ordinary, something short-lived and usually experienced in the peak of health.

Pauline signed in the staff book on Tayla's desk, noting the time which was now 07.20. She didn't have to do as was required of the staff perhaps but felt it set an example. "Everything going well?" she asked.

"I'm sure it is," surmised Tayla. "I haven't seen anyone much yet. Think there's some blockages on the A12 since I got in." That was a safe bet on almost any weekday. Tayla gently kicked her magazine into touch under the desk. Her morning shifts began at six am. On the days when she worked mornings, she didn't have time to do much before heading to work. Those were her dry shampoo, ponytail and talc days and she never felt quite right. "I'm lucky that I miss most of the traffic problems when I start on earlies," she tried to convince them both.

Pauline had already left the Reception area to unlock the adjacent Manager's Office door. She maintained an 'empty desk' policy, leaving her office spotless and papers unable to be read by wandering eyes each evening when she left. Now documents were emptied from the briefcase, computer turned on and she was already back in harness, moving out past Reception and towards the coffee machine in Ye Olde Tea Shoppe, before Tayla had even finished her customary patter on the benefits of starting early.

The chintz curtains had not yet been opened there in the café, as it was more conveniently known by the residents and the staff. Setting up this space each morning was part of the Receptionist's role. Tayla must have been on something of a 'go-slow' this morning, Pauline surmised. However, the coffee machine had already been kick-started by one or other of the as yet invisible staff members, so that she didn't have to wait long after pressing the button until it gurgled and spat liquid through its tubes, coughing up a frothy cappuccino. There was no time for her to open the curtains but to get back to her office, leaving that task to its rightful operator and certainly to get on with her own tasks.

She was on her way back to her office with her coffee to fire up all the administrative systems that sustained the 'platform' of her existence when she heard laughter coming from the Staff Lounge. She would investigate in a tick. More important at this moment was to send the Performance Appraisals of the Senior Team through to Head Office so as to ensure she was ahead of the ten am deadline and would therefore earn the required green lights on her own monthly performance dashboard. This in turn would go to provide evidence of her competence in the role that she had held now for eleven months. She watched the green-light flight of the appraisal forms sent from her computer and wondered if there would be anyone there at Head Office now, at 07.30, to receive the evidence of those hours of work that had gone into setting out the 'key performance indicators' for each of the Head Nurse, Office Manager and Sales and Events Manager who served with her as Gramwell's Senior Team.

The phone rang at Reception but had not been intercepted by Tayla within the statutory three rings. It then devolved to Pauline's line and had to be answered. "Good Morning. Gramwell Glade. Can I help you?" Pauline felt that she was entitled, as GM, to omit the required identification of the speaker since few people referred to her by her first name. It could then sound too informal or too demeaning to add, "Pauline speaking," she'd reasoned.

The milk delivery man was on his mobile and, although only a few metres away in the car park, mobile reception was so poor at this part of county near Senerwell on Sea that she could barely understand what he had to say. Since this was a common occurrence, she deduced that the kitchen staff, busy with breakfast preparations, had failed yet again to unlock the external door; consequently, the milkman was left unable to make his delivery. Time for him, as for everyone each morning in Gramwell Glade, was of the essence. She shouted down the phone, as though she were speaking to someone who lacked mental capacity, that she would notify the kitchen immediately, then hung up. There was little point in trying to phone through to the kitchen since they obviously weren't picking up and, although she had spoken at length to both chefs about this issue on numerous occasions, the best solution was to rattle their cage.

Pauline flew past the Reception desk that by now had been vacated by Tayla. She could then be found dithering at the noticeboard with the posting of the daily menus. With some annoyance, Pauline punched in her code at the security doors back of house and headed on clicking heels to the kitchen. Unlike all other visitors to the kitchen, she didn't stop to put on a white coat and hat or swathe her hands in anti-bac gel but stuck her head through the double doors as a reminder of this far too common event.

Peggy Hewson, morning chef, looked up red-faced from the vat of porridge she was stirring on the ten burner hob, immediately aware of the problem. "Oh, sorry, Mrs Graves," she spluttered. "Did Henry forget to unlock that door again?"

"Good Morning Peggy. Can you let the milkman in please? He's been waiting again."

The wafting, sweet smell of bacon immediately caught Pauline's attention. The diet was annoying but working and would be worth it in the long run. She couldn't afford to give in, she coaxed herself. She let the door close behind her and the kitchen continue with their stirrings before she had a chance to give in to temptation.

Heading past the Staff Lounge she could hear more laughter. Stan Novak and Malgosia Matkowska appeared to be in some sort of huddle together. Both Care Workers, they had come separately from Poland to look for work in England some years ago. Both married, they had also found that their long hours of work, mostly in night shifts, had led them to some irresistible extra-marital comforts that seemed to them to be a reasonable quid pro quo for all the inconveniences of the constant demands of the work. These days Stan continued to work nights while Gosia had been moved to the day shift in an attempt to provide fewer opportunities for the shenanigans that had upset others of the Night Team.

"Hello, Stan, Gosia," Pauline noted, looking around the conservatory extension of the room to see if other staff were also taking a break, "how are you both today?"

"Morning, Mrs Graves," offered Malgosia. "We are really good, thank you. We have a funny app. Do you see?" She thrust her mobile phone under Pauline's nose to show her a picture of Stan sporting a bird's beak and rabbit ears. "What do you think of Stanislaw? Do you think this suits him?" She shrank into a huddle of giggles. "It's an improvement, no?"

"Are you both on a break at the same time?" Pauline wondered.

"Ah, Mrs Graves. You are always the watchful one," Stan noted. "I'm just finishing night shift and Gosia is just starting. But I have to do some day shift too today. Someone else is not coming." They both giggled. "But we had a good night here. Hilda Matters was a bit naughty in Daffodil and walking around a lot but we put her back to bed. No sickness. All good, to be honest."

"That's what we want to hear," noted Pauline. And it was. She dreaded the mornings when she would come in to find that there had been a death in the 'family' through the night and was always relieved to know that things were running as smoothly as could be expected through all the trials of geriatric experience.

Gosia handed the phone back to Stan as she headed to the sink to wash her mug and deposit a banana peel. She had had her silent marching orders. "See you later, Mrs Graves," she added as she headed for the door and back to Tulip, the secure community in the east wing. Pauline walked with her to the door. Turning back on her heel, Pauline let Stan know, in case it had occurred to him, "and make sure you don't use that app on any of our residents."

Stan and Malgosia both giggled.

"You know I am the good one," Malgosia protested to Pauline as they walked up the corridor towards Reception and the Lobby. "You always say 'No phones on the floor,' and I always have no phone on the floor." She smiled dutifully and left in the direction of Tulip Community while Pauline headed back towards her office with the intention to check that the Performance Appraisals had, in fact, left the building. She'd been caught before when she thought she'd sent emails only to discover that they hadn't arrived with their intended recipient. These days she always included a 'notify when opened' command when sending emails.

Tayla had moved on the café to open the curtains which allowed bright morning light to flood the room and the corridors beyond. Red and black tables and chairs decorated the room in a 1950s 'diner' style which was anything but Olde Worlde but designed, apparently, to bring a sense of gaiety, youth and adventure to the octogenarians. However, this décor was not in any way reminiscent of their youth. The young designers commissioned by Empire had been unable to imagine or conjure the Essex or even the England of the 1930s and '40s. This café was now the setting of many of the social comings and goings of Gramwell Glade, somewhere where families could visit their old-timers in the shared task of spending time together without being confined to personal bedrooms. A chance to be jolly. Or a chance, at least, to try

Elsie Lister, one of the few early risers among residents, had already made her way to the coffee machine. Getting up early was just one of the things she could do for herself and, even though she didn't really like the taste of coffee, she had been delighted to discover by mistake one day that the machine also produced hot chocolate if you pressed another button. She nodded and smiled as Pauline passed by. She had been looking for the glass-covered stand that was filled each morning on the diner counter with cakes and biscuits. On this occasion, and most others, she was not aware of the time; the cakes were produced around ten and it wasn't yet eight in the morning.

She could have had breakfast first but hadn't remembered that and, even if she had, she liked cakes and biscuits and she hated porridge.

"Hello, Elsie! How are we today?" Pauline asked in passing.

"Good morning," Elsie responded, collecting her walking stick from the countertop where she'd hung it. "Where are the cakes?"

"Ah, plenty of time for that, Elsie. Breakfast first. If you go on down to the dining room, someone will bring your breakfast from the kitchen very soon."

"I don't like breakfast at all really," confided Elsie as she toddled off towards in the direction of the corridor that led back to her bedroom and to the dining room. Pauline, meanwhile, headed to her Office to start on the batch of reporting that was expected to be compiled each day in logs for random official inspections by the authorities. One of Pauline's own 'key performance indicators' was to improve on all the assessment ratings of her predecessor who, by all reports, had left quietly one evening never to be seen again. Apparently, no one had been around at that time to report back or at least no one was game to discuss the situation. One major tenet of Gramwell Glade was that no one spoke about staff who had departed whereas everyone talked – often – of the residents who had.

Elsie reached her room where the TV morning news programme was blaring. A blonde woman was smiling broadly. There was a guide dog beside a man they were interviewing. Some of Elsie's clothes were strewn on the bed. She wondered who had been in her room, having forgotten that she had tried on a few different outfits before settling on the pink cardigan and orange trousers in which she currently stood, lighting up the darkened room like a candle.

She had also forgotten that they had put her mobility scooter away under its cover on the patio outside the French doors from her room that led on to the manicured gardens of the Home. Elsie pulled opened the full-length curtains and found that the patio door was unlocked. Unaware that she had set off an alarm by opening the door, Elsie pulled the fitted cover from the scooter, threw it aside, climbed on board, turned the key and headed on to the sealed, wheelchair-friendly path that circumnavigated the entirety of Gramwell's expansive, manicured gardens. She loved to feel the breeze in her thinning, coiffed hair. She may have been a little chilly but that was to be expected in autumn. As she opened the throttle, Elsie took in the colours of the thicket that backed on to the Senerwell Links Golf Club. For years she and her husband Douglas had been mainstays of the Club. Douglas had been President four years in a row once. Douggie always said that he had a lot to give the club when he'd come back from the war, she recalled, and being busy there would "keep him off the streets."

Although Elsie had been allowed to play nine holes with her girlfriends on Thursdays, this far-flung part of the thicket had not been part of their journey so was unfamiliar even in those days. At that time it had been called The Glade: it was a tangled area of untended blackberry bushes and trees around the Old Folly. The Golf Club had not been permitted to bring down the old turrets that remained on the stone wall, so it remained without any use or value to the Club Committee, Douggie said.

Times had changed since Empire PLC approached the Club some seven years ago and paid a relative pittance for the unused land with a commitment to Council to preserve the Folly as part of their enterprise.

Elsie was transported to the woods of her native Suffolk where each autumn chestnuts, sycamores and willows all gave wonderful displays before giving up their leaves altogether. This particular glade reminded her both of the woods near her childhood home and the woods near the Army Base she frequented in her early twenties. Elsie used to fix engines during the war. She was a dab hand. She wondered now if that had been in another country because she couldn't recall where the war had actually taken place. She was a popular girl with the soldiers. With her even features, petite figure and beaming smile, company was always on offer. "Wartime and golf and autumn leaves." So much was familiar on this journey today, she thought to herself.

The alarm panel at Reception indicated that the external door to Daffodil 9 had been tripped. Tayla was on a call to the accounts person at Head Office who wanted to speak with Barbara Fenway, the Office Manager. Although Barbara's long work hours meant that she practically lived at Gramwell, oddly enough she wasn't here this morning so Tayla duly wrote down each word of the message that Olga Dean was spelling out. "I need the wage sheets and the sickness records entered into the system before 9.30 am. Have you got that?"

"Entered into what?" Tayla asked, mainly because she needed to know exactly where Barbara was supposed to put these sheets. Too many times she'd been counselled on ensuring that messages were taken accurately and in their entirety.

"Into Omega. The human resources system. Where she usually puts them," Olga spelt it out slowly and with annoyance. "Any problems, let me know. Bye."

Tayla wrote down the remainder of the information while the phone rang again.

"Good morning, Gramwell."

"It's me Tayla. Don't worry about the greeting."

The line was very muted but Tayla recognised her boss's cigarette-thick voice.

"Oh hi, Barbara. I was just writing a message for you from Olga Dean."

"She wants the weekly results." Barbara confirmed.

"No, she wants the weekly sheets in *home goer* or somewhere."

"That's the weekly results. Look, I'm on the side of the A12 with a flat tyre and I have to wait for the AA man to change the spare. Can you let Pauline know and call Olga back? Tell Olga that I will get the results to her just as soon as I can."

"Are you alright? AA?" Tayla quipped. She never really knew which side of Barbara's many temperaments she was going to encounter but she was keenly aware that her own success in the workplace depended on nurturing this relationship. Her mother reinforced this point as an essential of being a success in the workplace.

"Do you want someone to come and get you?"

"I have to wait for the AA man, Tayla." Common sense was not one of the girl's most notable assets, as Barbara was well aware. Stickability, on the other hand, was a rare commodity in this day and age and not to be sniffed at. "I'll be there as soon as I can." Barbara sounded exhausted.

"OK. I'll let them know." Tayla hung up, then phoned Pauline in the office next door to her desk, relaying as much of the news as she had fathomed.

Pauline was annoyed. Some of the tardiness resulting from Barbara's absence would now cause her own performance measures to slip. She watched the split-screen security camera relay that filmed various posts of the Home in black and white. It flashed from the kitchen where the trolleys were being assembled for the residential and secure wings of the Home with bain-maries of hot food and cereal packets on top. A number of large water drops on the next screen looked like a scene of an alien invasion. This was the steamed-up camera in the pool room, or Aqua Therapy Pool as it was referred to in the glossy Gramwell Glade brochure. This was a total waste of money in Pauline's view, as she reflected that no eighty-year-old wants to take off their clothes and go swimming in the autumn, never mind winter, and yet she had to keep it heated. As a result, the Utilities line of her budget was always about double the allocated cost. She'd get rid of the whole pool idea if it weren't part of the company's prize differentiators.

There was a flash of something in the garden down near the potting shed as Pauline looked up for the second time before the view clicked over to the nurses' station of the secure wing, Tulip Community, where the Head Nurse,

Brad Fletchley, was speaking with Gosia Matkowska, his second in command, Bessie Roberts and the new Senior Carer, Brendon Longacre.

Meanwhile, Elsie had put care behind her and was on her second circumnavigation of Gramwell Glade. Squirrels scuttled up tree trunks ahead of her wheels as they crunched through gold and russet fallen leaves. The feeling of freedom and the rush of oxygen reminded her of earlier days. She couldn't quite bring them to mind at present. There was no need. These sensations were sufficient to bring a wide smile to her pretty face.

A squad of morning staff had started to roll in, meeting in small groups while signing in at the Reception Desk. Monday morning was always a haul. Apart from seeing residents from their beds, there was the need to complete and submit the previous week's notes on the computer. Empire had moved to a new electronic patient management system over the past six months and, like other workplaces, the staff had been promised that the new system would save time. That proposition had yet to be realised. In fact, they had only just finished entering all the data for all the residents when a couple of shaky weeks in the summer heat had seen the demise of four residents in one week, so then they had to complete endless screens to report on the deaths before filling out even more forms to start the new residents that had been found to take their places. It seemed a never-ending task, one that guaranteed to bring substantial doses of Monday-itis.

Kayleigh Longbottom was signing in as Brian Petty arrived. They had been out for drinks with some of the older carers on Friday night and had tried not to say too much to one another lest anyone spot that they might be more than a little interested in each other. He was twenty-two and she was just eighteen. He did fancy her. And he wasn't sure what to do about it.

Her bosses thought that Kayleigh was extremely shy. Her pale complexion was prone to betray her. It had been noted in her last performance appraisal that she needed to be more mindful of the residents' needs and improvement would be welcome in her making conversation to put residents at their ease. It was a constant struggle for her to try to come up with conversation; she would rather work quietly and get things done than chat like some of the others did – constantly. Talking to people was hard. She just wanted to carry on without any chat.

Tayla finished a call. "If anyone else rings before I can get to the loo, I swear I'll wet my pants!" she whispered to Brian. "Babes, would you hold the fort while I go to the loo? I've been bursting for an hour." This gave Kayleigh the opportunity to deflect attention from herself as Brian was now chatting with Brendon Longacre who was on his way to Daffodil community. Brian sat in the reception chair and swung around. Brian was intrigued in the general chat that Brendon was a proud cross-dresser in his own private time and that his alter ego was affectionately known as Brenda by his friends and already by a few of the staff at Gramwell.

Brendon was a capable and respected Senior Carer. He had a way about him that the residents responded well to. He was warm and appreciative, able to lean into their needs, however small or even hidden. Then again, he had the authority of a headmaster (or headmistress, depending on the alter ego of the day) and they would do things for him that might otherwise drive them to tantrums and other carers to distraction.

Brian was thankful that the phone hadn't rung while Tayla was away. Pauline Graves had stuck her head around the side of the desk, apparently with some request in mind, but, on seeing Brian in Tayla's place, had immediately returned into her own office, knowing that explanations would take longer than the actual task she had in mind for Tayla. She may as well get on with it herself.

Henry Pratt, the portly redheaded Kitchen Hand, pushed the large trolley up the corridor towards Daffodil Community and the dining room. Like Henry, it was both wide and heavy, a collection of bain-maries containing Mrs Hewson's porridge in the largest and the components of a 'full English' breakfast in the other sections. A number of boiled eggs in egg cups wobbled atop, wedged in place by cereal packets, a large stainless steel jug of milk and a plastic container of orange juice.

Carers assembled in the dining room holding trays to collect orders for those residents who chose to eat breakfast in bed. Many residents were still asleep. In those cases it had become a matter of guesswork as to what they might choose this morning, although their carers generally ordered the same thing on most days, that being whatever was easiest to feed and clean up. They had to attend to all the other tasks, especially the paperwork, and since the new system had been in place, they had to go searching for one of the few available tablets to enter that data.

Henry stayed on in the dining room to serve the carers, including those who were assisting early risers to the tables in the room.

Hilda Matters headed towards her usual table with the assistance of her walking sticks. After a night on the wander, she had built a healthy appetite.

"Morning, Hilda lovey," said Stan as he held her seat away from the table for her. "You've had a busy night, haven't you?"

"Busy dreaming of you, Stan my man," Hilda replied with a stage wink to deflect from her night walking but, on looking up to see something moving past the French doors to the garden, added with excitement, "there's Elsie!" She pointed her walking stick in the direction of the garden.

"No, Elsie's not here yet, Hilda. She'll be down in a minute. It's not like you to beat her to breakfast. You must be hungry. What would you like today?"

"I'd like a party. Perhaps some steak and chips?" She answered sarcastically because the staff didn't seem to have their eyes on the main game. "Elsie's gone out!" she pointed out again.

"Elsie will be in her room, dear. How about some bacon and eggs and, if you promise to eat it all, a sausage too?"

"And beans," Hilda's hunger was getting the better of her. Stan had brought her cup of tea which she sipped, her eyes moving from side to side, taking in the room and the other residents who had joined in.

David Jack was one of the few who was game to sit at the same table as Barney Perry. They both lived down the Daffodil corridor. Now 91, Barney was known by one and all to be a cantankerous old boy. No one really knew how to appease him but he'd been trotted out quite successfully each year to celebrate war commemorations such as the Battle of Britain and Remembrance Day. He loved a crowd. On those occasions, Barney's impressive collection of medals were always pinned to his clothing, even if that was a windcheater on those days when his daughters hadn't come in to smarten him up with his shirt and suit jacket. Most of the carers felt that there must be some degree of post-traumatic stress syndrome involved in his old bones. Most of the residents gave him a wider berth than his wheelchair demanded.

"Morning, David and Barney," Kayleigh said, pouring tea for both. "How are we this morning?"

"Very well thank you, Kayleigh, never better!" offered David.

"Sugar?" demanded Barney. "Elsie's on the run again."

"Sorry?" asked Kayleigh, adding two teaspoons of sugar to Barney's cup.

"That mad woman who lives down near me. She's off on her motorbike again."

"Elsie? Elsie doesn't have a motorbike! You mean her scooter?"

"If that's her name. Crazy dame. Elsie Scooter. Flying around. Scaring the chickens. Surprised we've got any eggs this morning." Carers had explained to him many times that the eggs produced by the Home's hens were not certified and so couldn't be served to residents. Instead, that bounty, with their large yellow yolks, was one of the few perks that the staff were allowed to enjoy. Either Peter Spence, the maintenance man, or his son Eric would leave the eggs in the Staff Lounge after collecting them each morning. They were quickly snaffled and enjoyed on a 'first come, first served' basis.

Kayleigh brought bacon and eggs to both David and Barney before leaving the dining room to find Brad in the nurses' room to pass on the news that Barney had reported Elsie was running loose on her scooter in the garden again.

"Can you let Brendon know, please, Kayleigh? I'm in the middle of medications." Brad deflected.

Kayleigh knew that she was needed in the dining room: they were always 'flat chat' at meal times, ensuring that everyone had what they needed, but it was also going to be important to check on Elsie. The temperature was much cooler this morning than it had been of late. Elsie had been prone to ride around on her scooter in the summer but she'd been told recently that it had now been put away for the colder months.

Kayleigh saw Tayla coming down the corridor. She was on her way to bring today's newspapers to the sitting room. "Tayla, Barney reckons that Elsie is scooting around the garden. Can you get someone to check?"

Tayla slapped her forehead. There had been an alarm showing for Elsie's door. But that was about three-quarters of an hour ago. It'd been so busy since, she'd forgotten. Elsie must be frozen if she was still out there.

Without admitting anything about the alarm, Tayla headed to Brendon in the nurses' room to ask him if he could send someone to find Elsie. "Can they check in her room because Kayleigh says Elsie might be in the garden on her scooter? Sorry, I've got to fly." She left quickly to get back to the front desk before she missed any phone calls or other demands from the office. "Dearie me! If a girl wants something done she'd better do it herself," Brendon flounced out of the room in search of Peter or Eric. They were going to have to store the scooter in the shed if Elsie couldn't leave it alone.

Just as the dining room carers were packing up the remains of breakfasts, largely uneaten, Peter Spence escorted Elsie in for breakfast. She was smiling from ear to ear.

"We found Elsie down near the chicken coops," he explained as he showed her to her usual seat. "Get your death of a cold, Els, if you're not careful, my love," he added as she shuffled herself into the seat, smile beaming. Elsie's cheeks were red with cold and excitement. Clearly she was exhilarated with her morning's adventure.

Henry came over to take her order, hoping that there was something left in the trolley for her.

"Eric's packing the scooter away." Peter raised his eyebrows in exasperation. "For the third time."

"Elsie, Peter will have to take the scooter away to the garage for the winter if you won't stop this." Henry tried to explain the gravity of the situation as he hastily swept crumbs from the table cloth with the side of his hand

"Oh no he won't!" Elsie confirmed. "You know I like to look at my scooter – and check that it's got its winter coat on." Elsie's winning ways still worked a treat on anyone who came into contact with her. It was impossible to say no to her. She savoured her tea as she patted her hair back into a shape that she imagined might neaten it up. "Just the thing after a morning drive, thank you, Henry dear. Have you got any sausages this morning? I'm really hungry today. I could eat a lion."

Henry went to the serving table to see what he might put together for her. So many of the residents imagined that they had an appetite but it was almost always the case of having eyes bigger than their stomachs. This was not something that Henry could be accused of. He was always pleased to be taking leftovers back to the kitchen where Peggy would let him eat his fill once breakfast service was over. She told him that he had hollow legs. Truth be told, she loved feeding him up.

There was a sausage in the bain-marie, half a grilled tomato and some scrambled egg still there too. He arranged them as prettily as he could. Mrs Graves was always telling them in the kitchen that "Presentation is half the battle." On the other hand, they always thought that it was the smell of the cooking that rallied the residents to the table and that they were able to order the comfort foods of their childhoods. All of which were called by really posh names on the menus at Gramwell: this for the benefit of the families who needed to be convinced of the value for the thousands of pounds laid out each month for the care of their relatives when other care homes in the district could cost as little of half the tariff commanded at Gramwell Glade.

Tayla was now sitting in the upright position at the Reception Desk. The morning was well underway. Visitors had started to arrive. The Home's GP, Dr Evelyn Dunwoody, a hale and hearty rambler in her fifties, was something of a fixture around the place, part of the furniture, and, even though she didn't have to drop in unless there was a specific call, Gramwell Glade was on the way to her own medical centre in Senerwell on Sea so she often called in on Monday mornings on her way to check on those residents in the nursing unit upstairs and to tend to any other soul who might need her ministrations.

She was checking in with Brendon who was at the Nurses' Station. Nothing to report other than Elsie breaking loose again. At least it was only in the grounds and not along the road, which had been known to happen in the past with other stray residents. The duty receptionist on those few occasions had been the first to know about the oversight when a local resident would phone to report a wandering elder. They were also the most likely one to be blamed, having been the distracted culprit to allow the escapee to pass the main doors unassailed.

Tayla's boss, Barbara – Mrs Fenway – had finally arrived. She had looked completely flustered as she dashed past the Reception Desk and into her office to the rear of the foyer, digging in quickly for the onslaught of Monday admin duties. For the most part, reception staff were left to their own devices so that contact with Barbara was more or less limited to those times when they needed to be reminded, hurried along, put upon to stay longer or simply told off.

Henry had pushed the trolley back to the kitchen. The smile he threw to Tayla on his way past belied his disappointment in the slim pickings that were going to be on offer today. Elsie had only nibbled at what was going to have been his treat but it was now in the bin. He didn't feel much like the load of tepid porridge that was the only real leftover of any substance this morning.

Amity Leighton, a tall, angular woman, had a job that Tayla never really understood. They exchanged greetings somewhat formally as Amity signed in. Amity's healthy escapades with horses on the farm she shared with her solicitor husband, Giles, had her looking some ten years younger than her actual forty-six years. Although that could have been down to her frequent holidays abroad or, most likely, her indulgence in regular beauty treatments. Whatever it was, she was called the Sales and Events Manager in the staff listing which meant, it seemed to most, that all she did was schmooze visitors who came to the home or boss the team and volunteers into spending time doing crafts and quizzes with the residents. That and go out for long lunches. The only activities she seemed to participate in were Happy Hour cocktails and the Book Club which was only ever frequented by two or three of the gentlemen residents, which was just the way that she liked it.

Amity shared office space with Barbara Fenway but was closer in age and interests to Brad Fletchley, the Care Manager, whose office was based upstairs in the Nursing Community, euphemistically known as Rose Community. Gramwell Glade was made up of Daffodils, Tulips and Roses. A garden of spring and summertime blooms now well past the autumn of their lives. Or perhaps an air freshener.

Chapter Two

CARPE DIEM

Opinion varied as to whether Elsie had done a brave or stupid thing by riding out on her scooter on that crisp autumn morning, but it had certainly caused a stir. Hilda Matters was Elsie's neighbour, her room being Daffodil 8, but that was about as close as they managed to be in most things. Elsie was petite and flirtatious; Hilda was a big-boned lady who called a spade a shovel and was as likely to devour the staff with her bold sarcasm as Elsie was to flutter her eyelashes. Hilda had no patience when it came to Elsie's creating her own rules. It was that she got away with it that really was the issue. There would be no such lenience lent to Hilda and, now that she felt compelled to walk the corridors at night, they had threatened her that she might move over to Tulip, the secure community. Much as she would prefer a different neighbour and have Elsie well out of sight, there was no way that she was going to the secure community and, in her view, it was Elsie that was clearly the more obvious candidate for locking up. Hilda had all her marbles and was the brightest of the lot, she thought. This was evidenced mainly by her supremacy when they all played Giant Scrabble together in Ye Olde Tea Shoppe. While three-letter words characterised others' stock in trade, Hilda knew how to optimise the double and triple word score opportunities, always beating the men, sometimes even David Jack who also showed tremendous ability at most competitive activities. David was still secretly waiting for a new resident to arrive one day with whom he might play chess, having given up completely on the idea of ever again being able to put a bridge four together.

Elizabeth Hollick, who lived in Daffodil 3, had been taken to the hairdressing salon. She'd had her weekly wash and set in the humid atmosphere of the little room at the end of the Tea Shoppe. The room had been set up with two salon sinks and two chairs with mirrors, just like the real thing. Sometimes there were two stylists in at once. Today there was only Chantelle, a glamourous blonde who always treated the old ladies as though they were as beautiful as the young clients she worked with in the proper salon where she worked in Senerwell on Sea. She valued this work at Gramwell because the population at Senerwell varied significantly from summer to winter when demand was so reduced that the salon was only open on Thursdays, Fridays and Saturdays.

"Hello Hilda!" she exclaimed with enough enthusiasm to have Hilda believe that she truly was pleased to see her. "How are you today?"

"Tired, as usual," Hilda complained as she struggled through the wall of humidity that choked the tiny salon. However, Chantelle wasn't discouraged. "Shall we do the usual?" she asked. "You always look so glamorous when we've done your shampoo and set."

"You do cheer me up," Hilda owned up. "There are so many around here that I could do without but I'll keep you because you always have a lovely smile." Her body visibly relaxed into the chair. As Chantelle massaged her scalp, Hilda fell asleep briefly, waking herself with a loud snort.

Old Grace Garrett from Tulip 4 had been waiting for a carer to collect her and take her back to her room after her manicure. She sat at the other end of the salon table, watching the newly shiny pink polish dry on her fingernails, apparently without a thought in mind, but she giggled at Hilda's loud snoring until she saw Hilda glaring back at her. It was at that point that Hilda made a final judgement about the potential problems of moving to Tulip community and vowed that she was going to avoid any further speculation on the possibility of a move. She didn't yet know quite how she would manage to change their minds but her steely determination was evident in her tightening facial expression. Chantelle looked at her puckered upside-down face while rinsing her hair.

"Are you OK Hilda?" She worried that the water may have run a little cool.

"Never better dear," Hilda replied with grit as Elizabeth Hollick, head held high, swanned by with her coiffure.

Just outside the salon doors, waiting for her glamour session, Delphine Thomas was full of the joys of anticipation, even though there were two clients booked before her. Music was piped through speakers in the Tea Shoppe on a loop tape. The music also leaked its way to the Reception area, much to the annoyance of the team on the front desk. However, the familiarity of these choices pleased Delphine. She had been joined on the upright settee by Maisie Dunstable. They were both from Tulip community but were able to spend some time each day in the Daffodil community owing to their generally more competent ways.

"Did you hear about that Elsie Lister this morning?" Delphine asked Maisie excitedly.

"Was that the one who got out on a scooter?"

"Too right!" Delphine was full of vicarious excitement. The skulduggery of it all was a thrilling departure from bingo and fish tanks.

"And they keep *us* in a secure community. To think of it!" Maisie's frustration was a product of her loneliness. She was still a newcomer to Gramwell, having only been resident since February following her husband's passing in January. There were about a million things that didn't really suit her about this new life.

"I don't know how she got out," continued Delphine. "There should be staff keeping an eye on the ones who want to get out. 'Leave your troubles on the doorstep'," she echoed the piped music.

"She was in the garden, wasn't she?" quizzed Maisie. "I don't think she got *out* out. How did she do it?" Perhaps there were things to be learned, Maisie thought to herself.

"She's got a scooter. It's parked outside her place down at the end of Daffodil. On the patio. She uses it in the summer on all those garden paths. 'Just protect your feet on the sunny side of the street.' I don't know if I want a scooter." Delphine reflected. At eighty-nine she was quite content for carers to take her for garden strolls in a wheel chair on pleasant days.

"Respect," corrected Maisie. "Just 'respect' your feet." She looked down at her red slippers and wondered if she'd ever get used to being here.

Morning tea was served in the Daffodil Lounge for those residents who needed sustenance or company between breakfast and lunch. On Tuesdays it was also an opportunity for the majority of female residents to show off the newly swished hairdo. Chantelle also provided services to the gentlemen who appeared more dapper with hair, beard and moustache trims than they seemed to on other days of the week. Therefore more gathered on this day other than Sunday when a Baptist minister came in to see to the Anglican congregation to their 'happy clappy' strain of worship which, for its energy levels if nothing else, brought about many apparent conversions. The local vicar was missing a trick.

Within the Daffodil community, there was a general consensus that the most eligible single man was David Jack who lived in Daffodil 5, a room that was central to the east wing of Gramwell. Among his neighbours, Mildred Absolom, Elizabeth Hollick, Elsie Lister and Hilda Matters were all widows. Dot Baker, David's nextdoor neighbour, had never been married and was quicker to blush than her neighbours at any suggestions of dalliance or discussions on who was the most attractive squire at Gramwell Glade. Some were more interested than others in the idea of being noticed by the opposite sex. Others felt that ninety-one-year-old Barney Perry in Daffodil 7 was in fact the most eligible specimen in the game owing to rumours of his having been an extremely wealthy farmer in his day. Certainly there was little evidence of that these days if one took out of the equation the cost to each and every one of them in exchange for their 'home away from home' which was the Empire logo. Barney was no dapper dresser and his personal hygiene wasn't always top-notch. He was one who shunned the hair salon, resulting in many stray hairs from every aspect of his face – eyebrows, ears and nose.

Today David was sitting at the easterly window of Daffodil Lounge which overlooked the meandering gardens which, at that point, sported a long pond complete with waterlilies watched over by a steel statue of a heron. The pond had been filled with goldfish four years ago and those that had braved the three subsequent winters had grown substantially in size. It reminded David of a painting of Winston Churchill's that he had once seen. A pond in a stately garden, Churchill's home, had flashing brushstrokes of orange, suggesting an active population of goldfish beneath. The inclusion of these little touches, whilst something of a burden to Peter and Eric who often needed to free the pond of weed and to feed the fish, was appreciated by David. His thoughts were interrupted by Stan who had approached quietly from behind, carrying a supply of towels apparently diverted from his journey to the bathroom to replenish the stock there.

"Looking at the fishes, David? We had some fishes like that in a pond in the park near where I lived in Krakow."

"Really? How did they manage in the winter time?" David put down the piece of sky blue jigsaw that he had been hovering over the puzzle. "I would have thought that a Krakow winter would be too cold."

"Ah, we're tough in Krakow!" Stan looked at the picture coming together on the table. It appeared to be a Tudor house in a wooded area. The sky had holes at this stage. "This is a rich man's house?" he suggested.

"It's a country pub in Wakefield called The Coy Carp," David explained in the manner of a gentle tutor.

"Carap?" the word had made little sense to Stan but sounded dangerously like a word that he knew should be avoided in Gramwell Glade, at least by the staff.

"Coy means 'shy' and 'carp' is a fish."

"Carp. Yes carp. I have gone fishing with my friend for carp. They are big and ugly fish. No good for eating here, they said, but I think that we do eat carp at home in Poland," he mused. "Not pretty like these." Stan tapped on the tropical fish tank beside the table, scaring them into their rocky hideaways.

"Carp can be big and ugly but they are the big cousin of the goldfish we have here in the pond." David explained. "They are called Koi carp." He indicated to the pond. "They generally grow to the size of the bowl or tank or pond that they live in."

"But they are shy?"

David wasn't sure that Stan was on the same track.

"Coy carp like in the picture?" asked Stan.

"Oh, I see," laughed David but in fact he was not sure how he would begin to explain this through the language barrier he and Stan tried to brook. "The Coy Carp is a pub in Uxbridge. These are koi carp. Different spelling. Different meaning." He looked at Stan's puzzled face, hoping that he wasn't proving too tricky since the man really did want to master the language and he was keen to help him. "I know. English is such a difficult language, Stan. Most of the English don't even manage it. You do well. Really you do," he assured.

Stan left him, punching the stack of towels as though it was all too difficult but with a smile that indicated he appreciated the efforts that David made for him.

If one was to manage a sighting of David Jack in the living room after having visited the hairdresser, luck was in for those who were still in the mating game and it was time enough to seize that day. As life's numerous ironies would have it, the person that David related to most easily was Hilda Matters, that large and fairly unattractive martinet who frowned on most of her neighbours for various reasons and, as was much discussed between the other ladies, especially when she had been known to have had the odd hair removed by Chantelle from the moustache and chin regions of her stern face. David and Hilda shared both the crown and the verve for competitive Scrabble. Between the two of them they held the competition at bay when Fenwell Lodge's team came over on Tuesday afternoons for a game of Giant Scrabble in Ye Olde Tea Shoppe. While all the girls thought David clever and attractive, they regarded Hilda as having far less ability and very little attraction but were jolly glad that Gramwell continued to take the honours in the rival Scrabble tournament. David left the puzzle in place on the table while he made his way to the dining room for lunch.

Janette Gosling, Peggy Hewson's kitchen hand, struggled to push the lunch trolley down the corridor and around the corner to the Daffodil dining room. The hearty aroma of steak and kidney pudding dominated all the other offerings of the day: it was bound to strike up an appetite with the fussiest of eaters since it harked back to the familiarity of their younger days. Carers were waiting in the dining room to launch the lunch service. On most days there were more takers for lunch in the dining room than for breakfast. Attendance was encouraged on the basis of social interaction. While it suited the Care Team to serve breakfast in bed to some of the slowcoaches, allowing themselves more time to attend, one by one, to those who needed help to shower and dress, by midday, they were all out of bed and easier to manage en masse in the dining room.

Each resident had their usual spot. The one thing that would alter that predictability was that Barney was not always ready to share his company with David Jack and Ronald Storrick, choosing to order lunch in his room as he did today. Ronald lived with his wife Marie in Daffodil 10 & 11, a unit that was purpose-built for accommodating a couple. There were two double suites on this floor. The other was in Tulip community and there was a double nursing room in the Rose community upstairs. Amity Leighton had a long waiting list for double suites and had often given Empire the feedback that they could sell the double suites ten times over which may have been something of an exaggeration but often doubled as a good excuse as to why single rooms were not 'selling' quickly in times of higher vacancy. Not that Amity often needed an excuse: her sales figures were the best in the Empire portfolio of care homes.

Ronald and Marie would sit at the 'men's table' along with David and Barney on the days when they felt up to the clatter of the dining room. In truth, their suite, which had a larger living space than the single rooms, was a lovely place to be, especially when their meals were served to them there on the small dining table near their television. This meant that David Jack was the only constant at the 'men's table' and that there were irregular vacancies there to be filled by any of his admirers who was keen enough to shuffle the usual arrangements. Most often this was Hilda who preferred male company because, in general, they shared a more erudite background than most of the women. Both David and Hilda had been teachers until some twenty years ago. It was evident that David may have been more the mentor while Hilda's commanding presence reminded more than a few of the other ladies of their own trepidatious school days. Under the guise of discussing Scrabble strategies, Hilda would take an empty seat at David's table without any of the trappings of politeness or shyness that struck other candidates brave enough to venture there.

Soup had been served to those ready for a heartier meal. Today Dot Baker and Mildred Absolom had also taken advantage of the absence of Barney and the Storricks to take a place at the special table. Both had chosen the smoked mackerel paté starter before Dot started worrying that the strong fish smell may have overpowered David.

David's daughter always ensured that his stocks of toiletries were never in short supply. David had used aftershave all of his professional life. He'd started fifty years ago with Old Spice and would have been very happy to have stayed with it but his daughter Sarah had had different ideas, supplying him with a few varieties of the more subtle perfumes available on the market. Swathed in pheromones, David's inherent attraction was multiplied many times over. It was the lovely way that he smelled that was perhaps the most significant factor in determining who would run the gauntlet of gossip and examination to spend time at his meal table.

For Dot, never married, David's attraction was a mystery. She had seldom found herself in close proximity to the male of the species, having worked in a haberdashery for most of her early life in Colchester and for the latter part of her career as a bra fitter in a select gentlewoman's outfitters until her retirement four years ago when she came as one of the first residents to Gramwell. She wasn't practised at rubbing shoulders with men although there had been an episode about fifty years ago which was occasionally referred to but it seemed that an engagement had not come to its rightful fruition and the matter had been laid to rest then. When she had encountered workmen at her flat, on an *as needs* basis through the years, she had not enjoyed them coming too close to her. They did seem to have a shared smell, one that was not particularly enjoyable. David Jack, on the other hand, always had a gentle but irresistible aroma. Dot found herself looking for reasons to look over the menu with him, helping to arrange the table when things were a little array or passing the salt and pepper so as to be a smidgeon closer, to ingest the puzzling elixir. "What's *roulade*, David?" she would ask or "Have you ever tried Thai *green* curry before?" Her need to do so annoyed her intensely. For the longest time Dot had had complete mastery over her own composure. Now she appeared to have met her denouement.

Darragh Slattery, Brian Petty and Naomi Page were the carers assisting with the lunch. It had been an easy service in the dining room since a number of residents were choosing to eat in their rooms today. Darragh, at thirty-seven, had a comfortable way of relating to all the residents: he was comfortable in his own skin. Naomi, originally from South Africa, had moved to England as a twenty-one-year-old a decade ago and made it known that she would never move back there. Her accent had remained as strong as the day she had arrived and was not always clearly understood through her sharp vowels. Darragh had a West Country Irish brogue. The running together of his words was also challenging to the Essex patrons for whom he cared. Brian was a local and well understood by all and so was called on more frequently when assistance was needed. This didn't faze Darragh and Naomi who made as much enjoyment of the experience as they could muster. To their patrons, their various accents constituted a veritable Tower of Babel.

Carers, when asked at interview why they wanted this job, would reply that they 'want to make a difference' and claim that they are 'happy to do whatever is needed to make sure my resident is comfortable'. This allusion was primarily to toileting requirements. In fact, few were totally comfortable with taking up waiter or waitress duties because it seemed a task well below their level of training. Darragh and Naomi had worked up a happy routine between them that removed them from the humdrum of plate-scraping. At least, they consoled one another, there was little spoon-feeding required in Daffodil dining room. On the contrary, not only the 'men's table' but most of the other patrons demonstrated the epitome of sterling table manners.

Naomi swanned over to table four to ask Elsie Lister and Elizabeth Hollick their choices for main course. "Just the two of you here today, ladies? But both so glamorous."

Much as Elizabeth Hollick did not want to be put into the same basket as the troublesome Elsie, she did pride herself on keeping up with the spotless manners for which they were both known.

"Well, it's musical chairs around here, isn't it?" asked Elsie with a twinkle in her eye. "Mr and Mrs Storrick are away again so Dot and Mildred have left us out to dry here with no one to talk to."

"I'm not *no one*!" countered Elizabeth, touching the curls at the nape of her neck. "Speak for yourself, Elsie!"

"And I hear that you had them all worried when you disappeared this morning, Elsie. Now you mustn't run away again. You'll catch a cold out there now that autumn is with us," warned Naomi.

"Just a little drive to see how the garden is looking," Elsie explained while Elizabeth engaged Naomi with a glance, her eyes rolling heavenwards to protest that *she* would never be so foolhardy.

Darragh collected the plates from David's table and returned with the dessert menus. Ice cream was rapidly melting in the bain-marie. Darragh had often pleaded with Peggy that they should keep the ice cream in the kitchen until it was needed because it too often melted with the ambient temperature of the dining room which, like all the other common rooms, was kept at a constant twenty degrees. Peggy saw it as a reason for the staff to be coming backwards and forwards to the kitchen many more times than they currently did or needed to and had convinced Pauline Graves that this would be a counterproductive move because they would likely take their chance to skive off for a quick cigarette. So the decision had been made, leaving them continually apologising to the residents who chose ice cream for pudding when serving them something that was more reminiscent of custard.

"I think I'll have the jam roly-poly today," David told Hilda, "in keeping with the changing season."

"Need to keep up our strength for the tournament this afternoon," she agreed. "Have you got a new aftershave?" She twitched her nose and made a show of inhaling.

Dot was mortified to witness Hilda's bold and, frankly, embarrassing examination of something that should, after all, be a private matter.

"Sarah's brought some new one," David offered without compunction.

Dot was slowly blushing while convinced of Hilda's having reached a bridge too far but it didn't seem to faze David at all. Dot realised that he and Hilda were comfortable together which was something she was never likely to be.

"She's very sweet, my daughter," David added. "I'm not sure that I would be bothered if she didn't keep up the supplies the way she does but I can't complain when she tries so hard to make sure that I have everything that she thinks I need, at least." He and Hilda laughed together as Darragh brought their jam roly-polies. "And for you, Dot? What can I get you?" Darragh asked gently.

Dot couldn't quite bring herself to say the words 'roly-poly' so gave a dismissive hand gesture and a shrug to Darragh to indicate that there was nothing that she needed at all.

When Daffodil lunch was over, Brian despatched the trolley back to the kitchen to start the clean-up. Some of the Tulip residents had already taken up their seats in the Daffodil Lounge to witness the Scrabble Tournament. Even though Maisie Dunstable and Delphine Thomas had very little interest in Scrabble, they were always glad to take up the opportunity to go for a wander to Daffodil community and absorb the more gregarious atmosphere, especially when their hair had just been done.

Stan and Ronnie had also brought Marie Taylor and Dorotka Gryzyna down from Tulip for a little outing. Maisie and Delphine took pleasure in demonstrating their greater familiarity with Daffodil community by taking up their seats in the audience area of the set up and chatting amongst themselves. The giant Scrabble board took central place; two desks were placed in front each with three chairs for the rival parties and beyond was the auditorium for onlookers. Ye Olde Tea Shoppe was decorated with vases of autumn leaves. Lights were shining from above and also from table lamps around the mirrored bar. All of this spelled *PARTY* to Marie who clapped her hands and shouted "Booty full! So booty full! Let's have a party together! Happy Birthday!"

By the end of the hour long Scrabble contest, David Jack and Hilda Matters had restored Gramwell's superiority yet again. If things didn't change soon, it was possible that Fenwell Lodge mightn't keep coming back for more punishment. Naomi had led the session trying to acknowledge the Fenwell group for every one of their little successes while in reality they were unlikely to unseat the reigning champions. Hopefully, she could persuade Peggy to keep up the cream teas; her scones were beyond competition.

David Jack made his way back to the table at the far end of Daffodil Lounge to resume work on the sky above the Wakefield puzzle. There were no other residents around. The tropical fish drifted up and down the height of their tank in the corner as he took his chair in the peace of the large room that had been modelled on an old-fashioned gentlemen's club. Life had become so quiet since he'd been encouraged by Sarah and her husband Colin to leave the marital home where he'd hung on alone for twenty years. They were certain that he could continue to read, listen to the radio, enjoy all the things he'd previously enjoyed. When the time came, later on, he would have constant care in a familiar environment and, for this, they would buy peace of mind. This they did when they entered into a contract with Empire's Gramwell Glade.

Something caught the corner of his eye. He looked up to see a real heron standing beside the steel heron at the edge of the goldfish pond. He had to check himself. They were of almost identical proportions; however, one was metal and the other flesh and blood. The sculptor had done an impressive job. He wondered if the real heron thought that the steel heron was somehow related.

David had not heard Dot Baker come up behind him while he stared at the odd phenomenon. He turned to acknowledge her with a smile. She had spotted the heron too. It was transfixing. She had forgotten her inhibitions about being close by David. They remained perfectly quiet as they watched the graceful bird cock its head to look around before dipping its pointed beak into the water between the waterlily pads and bring out a large, orange fish. With a jolt of its long neck it threw the prey from beak to throat.

Neither David nor Dot spoke. They were taken by both the elegance and the savagery that they were witnessing. The bird stood on one leg, shaking its slender neck to move the tasty prey down its gullet. There was no need to be coy with David, thought Dot, when they both found this to be as marvellous and as ghastly as the other "*Carpe carpem*," expounded David as they watched the long legs of the bird pick up from the ground in front of them and fly over the autumn colours of the trees beyond the gardens.

Chapter Three

MAISIE AND THE MAN DOLL

Daily update meetings for all Seniors were held in Pauline Graves' office. Even on her days off they continued there without her as though she were omnipresent. Wednesdays were the allotted time for Brad Fletchley, Gramwell Care Manager, his Seniors and as many of the Carers on rota who could be spared from the floor for the weekly Carers' roundup. Brad had held this post at Gramwell since its inception, "B.R."(before residents), so in many ways was more senior than his boss, Pauline, who had come from a hotel management background. He had helped her time and again to get to grips both with the rigours of care sector management and with Gramwell itself without being certain that his efforts were always appreciated. While she tended to pander to the demands of Head Office, he kept the residents' safe care firmly in his view.

The Carers trickled in to the Daffodil Lounge to take up the damask armchairs. Each was armed with a tablet that contained the electronic records of each of the residents who were notably missing from this meeting. Many of them had instead been dragooned into the seated exercise class that was held at this time each week in the café. Others were in their rooms, glued to the television or deep in thought, catching and letting go of ideas as they slowly filed past like dust motes in shafts of light. For those who kept their doors open during waking hours, there was a constant passing parade of staff, visitors and residents up and down the corridor to interrupt their trains of thought and remind them that life was busy.

Brendon Longacre was the first to join Brad in the room. Brad took advantage of their time together to have a quick word about the team performance appraisals that were falling due. Both men were exact in their time keeping. Brendon, some six years younger than his supervisor, was quick to identify Brad as his role model: he truly wished that, by the time he was thirty-eight, he too would have the seniority and competence that Brad so easily displayed, if not the good looks. However, Brad would never have the thick, blond curls that brought Brendon so much attention since his own hair was already greying and very much thinner on top than it had been when he first came to Gramwell those four long years ago.

None of the residents had been here longer than Brad. They saw him both as a piece of the furniture but also as a steady, reliable and empathetic professional. Because Brendon was just as likely to trot Brenda out, especially when they were having a social in the café, they took him less seriously and this was something Brad meant to bring up with Brendon in their next review of his performance. What he hadn't yet worked out was that he needed to keep Brenda as entertainment rarely and only for his colleagues so as to shore up the impression held by residents, families, staff and Head Office. But that didn't mean that he wasn't just as strong and steady as Brad. And Brendon hoped in his heart of hearts that, one day, they might be strong and steady together, perhaps with a house, a dog and a couple of kids.

Nurse Bessie Roberts, the part-time Assistant Care Manager, was the next to join them. Bessie's mid-life mid-waist expansion put paid to Brendon's reverie the minute she pushed into the room. He knew that Bessie and Brad got on well together because of their shared nursing backgrounds but only professionally. In all other regards Bessie, bosomy, loud and touchy-feely, was the antithesis of attractive in Brad's view. He could always hear her coming along the corridor before she'd arrived because of the rasping noise her stockings made as her thighs rubbed together.

Morning Chaps!" hailed Bessie. "How's it hanging?"

Brendon's stomach flipped, reminding him in the process that he had skipped breakfast because it had taken so long to convince Harold Sherry in Tulip 18 to swallow more than a couple of teaspoonfuls of porridge with his morning tablets. It was important to try to encourage Harry to eat. His weight was tracking down. Questions would be asked.

"Kind of you to join us, Bessie," Brad observed. Now, if Brendon had said that, it would have been regarded as a sarcastic comment but somehow Brad could be charming when he was also being cutting. But only he and Brendon would know his real meaning.

Bessie plopped down on the large red sofa beside the enormous television that dominated that end of the residents' large sitting room. "We'll have to think of something to talk about if no one else shows. Or someone?" she suggested with a guttural laugh.

Neither Brad nor Brendon was biting at this obvious reference to Barbara Fenway who, it had been established yesterday, had had some kind of drama coming to work and had not spoken to anyone since. This had led to speculation that she had something to hide. Since yesterday, forays into the admin office to see her about rotas or petty cash had resulted in her picking up the phone and, with her back to them, waving the interuptee away.

"Downright rude – as usual," added Bessie, annoyed that she was not going to be able to have a little gossip. Looking at the raised eyebrows of her colleagues she hastened to add, "No, not you. Her." She then realised that she had best leave it at that. She plopped one of the many cushions on the sofa onto her adequate lap to form a portable desk for her tablet. Edging back into the deep seat, her lace-up shoes swung at the end of short legs that could no longer reach the bright red and blue patterned carpet.

Marigold Pratt and Phoenix Kennedy, both twenty-four, both with long brown hair tied up in identical topknots, came through the door, bumping each other and laughing as they moved to the blue sofa across from Brad and Brendon.

"Glad to see someone's got the happies today," noted Brendon.

"Hi ya," Marigold spoke to everyone and no one. "Alright?" she asked. Both girls were glad to have a chance to sit down. They'd been on since seven, stood through a handover meeting with the night team and been on their feet ever since delivering breakfast trays, trying to coax still sleepy old-timers from their cosy beds and seeing them to the toilet, whether or not it was too late. The meeting was a relief, a chance to take the weight off their feet but, as they'd been saying to each other, "pretty much as boring as batshit" to go through the list of residents and their current situation because nothing much changed what they actually had to do, day in and day out.

"OK," led Brad. "Are we expecting anyone else this morning?"

"Darragh's bathing Millie but he said he'd be here when he can," chipped in Phoenix as she unwrapped a peppermint.

"Only if you've got one for the rest of the class!" chastised Brendon with no effect.

Stan and Malgosia were next into the room. Although working with different communities and Stan having worked the night shift, which was a deliberate rostering decision requested by Brad to Bessie, they still had a knack of finding their shifts and their breaks match up so as to be found more often together than apart.

"Stan, Gosia," Brendon nodded at their attendance and made a note on his tablet. "I guess we can start. Darragh can pick up from the rest what he's missed when he gets here. And I'll write up the outcome of our session today on the system calendar so you can check back on decisions made. OK? Let's begin."

The format of the meetings had been changed some time ago. Before Gramwell Glade had filled up, each of the residents was discussed in detail at the Wednesday meetings. As numbers grew, they decided to work on only those who showed presenting issues and leave the rest, otherwise they would have filled half a day. The nursing team upstairs, on the other hand, were required to review each and every resident on a weekly basis at a minimum and more frequently for those who were closer to the end.

Stan was the first to pipe up. "Hilda has been walking at night and trying to sleep in the day. I don't like to see her so tired in the day but I can't stop her walking at night. That wouldn't be right. What do you want me to do?" His genuine concern for Hilda Matters from Daffodil 4 was palpable: the hindrance of his having to use a second language made it sound as though he found the situation tiresome. Gosia had picked up on this, coming to his defence. "Stan really cares about Hilda. He tries too hard to keep her awake in the day."

"We know, Malgosia. We all love Hilda. You're doing a good job, Stan. Maybe try to take her for a walk in the garden some mornings? The oxygen might wake her up. If we all make an extra effort to speak with her when we go by, just have a little chat, we might be able to do something about her body clock, but we all know that eventually there won't be a 'clock' to keep her ticking. She won't know the difference between night and day and then we will have to talk about moving her upstairs."

Brad had pronounced what they all expected. It wouldn't be long before Hilda Matters had to be moved to Tulip or Rose Community. Besides, this always created a vacancy in the downstairs community and Amity always had families waiting in the wings to bring their loved ones to Gramwell Glade. This was the lifeblood of Empire Homes and they all had to keep in mind who paid their wages.

"I'm having a family meeting next week," Brad concluded. "Family Matters," he chuckled over the pun, allowing only a second of frivolity before getting back to the plan. "I will have a discussion with her daughter about the options and I will let you know." He quickly made notes on the tablet before raising his head with the invitation for another topic of discussion. The team was well aware of Brad's signals and requirements. He had cemented his leadership role over time with the backing of Head Office. No one was in any doubt.

"Barney Perry, Daffodil 6," noted Brendon. "He seems to be having a lot of trouble concentrating. He's been reading the same book for about four weeks. When I asked him if he'd like me to find something more interesting for him, he snapped. His vital signs are all in order. I really don't know what to do with him."

"He is cross nearly every day," confirmed Marigold under her breath, shuffling down into the plump cushions of the sofa.

"Barney had his ninety-first birthday last week, didn't he?" Brad observed. "I imagine he has every right to be as grumpy as he wants to be but I've been wondering, when did he last have his eyes tested?" He swiped the tablet to look into the resident record section. "Two years ago!" he gasped. "How did we overlook this?" His intention was not to be as inclusive as his question might have indicated. Brendon knew that this was something that he should have had in mind.

"Right. This is blindingly obvious. We'll see to that this week," Brendon's voice was stern as he made notes on his tablet. Barney's eyes had to be tested immediately. They would get the spectacle people in.

"I think that, if I couldn't see or see to read. I'd be really grumpy too." Brad gave meaning to the blindingly obvious.

Bessie made her first observations of the meeting, having calmed down about her colleagues' downright refusal to gossip about Barbara Fenway. "Maisie has been crying a lot, particularly at bedtime and when she wakes through the night which is becoming more frequent. She's just not used to sleeping alone."

"Well they all sleep alone." Stan was puzzled as to why this would be raised as an issue. Each room in Gramwell was generously fitted with a wheelchair-accessible, en-suite bathroom and a small sitting area but was dominated by the ergonomically-approved, electric single bed that allowed the staff to raise prone residents up and down or sit them up as required.

"Let's not forget that Maisie's only been with us since the beginning of this year, since she was widowed in January. Think about it. Maisie's not used to sleeping alone," explained Brad. "That's a lot to get used to."

Brendon picked up on this plaintive observation, aware that Brad had been in a long-term relationship until last year when his overwhelming commitment to his work had, in turn, overwhelmed his partner. Their social life had dwindled and, with it, any excitement they had once shared. Brendon knew that Brad was speaking from experience, one that he dearly wished he might change.

"So what can we do about it?" Stan asked the group rhetorically. "We go in to see her through the night if she gets out of bed. I know a few of us have sat with her until she goes to sleep. And she likes to have the TV on while she sleeps. I suppose she thinks that's some company? We do try. Poor Maisie."

The pocket in Malgosia's tabard began to move as though she had hidden a small pet in it. She tried to pretend that she hadn't brought her mobile phone into the meeting which, even though it was only on 'vibrate', was a no-no. Brad's face registered his disapproval. He had a silent debate with himself as Phoenix and Marigold giggled at Gosia's moving lap. Staff were not allowed to have their mobile phones with them while they were working. Technically, Malgosia had finished her morning shift and had stayed on to contribute to this clinical meeting so he decided in a flash to let this go since most of the gathering was now aware of the indiscretion.

"I have a few ideas." Brad seemed inspired as he changed the subject in his own mind. "There's a family meeting next week. Bessie, Pauline and I will speak with her son- and daughter-in-law and see if there's anything else we can do. We must realise that it takes a good year for residents to settle in, especially those who have lost loved ones. There's that saying, you know, that you have to pass a whole year, to see out all the anniversaries, birthdays and Christmas before you settle into a new pattern of relationships after losing someone you love."

And I'll try to make that as painless as possible for you, Brad, committed Brendon silently.

Darragh had only just come in to the Daffodil Lounge to join the meeting when Brad pronounced it over and done with. He thanked all in attendance. The action items for each case discussed were already noted on their own electronic records, thanks to the new system. In the 'old days', last year, the minutes of the meeting had to be taken, typed up, distributed and then actioned. They were lucky to have tackled half the actions needed by the time the next weekly meeting came around and, if there had been any hitch in the process, it was a matter of repeating the chain of events all over again. Brad and Brendon exchanged smiles of congratulation on having seen the meeting over and done with in under forty minutes with all their staff knowing exactly what was required of them, at least for the next day or two.

They headed down the corridor together towards the central reception lobby. A tide of noise was flooding from Ye Olde Tea Shoppe which had been set up by Brian Petty and Naomi Page with a semi-circle of chairs. The circle was completed when Brian with the help of Veronica (Ronnie) Chan had brought a few more residents in their wheelchairs to join the morning's Armchair Aerobics class, better known to all as *AA*. The puns were never ceasing when it came to who needed *AA*. Some of the ladies – it had started with Elizabeth Hollick when her hearing aid had been playing up – called it *Hey, Hey*.

Towards the end of each session, the volume was increased so that the old tunes, always played in the same order on the one and only *AA* tape that Naomi had ever recorded, became ever more raucous. Tayla, and the other receptionists, loathed *AA* because the noise meant that they couldn't hear what was said on the front desk phone while 'The Music Man' and 'Ten Green Bottles' belted out. Sometimes they could barely hear that the phone was ringing at all and this caused no end of problems for them if they missed a call.

Dot Baker and Mildred Absolom waved their pink pom-poms in time to the music. Naomi was in the centre of the ring demonstrating higher pom-pom shaking and wider leg kicks than her charges could manage but the rush of blood to their extremities that *AA* afforded filled them with the sort of excitement that was otherwise fairly elusive in a day when other activities on offer – jigsaws, knitting, bingo and card games – were far more sedentary and sedate affairs.

Andrea Wallace headed out from Daffodil Community holding hands with her young grandson Archie who was overheard in his accusation: "Those nurse people just lied, Gran."

"Can you use your *indoors* voice please Archie? What do you mean that they just…?"

"They all said that your Mum is looking well today but she looks like the horriblist, oldest person in the world."

Andrea tried to hurry along the corridor in order to sign out and leave the building before anyone else heard Archie's current theories. "She *is* Gran. Her hair is see-through like spiders' webs and her skin is more wrinkled than them dogs. What are they called again?"

"'Those', Archie, not 'them dogs'."

"Well them elephants then. Her skin looks like them elephants."

Tayla had cottoned on to the conversation by the time that Andrea and Archie had reached the desk to sign out in the Visitors' Book. She shot a smile to Andrea as she threw in: "Out of the mouths of babes, then?"

Andrea returned a wan smile before reaching again for Archie's hand when she'd signed out. "My skin will look like that one day, Archie. You'll still love me though, won't you, like I love my Mum?"

"Maybe," Archie conceded. "As long as I don't have to touch you."

"That's not very kind," Andrea feigned hurt.

"But you didn't want me to lie to you, did you?" Archie asked as they left the building.

Brad headed into Pauline's office to brief her on the outcomes of the Seniors' meeting while Brendon headed in to the *AA* circle with Naomi to dance it up for the benefit of the residents. They always enjoyed a Brendon floorshow and he couldn't help himself. Immediately he was twirling in the centre, silver pom-poms seemingly flying through the air. He ducked down beside Barney Perry's wheelchair and in a loud stage-whisper told him and, in high volume, the rest of the group, that he was going to be on *Strictly* one of these years.

The finale of each *AA* session, the loudest recording of the lot, was a Mexican tune with a lot of "*Aye Aye Ya Yai*" in it. Residents had been encouraged to add their voices to the chorus which they did with gusto. The screaming crescendo came with a closing of the door to Pauline's office and Tayla rubbing her temples in an effort to get rid of the crashing headache that had built with every song over the past hour. "*Suco, Suco, I don't care*!" she belted out before picking up the phone for the umpteenth time that morning.

By Thursday, Barbara Fenway was ready to release her frustrations on someone. It happened on that day when her favourite receptionist, Donna Herbert, was on for the morning session to assist her with some of the backlog of admin. Head Office had issued a memo to all Empire Homes to augment the electronic records with all the staff training details. When she'd first read this she'd screamed at her computer screen, causing a walk-out by Amity Leighton who had more than once complained to Pauline about Barbara's hysteria and use of profanity in the office which she claimed was "totally inappropriate when I am on the phone talking to our clients." Pauline had put the issue of perhaps relocating one or both of those volatile women on the back-burner, mostly because there was little alternative space to offer a suitable solution but also because she felt that they really should try to sort it out between themselves.

Amity had left the building later that morning glammed up to the nines. She said that she was going to a lunch meeting with some local conveyancing solicitors who were going to be useful contacts since they met frequently with people who were selling property on behalf of elderly parents so could easily offer up 'warm' referrals to Gramwell.

Barbara had begun to explain the new requirements to Donna who'd taken up Amity's desk for convenience in her absence. The two had developed something of a friendship over the four years they had been at Gramwell together. Barbara had come from another Empire home in Newcastle and before that from a hotel somewhere in the centre of London. Donna lived locally and had worked in a call centre before giving up work to care for her babies. Even though she'd only been back in the workforce for four years, she was worth as much to Barbara as the three other receptionists put together because she was good with computer systems. It was as though they came naturally to her. Many had been the times when they'd sorted problems out together with Donna often leading Barbara through the mazes of statutorily required record-keeping or Head Office spreadsheets. They looked together at this morning's Head Office email for any key that might unlock the puzzle. In fact they knew on this occasion just how to enter the required records but the real issue was their incredulity at how long it was going to take to get the records that already sat on handwritten files into the system. That amount of data entry was going to take weeks.

"Why do they bloody expect that we can do this and keep all the other things going at the same time?" Barbara, her head in her hands, asked Donna. "Would they like us to stop work on the time sheets and have the staff go without pay while we focus on this shit?"

Donna knew that other Empire homes would be dealing with this task by requiring all the reception team to take on the data entry, to make it an urgent ongoing task to be spread among the four of them. She also knew that Barbara seldom delegated. When she did, it was only to Donna and, in many ways, this suited Donna perfectly. Her boys – Sam, now sixteen and James, eighteen – were becoming more rather than less expensive as they got older. She could always do with the overtime as long as it didn't clash with Sam's transport needs or James' uni holidays when she wanted to spend as much time with him as she could. She missed him while he was away in Bristol.

Barbara's head hadn't left her hands. As Donna looked up she realised that Barbara was now crying. She knew that she was the only person, at work at least, who Barbara would ever risk seeing her in tears.

Donna got up from the desk she'd commandeered and went to put an arm around Barbara's hunched shoulders. The spasms of sobbing were palpable but she knew from past experience that she had to wait until Barbara was ready to open up.

The office door opened. Donna moved to block the interloper's view of Barbara's demise and turned to smile.

Phoenix, ready to leave for the day, had reinserted her nose-ring. Like a bull at a gate, she blurted out, "Have you found me a new tabard, Barbara?"

"We're working on a difficult calculation on the system," Donna scuttled for a reason to get rid of Phoenix. "Can you come back after your shift tomorrow and we will look one out for you in the meantime?" she added.

"Righto," burbled Phoenix, pleased to be leaving off work and to have faced Barbara who could be so difficult about uniforms since she was always stuck in her computer and acted as if she was being put upon if asked about other tasks that were her responsibility. At least she could tell blinking Brendon that she'd been to the office about it if he tried to attack her again tomorrow for having a ripped pocket in the gold-edged burgundy tabard that was worn as uniform by all Gramwell staff other than the managers.

"I'm sorry," Barbara said to her handbag as she fished out a tissue to blow her nose loudly.

"No need to be sorry," Donna soothed. She was rather hoping that this issue, whatever it might be, would be left at this denouement because she was keen to get on with the task they'd been assigned. There'd been talk in the staff room about Barbara and that it looked like something major had gone wrong this week but no one really knew what it was, only to say that she was in perhaps the most foul mood they'd ever seen – and that was saying something.

"I've run out of fricking tissues," Barbara gulped, withdrawing her hand from her upturned bag, before she shot from her chair in the direction of the office door which she ripped open at speed, immediately crashing in to David Jack who had been taking a slow stroll down the corridor. His head had apparently been in the clouds and now he was obviously shocked from his reverie. Barbara patted his arm mechanically as she headed for the Guest Toilet nearby.

Donna followed in her footsteps just to see that David was not too shaken or stirred by the collision. He patted Donna's hand reassuringly and continued at a brisker pace back to his own, safer territory.

Maureen and Don Dunstable had signed in the Guest Book which was kept on a hall table across the lobby from the receptionist's desk. They knew the drill by heart and had performed the task many times, signing their names, time of arrival and registration number of their car lest it had blocked another in the limited spaces of the guest car park. Donna was still dealing with Barbara's drama in the Office and so there was no one at the Reception desk to greet visitors for the time being. Don and Maureen could go no further on this occasion as it happened because they didn't know exactly where they were supposed to meet Pauline Graves, Brad Fletchley and Bessie Roberts to have this specially-called meeting to discuss Don's mother's recent issues. In fact, they weren't even sure what 'issues' these were since she seldom had much to say when they came to see her. Maureen was certain that she'd ordered sufficient nappy pants for this month and was always really mindful to make sure there was soap, denture cleaner, her Lily of the Valley talc and Fox's Glacier Fruits in the drawers of her sitting and bathroom cupboards. They had to hope that there were no sinister developments to be announced. Maureen was keen to get back to her workshop as there was an order that really should have been sent off yesterday to a client in Birmingham but she'd been short of staff over the last two weeks and was running behind.

Brad came conga-ing up the corridor from Daffodil Community towards the lobby with Bessie in tow.

"Good morning Don, Maureen," he nodded with his best friendly smile as was his usual and most professional greeting, shaking off all traces of his playful self. He was nothing if not self-aware as he turned past them in the direction of Pauline's office, one hand behind his back in semi-subservience. "I'll just check that Pauline's ready to see us now," he explained and sallied away from them in the opposite direction, leaving the Dunstables still standing beside the Guests' Sign-In book wondering what was to come.

Bessie followed Brad into Pauline's office where they both briefed her about this morning's meeting in double-quick time to bring her up to date. Pauline had so many things to think about, so it always paid to bring her up to speed.

"OK. I'll kick off," Pauline decided, "and then I'll hand over to you Brad – for your clinical concerns."

"Of course," he assured, "and Bessie, I'll bring you in to give some personal experience of your work with Maisie."

They were all in agreement as Brad sprang to the doorway. He ushered the Dunstables into the General Manager's office where greetings and handshakes were exchanged again. It was then indicated, by a smile and a sweep of Brad's right arm, that the Dunstables were welcome to take their places on the pink stuffed sofa that Pauline had chosen for her office when she moved in almost a year ago. Pauline remained in her office chair, while Brad and Bessie took their places in order on the office chairs that surrounded the large desk.

"I suppose you're wondering why we asked you to come to a meeting with us today?" Pauline looked from Don to Maureen who both nodded in agreement, none the wiser at this point. "It's, of course, because Maisie is one of our most special residents and lately, well, Brad and Bessie have been somewhat concerned about Maisie and, specifically, the amount of time she spends awake now at night and, frankly, what that might mean in terms of her prognosis."

Brad immediately sought to hose this down. Pauline had gone in too heavily and too quickly for his liking. The results of having done so had landed like a blow to Don. Maureen kept a straighter face.

"Maisie has been quite tearful of late," he oozed with empathetic care, "and we really hate to see her upset. It mostly happens at night and so we wondered if you had even seen it and thought you ought to know so that we can find some solutions together if we knew what the problem really is." He encouraged their part in the problem-solving so that they didn't feel as though they had been sent to the headmistress's office. Pauline had the effect of projecting this, even though she didn't know it herself.

"No, we've seen Mum's been increasingly upset of late," chipped in Don, not wanting to look as though he had no knowledge of his mother, that he hadn't handed over all care and responsibility when he and Maureen had broken their promise and put her in a home soon after his father had died. There had been no option really when she was mourning, pining, but also failing to do all the things that he had been doing around the house, despite his increasing frailty. Her personal care, or lack of it, had given them all cause for concern.

"She does seem to be getting more upset. And tired. Maureen and I thought she would have been settled here by now. Instead, she seems to be getting more unsettled." The Team were well aware that the family's concern could and would be sheeted home to matters of their care for Maisie but were practised in diffusing such suggestions.

"And we wondered if it was that Harry Sherry next door to her. He shouts out a lot when he wants attention and she can't bear it when he's shouting," Maureen added.

The Gramwell staff realised that this was sounding more like a decision by the Dunstables to take Maisie away rather than their move to find some pacifying solutions to her distress. Brad gently eased his way in to cut that suggestion off at the pass.

"I think we've managed to explain to Harold that he can ring his call bell and that he'd been upsetting Maisie when he shouted. And he was horrified to think that he'd had that effect. He is a lovely gentleman. They both seem quite resolved to be very civil to one another these days."

Bessie agreed enthusiastically, for it was she who had spent a long time with Harry to explain the situation, to show him how to use the call bell and, with a greater degree of difficulty, to request the Carers to ensure that they responded *immediately* to Harry's bell so that he could see that this would in fact bring someone to his beck and call. In the same way, they began to ignore any lapses. When he shouted, no one came. Like the best Skinner experiments with pigeons or Pavlov with his dogs, Harold Sherry had learned that people came when he used the call bell and he liked it that way.

"I'd noticed that," Maureen agreed. To be agreeable was, she thought, going to be their best strategy even though she was still wary about what might be coming, what could warrant a special meeting, She really wanted to get back to the small premises she now rented on a Colchester industrial estate where her three staff members were putting the final touches to the bespoke soccer player dolls that had been expected in Birmingham two days ago.

"Well," Brad announced in a new phrasing that suggested he might now be coming to the point, "what we've noticed is that Maisie is still missing your father, Don, and most particularly in the middle of the night. Bessie has spent a lot of time with her and with the night team and it seems that this has been the root of all her upset of late."

"They were very close," Don lamented their separation keenly. "They'd been married since they were eighteen. He was eighty-seven when he died in January. They'd been married for sixty-nine years and not a night apart." Tears came to his eyes. Maureen reached for his hand. "And they always held hands in the night."

"They were totally devoted to one another," Maureen chipped in. "I suspect that she reaches for him in the night."

"And finds he's not there," Bessie chipped in empathetically. "That's exactly right. And then, instead of her being able to soothe herself back to sleep, she becomes more and more distressed because she can't find him. It's so sad and we're trying everything we can think of to help her get back to sleep."

"Not sleeping tablets, please?" Don interrupted. "Mum's never really taken anything more than an aspirin in her life and we don't want her to be drugged to sleep."

"Of course not! No." Brad insisted. "No, we're working really closely with her, aren't we, Bessie, to make sure we comfort her as best we can each time this happens."

"The trouble is," Bessie added shifting in her seat, "it's almost every night now and this makes her tired and upset in the day time too because she's just not getting the sleep she needs, which in turn leads to loss of appetite."

Maureen appreciated that the Nursing Manager had cut to the chase and, in a way, was relieved that it wasn't really something a lot worse. She'd often heard Maisie's laments when visiting so this was not really anything new or startling as might have been expected.

"I was wondering," Brad mused, "if she'd ever had a teddy bear or a doll as a child?" He looked around the room, realising that none of the present assembly would have any inkling of what eighty-eight-year-old Maisie had done as a child and, if he was suggesting that they give her a teddy bear, perhaps it was he who had lost his marbles?

"I think you might be on to something," piped up Pauline who had, until now, been silent, watching the dynamics, realising how well Brad and Bessie worked together and how tight Don and Maureen Dunstable were too. She was the odd man out, at a further distance from the situation and perhaps unlikely to be the one to have any solution to offer. "You make 'people dolls', don't you, Maureen? I recall your telling me about your growing business when we first met at the start of the year."

Maureen was always really happy to talk about her business which had done so well that it had moved from being something of a hobby set up in the spare room to now being a business with three staff members beside herself. "My business is called '*People Dolls*'. We craft realistic-looking portrait dolls from photos of people. We've done such a variety. I started off by doing some of my family as prototypes which I just gave away as presents but, from there, it's grown a lot. We're just finishing off an order of a soccer team that was ordered by their wives. I can show you the website with lots of examples of the dolls we've produced – politicians, other families, pop stars. Orders are coming in all the time."

Don smiled at Maureen's enthusiasm and the way she'd contributed so much to the family's coffers over the couple of years she'd been at her dolls. Truth be told, if it wasn't for Maureen's income that now exceeded his own, they wouldn't have been able to afford to put Maisie into Gramwell Glade.

"Did you ever do dolls of Don's parents?" Pauline continued on her line of thought.

"Yes, I did Grandpa and Granny D. They were some of the prototypes and they were a present for our daughter. Karen was always so close with her grandparents. She's working in New Zealand now and misses her Granny D so much."

"Would Karen let you have the Grandpa Doll back, do you think?" Brad and Bessie now saw where this was going and were both surprised that Pauline seemed to have come up with something that might ease the problem.

"Well, she's still in New Zealand but she's left all her stuff here. I'm sure she would let us have Grandpa D Doll if she knew it might help her Grandma."

"Shall we try?" Pauline looked at each of the faces in the room in turn.

"We have nothing to lose and everything to gain, I think," Bessie concurred.

"Absolutely! Let's give it a go!" chimed Brad.

Maureen and Don were delighted that the meeting had gone so smoothly but left with some questions in their hearts as to whether this was going to solve Maisie's apparently enduring and deep grief. She had laughed along with her husband John when the dolls were first shown to them by Karen. It was rather silly, they thought, to have dolls that were made to look like them but there was no doubt that Maureen had done a great job because there was no one who saw them who was left in any doubt that these twelve-inch rag dolls, worked in intricate detail, looked exactly the way even they saw themselves.

On their way back to the workshop, Maureen suggested to Don that she produce new dolls, based on the originals so that she could use some of the machined refinements that had since been developed by her company. That way, Maisie might think that it was something new, something for her, in case she recognised Karen's old rag doll – "And then Karen would still have her dolls, perhaps to pass on to her own children one day?"

Some days later the Birmingham soccer wives cooed over the shipment of their team of dolls and Maisie was proudly introducing everyone she bumped into to her 'husband'.

"I'm almost tempted to take a photo of her in her sleep. She sleeps with a smile on her face now with the doll tucked beside her on the pillow," Bessie told the clinical meeting the following Wednesday.

"Don't you dare!" ordered Brad. "But I must admit, it's a triumph. Aren't we clever?" he asked the team.

Chapter Four

LOVE

On first sight of the doll that had been presented to her, Maisie's face had lit up. "John!" she called out in amazement, as though her beloved husband had been returned to her. *People Dolls* now sourced human hair that was planted in place with precision, down to the eyebrows and lashes. His clothes, in miniature, were John to a 'tee'. Maisie had reached out, grasped him and hugged him to her the way a four-year-old might have greeted a dolly on Christmas morning. She made a low humming noise while she rocked him and herself slightly in the electric recliner chair in Tulip 1.

Don had been convinced by Amity Leighton, when they were making arrangements for Maisie to move in, that many of the residents felt especially comforted if they could have their own chair in their room to remind them of the comfort and familiarity of home. He and his son Richard had no end of problems getting the thing in. It was incredibly heavy despite coming apart in two halves. Even then it had been difficult to get the heavy base section through the door of Tulip 2. He'd wondered from time to time since if it had been a good idea after all because it had actually been his Dad's chair. He wondered if it still smelt a bit of his Dad. Not in a bad way, but perhaps to make a subliminal suggestion that he was still about.

Maisie had never stopped talking to her late husband John. These days she talked to the doll and took him everywhere with her. 'Everywhere' was turning out to be just that, Don and Maureen had noticed. Maisie had not looked back since the day Maureen placed the doll in her arms. She was now to be found at the *AA* exercises and had even joined the knitting group. The managers were having thoughts of placing her in Daffodil Community when the next vacancy came up. No longer waking and walking at night but peacefully cuddled up with her doll on the pillow next to her, Maisie's body clock was keeping impeccable time. Really, she didn't need to be in the secure community any longer. On the quiet, she had been encouraged to come into Daffodil on most days where she could take advantage of all the activities on offer and make friends with some of the others who were more sociable.

A wonderful change was evident for Maisie. Her eyes were sparkling, She was in love with life all over again.

"Have you met my husband?" she would boldly ask anyone who would listen. All the receptionists had been asked many times but were generous in making a full examination of him. They were also curious and half in love with him themselves. A few commissions had come forward from the staff to Maureen for creations for special presents. Amity Leighton was the first to have ordered a cuddly likeness of her Giles as a present for his upcoming fiftieth birthday. It would be something that was a delight among his friends at the lavish party she was planning for him at Haddington Hall but, then again, would be most unlikely to cross the doors of his legal practice in Colchester.

"Oh he's divine, Maisie," Alex Durwyn cooed as she traced the tiny buttons on his tweed waistcoat. Alex was the last of the receptionists to have seen the doll although, by now, she'd heard about him from Tayla and Donna. Even Barbara had mentioned him on one of the few days that she'd joined in a conversation by noting that perhaps every husband would be more attractive as a proper *People Doll* than a 'proper wally'.

"He's my John." Maisie retrieved her 'husband' and ventured with her walker down to the Daffodil Lounge to see what was happening today. As it was, she found the doors closed. Through the glass she saw that Brad and some of the carers were meeting in there. The residents had commented that they were pleased that Brad and Bessie and the others got to rest in the lounge sometimes. "Wasn't that a good idea?" they'd agreed and thought too that sometimes they were "working too hard". They "might just need a nice rest".

Maisie sat on one of the designer chairs in a niche in the hallway: she was brought into sharp focus by a bright shaft of sunlight as she contemplating how pleasant it was to be here. She told John that it was good that they'd moved here. "The food's good, isn't it? And now you don't have to mow the lawn and dig the garden. We'll be better off here. And Don visits more often too, have you noticed?" she laughed. "But I haven't seen Karen for a while. Have you?"

Just on the other side of the door to the Daffodil Lounge Maisie was unable to hear the discussion underway about the flipside of having John living with them.

"It was such a brilliant idea," Bessie sighed. "No one could disagree that it's transformed Maisie but look at the problem it's caused. Mildred Absolom practically ran Maisie over the other day to get hold of the doll. And Elsie keeps asking if she can have a doll too. And then Maisie wasn't too keen on hearing her call John a *doll*!"

"Maybe we can put some brochures of Maureen Dunstable's business on the Guest sign-in desk?" suggested Marigold.

"I guess that wouldn't hurt. We allow other people to put down fliers and the like. It wouldn't be a conflict of interest, would it?" Brad asked in Pauline's direction.

"Not at all," she replied, still pleased with her ownership of the strategy that had solved a big problem, even if it had created some spin-off issues. "Really, we could think about encouraging other families to invest in a *People Doll* as a therapeutic tool. Brad, can you mention it as a case study the next time we have a Families' Meeting? Let them know how it worked for Maisie and suggest that it might be a lovely thing for some of the others to have."

Brad made a note on his tablet. "Will do," he said without looking up. Pacifying the unsettled was his stock in trade. If *People Dolls* were to be another weapon in his artillery, bring it on, he thought.

The team left the room as *AA* was belting out old favourites in Ye Olde Tea Shoppe. Pauline had it in mind to finally tackle Barbara as to why she was slipping so badly in her punctuality and with the payroll errors that Head Office had brought to her attention this month. As they passed by on the way to their respective work stations, they saw Maisie in the group, her hands vigorously shaking yellow pom poms with John sitting on her lap, bouncing with every shimmy-shake.

The harvest moon that Wednesday had been spotted by so many of those warmly tucked away at Gramwell Glade as it punched over the eastern horizon to fill the end window of the Daffodil Lounge where, fortunately, someone had forgotten to close the curtains that evening. On Thursday morning there had been discussions amongst those who had seen and remembered a harvest moon as a startling sight. A gaggle of residents was shuffling in the lobby, chatting with Tayla at Reception whilst awaiting the arrival of the Empire Bus. All swaddled in overcoats, hats, scarves and gloves in the full twenty degrees of central heating, each minute of the wait led to increasing numbers of them heading back to find seating in Ye Olde Coffee Shoppe, whereupon they had forgotten why they were there.

Since staff had been trained never to refuse any reasonable request, when Joan Fairs and Molly Tipple started to play with the coffee machine as though it were a free slot machine, they were not to be deflected from their game. Residents and their guests were always delighted that the machine would give out swish-looking drinks without the requirement to put in any money. The sucking and gurgling noise of the coffee machine reminded some of the group that this was the usual reason that they came to the café so the prospect of an excursion was immediately put out of mind. Having given up on waiting for the bus, attention was now focused on forming a queue behind the giggling Joan and Molly as coffee wafts enticed.

"Ladies! Ladies!" belted Brendon from the doorway. "No time for coffee here! Don't forget that you're waiting for the bus and we're all going to head out for a wonderful walk on the Prom at Senerwell on Sea. We'll have a drink there." Already he and the other staff members Stan, Darragh and Marigold, together with Nurse Nwaoma Katsina who had been rostered to take the crew for the outing that morning, were planning how they would manage toilet stops or the discomfort that might entail if few or no public loos were to be found and someone was *caught short*, even for those of their charge who were wearing protective underwear.

Elsie was certain that no one had seen her lift the glass lid of the cake stand, whip out a flapjack, wrap it quickly in her embroidered hanky and secrete it in her handbag.

A cheer from some of their company who had dutifully remained in the lobby together with staccato reversing beeps heralded the arrival of the Empire bus and its driver Mobo Tarfa. Mobo was among many Nigerians who were employed by Empire throughout their homes since the Managing Director and owner of the company, Akin Akindele, looked to support his parents' countrymen.

Nwaoma had come to the UK with her family as a four-year-old from Nigeria. Her Essex accent was authentic but went little way to convince some of the residents that she was a fellow countrywoman. She was a much loved and well-respected nursing sister who worked mostly upstairs on Rose Community but was always keen to schedule a morning at the seaside when Mobo's bus was on duty at Gramwell. Brendon encouraged her to come along so that there were nurses of both genders in case there were those bathroom dramas or worse to be dealt with while they were out. Carers were capable, dealing first-hand with any and every eventuality, but they always deferred to trained nursing staff, particularly in cases of emergency.

The automatic doors opened for Nwaoma, her great coat flapping out behind her as she went to greet Mobo. He had reversed the bus from the circular drive right up to the front door in the castle wall so as to make things as easy as possible for those who were walking with frames or sticks as well as to align the bus's rear wheelchair access door for the ease of the carers who needed to organise Barney Perry, Marjorie Simmonds and Albert Watts in their wheelchairs on this occasion. Mobo was always astounded to see the folly castle wall at the end of the Gramwell driveway. All the other Empire homes were purpose-built, modern structures which he regarded as more *run of the mill*. This one was a corker. He stood back in the morning sunshine to admire it again as the sun bounced off the stonework, and he grinned as he saw Nwaoma approach for a collegial hug.

"The Lady of the Castle Oma, in'it?" he greeted.

"Yeah, can you imagine?" she asked. "A Nigerian Lady in a Castle. That'd be a first! Are you alright?" she gave him a big hug, reaching up to his broad shoulders as he twirled her in a semi-circle. She was only a little embarrassed. *When you spend your working life holding and lifting up others, it's nice to be made to feel that someone might do the same for you,* she thought.

"Always alright, babe. Good to see you. How many have we got today?"

"I think it'll be about twelve. Brendon's got the list. Three wheelchairs."

"Cool. A piece of cake," he replied.

Elsie held on to her handbag tightly as Mobo removed his hat with a flourish, liberating what seemed to be hundreds of tiny plaits. He took Elsie's tiny, manicured hand and walking stick to help her gently onto the bus. She was never dressed without a winning smile. "No, I haven't got a piece of cake!" she offered by way of defence and pleased that, technically, the secreted flapjack could not be categorised as cake, so, in effect, she hadn't told a fib.

Just as in her childhood, Elsie always loved being the first on the school bus. She used to head for the back in those days, but no longer. The back of the Empire bus was reserved for wheelchairs. These days the best idea was to sit right behind Mobo where she could join in with his singing and chat.

"Ah, the lovely Elsie!" he flattered, helping her to her usual seat. "My favourite girl." Elsie's smile beamed as she settled herself into the seat behind the grab rail, shuffling her bottom as she moved across to the window seat.

The main phone in Reception rang constantly during the loading operation. Tayla was trying to maintain the required smile and answer each call within three rings as she dealt with the conversations and questions at the desk while she'd been surrounded by the increasingly excited crowd. Noise volumes had increased significantly just as they do among schoolchildren embarking on an excursion to mark a release from the daily grind. Tayla wished for an end to the babble and perhaps a rare break so she could catch up with herself.

Brendon held Barney's chair back at the entrance to the café from where he directed traffic, acknowledging each resident as he managed the two-by-two embarkation of Joan and Mollie with their walking frames, Grace Garrett with hers, then those others with canes – Hilda, Elizabeth and the Storricks – before the progressing, one by one, of Barney, Marjorie and Albert who were raised in their wheelchairs by the hydraulic platform into the back of the bus. The whole exercise took about twenty minutes but, just as Brendon was about to get on board he saw that Joan was shuffling her walker down the aisle towards him and with little success as the contraption was bashing into the back of each seat consecutively.

"You're not leaving us already, are you, darling?" he quizzed.

"Just a quick visit to the *little girls' room*," Joan giggled apologetically into her red tartan scarf.

Brendon helped Joan straighten the walker so that it didn't bump into every bag, seat and knee it encountered. "Off you go then, sweetie." Standing on the driveway below holding her walker with a deep sigh, he held her hand as she negotiated the steps from the bus and pushed her walker through the automatic doors in the direction of the Guest Toilet in the lobby.

This lavatory had been opulently decorated to resemble a ritzy hotel powder room. It was Joan's favourite room in all of Gramwell Glade and she made a point of leaving her own suite to make use of it at least once each day because it had terry towelling hand cloths to dry one's hands after using a luxurious hand-wash. There was even hand lotion to use afterwards. Joan regarded this facility both as luxurious and something she was entitled to and, since she hadn't visited it yet this morning, had decided that the time was now.

Some five minutes later, her lotioned hands slipping slightly on the handles of the walker, Joan had been escorted back on board and the bus moved slowly out of the circular driveway, turning left down the leaf-strewn lane to head for the sea.

When he had residents on board his bus for excursions, Mobo played a selection of tracks he'd carefully put together from the 'thirties and 'forties. No matter where he was in the country taking Empire residents on excursions, they all knew and loved the music he played and would invariably join in. Mobo was the one staffer who was known and universally enjoyed by Empire residents throughout the country, apart from Akin Akindele. Consequently he had won more than his fair share of Empire Employee of the Year awards, miniature silver trophies which were stuck on the dashboard of his bus with Blu Tack.

Barbara Fenway hunched over her computer. She was alone in the office since Amity was taking a couple through the home with a view to winning their custom when it came to choosing a nursing home for the husband's mother. *That was a doddle of a job*, Barbara thought, *which could be done by anyone*. It didn't help that she was aware of the salary that was attached since it was some twenty per cent higher than her own. To add insult to injury, Amity received a commission payment on each and every admission to Gramwell which meant every prospect was worth money to her even though it was Barbara who was responsible for the copious amounts of record-keeping that admitting a newcomer entailed. No wonder bloody Amity was so over the top with her schmoozing. The inequity of it ate at Barbara. As she saw it, basically, Amity was up for a commission each time a resident died at Gramwell and was a lesser being for being open to accepting a *death bonus*.

Barbara had been in since seven-thirty to make sure that the time sheets were entered into the system and would be at Head Office before close of business tomorrow. The never-ending list of time-constrained tasks that beset her were a constant source of anxiety but not the same as Amity's *key performance indicators,* which were marked by bonuses. There were no commissions for processing purchase orders, reconciling budgets, managing staff uniforms or trying to remember the ever-flexible lists of names of residents, not to mention their Powers of Attorney. This was a major issue for Barbara when it came to Performance Appraisals because, even though they all spent long days together under the same roof, Barbara seldom left her office and so, unlike most of the staff, wasn't terribly well known to those who made Gramwell their home – or to their families either.

Having checked off the last of the time sheets for Care staff, she started work on those of the Reception staff, her own team. Donna Herbert had worked almost double the hours she was contracted for because Barbara had needed her skills to enter all the data required on the new system. With far less of the responsibility she shouldered, Donna's remuneration this month was going to approach Barbara's own take-home pay. This too rankled with her, even though she was the one who needed Donna to do the work that she couldn't face. She couldn't exactly blame Donna. The fault lay with the clowns at London Head Office who had no idea of what was involved in the constant decrees they issued or even what it was like to be in a care home. She felt anger rising.

Tayla's timesheet was a complete mess. Days had been changed. There were arrows supposedly indicating how the changes were to be tracked. Crossings out in different-coloured pens had the page looking more like a child's painting than a time sheet. She lifted it from the corner of the desk as she swung out of her seat and grabbed the door, almost pulling it off its hinges.

The foyer was empty and quiet now that residents had left for their excursion. Barbara spun on her heel around the corner to the desk to find Tayla holding a small mirror, topping up her very pink lipstick. "Brian on today, is he?" came her barb. There was no disguising the fact that Tayla had taken her eye off the job so she fixedly held her determination, mirror and lipstick while she smiled at Barbara.

"Hi, Mrs Fenway. Got to keep up appearances," she encouraged with a mealy smile while knowing, in the pit of her stomach, that appearances, in most cases, could be deceiving.

"What the bloody hell do you call this?" Barbara bellowed as she slapped the decorated page on to the desk in front of the girl whose smile had quickly changed to a fearful subservience. Mrs Fenway's temper was legendary, especially in the mornings. There was speculation as to what might be the cause but it was perhaps best not to go there. The possibilities were ugly: the simple reality was that she was the boss and had to be pleased.

Tayla looked at the sheet. "That's my timesheet," she felt rather silly stating the obvious when she already suspected what the real issue might be. "Sorry for the crossings out." She confessed, shifting in her seat. "I had to move the days around because you changed things – you know, when Donna came in for the extra in the back office and you needed me at the front." She was pointing to the arrows and crossings out, feeling less sure now that Mrs Fenway would remember the rota changes that she herself had made because she actually seemed to forget a lot of things lately.

Barbara's voice reached a crescendo, filling the lobby. "Do you mean to tell me that you fill out the timesheet at the beginning of the week and then make changes later?" she boomed.

"Yes," replied Tayla sheepishly, looking up from her desk to meet Barbara's glowering eyes. "Isn't that right?"

"Does it look fricking right?" Barbara knew that she was betraying her position and herself.

Both women pulled up sharply as Pauline Graves intervened. She had been alerted by the shouting which, having reached her office, was obviously

way beyond The Pale. Barbara spun around and tried to change her gaze from furious to collegial. It didn't work and it didn't wash.

"Barb, can you come in here for a minute please?" Pauline commanded quietly. Suddenly things seemed grim to Tayla. She didn't know who to please, Mrs Graves or Mrs Fenway: she was obviously in a heap of trouble. She felt sick in her stomach and wanted to go quickly to the toilet but there was no one around to relieve her so she remained, wondering if this was the job for her after all. She put her head down and continued with her computer work on the hair salon appointments for next week, willing the knot in her stomach to loosen. Barbara ripped the timesheet from the Reception desk, spun on her heel and followed Pauline into the GM's office where she sank into the pink sofa opposite the large desk, her ankles flying upwards as she sank into the feather cushioning. Pauline went back to close the door behind them which was a known indicator that this was likely to be something of a significant meeting

"What's going on, Barbara?" she asked bluntly.

"Tayla's timesheet looks like it was done by a monkey with set of coloured pens." She held the page aloft but just as soon as the words had left her mouth, Barbara recognised that Pauline may not have seen this as the catastrophe that she'd labelled it so she went on to explain her own take on it. "I ask them to be neat so that I can read it and enter the information without having to go back to ask for a translation," she faltered.

"And is shouting going to achieve that?" Pauline reflected the obvious to her. "What if Amity's new family had been down here when you were attacking a staff member, *your own* staff member? What if some of the residents had been around? Do you think that this is the way?"

Before Pauline had finished her rhetoric, Barbara dissolved into shuddering tears.

"I'm sorry Pauline. I'm finding it hard to hold things together." She held both hands to her forehead. "It hasn't been affecting my work until now. I just lost it. It won't happen again, I promise." The tears fell from her chin to the scarf around her neck. Mascara streaking, she looked all but broken.

"What is the 'it' that *hasn't been affecting your work*, Barbara?"

Clouds drew stripes of dark grey across the sultry North Sea between silvery sunlit patches of aqua blue. The sun was strong today and the temperature, surprisingly, given that it was October, was in the high teens. Salt air rattled through the papery lungs of Gramwell's excursioners, reminding them of times gone by, away from the cosily-heated cocoon of their home. The air was so clear and fresh, they felt quite dizzy and a little dazzled, being members of a generation which seldom wears sunglasses, even in the height of summer. Wrinkles gave way to squinting as the assault of this clear, bright place both enveloped and invigorated them.

The male staff gallantly rallied to take responsibility for the wheelchairs, Mobo brought Barney, Marjorie and Albert down in turn on the hydraulic lift. Darragh took Marjorie, Brendon reinstated himself with Barney and Mobo then took the handles of Albert's chair to head up the pack after locking the bus. Ahead the line of the seafront pathway followed the line of beach huts, snaking between the flinted ochre of the beach and the greenery of the Victorian gardens.

Nwaoma, Phoenix and Malgosia organised Joan Fairs, Mollie Tipple and Grace Garrett with their walking frames on the flat pavement of the Prom. Hilda Matters, Elizabeth Hollick, Elsie and the Storrick went ahead with their walking sticks. Dot Baker and David Jack needed no assistance with walking so they trailed behind the Gramwell staff to complete the squadron.

"Did you have to walk in 'crocodiles' at school?" David asked Dot as he looked ahead, the sun triggering his eyes to blink.

"I was just thinking the same," she smiled at him. "You don't really see that these days, do you?"

"I'm not sure I've seen a school excursion for a long time," he reflected. "I didn't take my pupils on excursions because I was Mathematics, but there were visits to the art galleries in London when I lived there in the sixties. They generally seemed to go 'two by two' in a fashion and they were usually very noisy, I remember," he added with a smile. Dot had seldom seen David smile. He was a thinker, one of the most knowledgeable members of her Dining Room cohort and certainly the most engaging. His attention to grooming had attracted her from the moment she'd started her stay in Gramwell Glade. He appeared to be admired by all of the ladies there and thought of as something of a 'catch'.

The group ahead of them had become a blob as they stood to attention, hands to foreheads to shield the glare as they looked out to sea at an enormous container ship, bathed in silver light, heading up the coast.

"'Never smile at a crocodile', they say," Dot glanced at him, a shaft of sunshine causing her to wink which, being so out of character, then caused her to blush. " I wish I'd lived in London. I love it. Do you ever think of going to galleries anymore?"

"I suppose I haven't thought of doing that now I'm so *tucked in* at Gramwell," he mused.

He seemed so easy to talk to. "I'm sure we could think about excursions further afield. Maybe I could ask one of the carers to take us?"

"Or maybe think of going it alone?" David observed.

Dot wasn't sure whether he was suggesting that they make a day-trip together to London or whether he was letting her know that he would prefer to go by himself. By now they had caught up with the others who were in awe of the gargantuan ship.

"Breathe in deeply," Brendon urged the coterie around him. "That fabulous rarefied aroma of fish and chips!" he quipped. A gentle breeze was coming onshore from the south, blowing past the entertainments and cafes down near the pier. "The wonderful smell of the seaside. Makes you feel so hungry, doesn't it?"

"Stop it, Brendon!" Nywoma insisted. "We're not here for lunch. Don't be putting ideas into our heads. I hate that smell. It's not even a fish smell. It's the beef dripping they fry them in."

"Too right, Oma," chimed Mobo. "No taste to it. Nasty things, in'it? Soggy chips."

Brendon's face creased with distaste and he made a flurry of pushing Barney off in the opposite direction from the crowded pier along the Prom gardens of Senerwell so as not to lead them into temptation.

"I like watching those tugs," Barney muttered to Brendon behind him. "My father used to work on the tugs at Harwich. When I was a boy, that's where we lived. Hard work. In all weathers. Same today. They can't use machines for that work, can they? I used to love going down to the tugs with my father. They'd let me come aboard and sit in a little space in the wheel-house."

"Angels!" shouted Grace, piercing the air. "Look at the angels on the sea!" She pointed to the windmills on the horizon, lit up like translucent bodies pointing towards heaven.

Phoenix peered out to sea while holding Grace's arm. "What are you looking at?" she quizzed. "You must have really good eyesight, Grace. For a lady of ninety-three you are amazing." The sunlit windfarm gradually came into Phoenix' view. "So pretty. I can see them now."

"Angels," Grace repeated. "I love coming to the seaside. You never know what you might see."

"Hey Oma," called Mobo as he pushed Marjorie along. "I've got an angel here. Can you see angels on the sea?" Marjorie was gleefully taking the compliment: her mother used to call her 'Angel' sometimes when she was little. A warm feeling for the old house where she grew up mingled with the delight she felt today on the Prom.

Malgosia, walking between Hilda and Elizabeth, bumped into Nwaoma as she had slowed down to answer Mobo behind. "Oops, Nwaoma, sorry,

sorry," she insisted. "Why does he call you Oma? Isn't that the Dutch word for 'Grandma'? Are you a grandmother?"

"Give me a break!" Nwaoma choked. "I'm only twenty-seven! And I'm not Dutch! It's just short for Nwaoma, i'n'it?"

"I'm a grandma!" Mollie chimed in which encouraged a bolt of similar declarations from Marie and Joan.

Brendon, with Barney, had by now taken the lead, heading along the garden walk beside the sea at a slow and sensible pace so that the group could keep a semblance of togetherness while enjoying the sensations that the North Seascape offered up in the warmth and sunshine.

"I'm not going to lie, Barbara. Quite a few people have mentioned to me that you have been short with them. You seem to have buried yourself in your work and we haven't seen you smile for weeks. Perhaps more concerning is that Head Office have reported to me a number of payroll errors needed correction last week." Pauline paused the flow of accusations to allow Barbara a chance to open up but she remained in a slumped position, looking to the front of her boots which she had noticed were quite scuffed. Her foot moved from side to side so she presented as a petulant child in tantrum. Finally, looking Pauline in the eye, she offered: "Things have been going badly at home but I've been very careful not to let it affect my work. They told me about a couple of little mistakes last week and I made sure that I re-sent the proper information before deadline. So that's not really a problem."

"I mean," Pauline interrupted, "we can't really agree then that it isn't affecting your work, can we? You've just been shouting at Tayla in Reception as well." Both women looked to the coloured page that Barbara still held in a tight grip. "OK, that's not a great recommendation for Tayla's admin skills," she continued, "but you have changed all of their rotas so many times this month." Pauline appeared to be mitigating Tayla's messed-up timesheet. Barbara's gut registered sudden discomfort. "And you can't say that you've been yourself? For quite a while now?"

Barbara continued to watch Pauline's expression as though to gauge which disclosures might be avoided, trying to contain the avalanche she felt inside.

"My work's up to date. I'm always in early," she began to grab at the plus points she could muster.

"But you have missed a morning recently which meant that we missed important deadlines." Pauline could see that Barbara was shifting in her seat, her feet moving quickly from side to side. She needed to hold this situation, deal with it by the book, because there was already the prospect that some of the admin team might be raising issues of Barbara's bullying behaviour and she didn't want her own name to be added to any bullying list, for any reason. As she sat hunched, looking at her shoes, Barbara was giving the impression of an unloved child.

"Something's been going on. You talked about '*it*'," she coaxed.

"OK. It's not really any business to do with work so I don't want it recorded," she blurted as though rehearsed. "My marriage has finished. It's over!" Her hands wrenched at the sodden tissues she'd been holding.

This was not what Pauline had expected to hear. As far as anyone knew, Barbara had been married for over thirty years. It might have been more than that because their eldest son was around thirty-five.

"I'm so sorry to hear that. You should have told me. We could have looked for you to take some time to deal with things."

"And how would we meet our deadlines if I did that?" she snapped back. "Work's the only thing that's keeping me sane," she sobbed "and now you're saying maybe that's not even working. I don't want anyone else to know," she insisted.

"Is that why you were late that morning? Did it happen then?"

"No, it happened the Friday night when I got home. He told me that he had had enough of me working all the time. That we had nothing left between us. That he'd found someone else. That he was taking what was left in the bank and I could keep the house." Barbara dissolved into heaving tears. Pauline went to sit beside her on the settee and put an arm around her shoulder as she sobbed. She smelled strongly of cigarettes and there was a suggestion of stale alcohol. This was going to be tricky. "Keep the mortgage more like." Pauline reached for the tissue box on the coffee table and grabbed at a few to hand over.

"Barbara, have you been drinking?" she put to the sobbing woman, perhaps more forcefully than she had meant to. This would not look good in a complaint.

"Last night. Yes. Not this morning," Barbara admitted candidly. Now that Pauline was close to her she felt that there was little else to do but to cough up. "But I'm going to lose my licence." There, she'd said it. She now felt as though she herself had joined the line of people who were betraying her.

Pauline held her at arm's length in order to focus their gaze. " Lose your licence?" she gasped. Both knew that this meant that Barbara was not going to be able to work as she was used to if she were to depend on public transport since she lived near Ipswich. This was going to make it a geographical impossibility. Besides, it was a condition of working for Empire that the senior staff held current driving licences in case they were needed to go to the bank, the supermarket for last-minute supplies or to deliver blood samples to the hospital.

"For how long? When?" Pauline asked in rapid fire.

"I know." Barbara wrung the tissue between her hands. "It's going to mean that I have to leave. Because the Empire rules say that I have to have a licence to do this job. It's all over," she continued to sob.

A knock came at Pauline's office door. She went out to see to the intruder, holding the door behind her as Barbara got up to reach for more tissues. Nurse Amadia Stokes had come to let her know that an ambulance had been called for Meg Hardy in Tulip 14. In whispered tones Amadia trotted out her professional case notes, "Because she's had a fall and there's a suspected broken hip, Meg is still in the place she fell. We have covered her with a blanket but will not be moving her until we have the *say-so* from the paramedics." Her African accent made the assessment sound all the more formal. Both Amadia and Pauline were well aware that a broken hip could take Meg into a new category of care, if not down the road to further frailty. Pauline's own background in hotel management meant that, in matters of medical care, she had always to defer to her clinically trained team members for their greater understanding so she took their expertise very seriously, since she had little or nothing to offer in that regard.

Pauline thanked Amadia for letting her know about the impending ambulance visit and moved past her to go to the café where she made two cups of coffee, perfunctorily stabbing at the buttons of the machine while double-checking next steps.

After letting Tayla know that they were now expecting an ambulance, Amadia looked back over her shoulder towards the café as she waited for the lift to return her upstairs where she would wait he paramedics. It occurred to her that Pauline's was about the most casual, perhaps even uncaring, reaction she could imagine when told of the crashing fate of a ninety-one-year-old resident.

With two filled coffee mugs, Pauline came backwards through her office door. She placed one of the mugs on the low table beside Barbara and resumed her place behind her desk, letting Barbara know subliminally that sympathy-time was at an end. Barbara had had sufficient opportunity to pull herself together and thanked her for the coffee which she cradled for comfort.

"How is it that you're going to lose your licence?" Pauline asked with severity sufficient to match the situation.

"When I came home on the Friday and he told me that he had packed and was leaving, I didn't know what to do. I had a glass of wine, thought about things, wondered why we'd stayed together for so long if he'd been so bored. I'd gone through almost three bottles and passed out because, first I knew, I woke up on Saturday afternoon. Then I went out to the supermarket to get some food and tried to withdraw some money at the *hole in the wall*. He had done what he said he would. There was no money there. We only had a joint account you see. My pay goes in to that. I don't have any money. Well, not now. I bought some food and some wine with what I had left in my purse and went home and then I think the same thing happened again. I slept through another day. I was late out of the house on Monday morning and was speeding a bit when I was pulled up. They breathalysed me and I was still over the limit on the way to work apparently. Although I think that must have been a faulty reading."

"So you were coming to work *drunk?*" Pauline asked in amazement.

"Not drunk! Only registering from the night before. I didn't have anything in the morning. It was left over in my system, I suppose. If the reading was right," she added tentatively.

"It must have been a huge binge, Barbara, to be still in your bloodstream the following day." It seemed that Pauline was not going to entertain any flaw in the breathalyser testing. She shuffled with some papers on her desk. "I am going to have to talk with HR." There was an edge to her voice.

"On no! I don't want anyone to know," Barbara pleaded.

"I'm afraid that everyone will know, Barbara, and it won't be me who tells them, will it? Don't forget it will be in the papers. I am duty-bound to let Head Office know of any impending legal cases involving staff. And of any concerns."

"But I can't lose my job! No one here knows how to do what I do. And they wouldn't work all the hours that I do. Surely you can work something out to help me?"

"I'm not sure that anyone needs to work all those hours, Barb. To be honest, I think that if you worked smarter, you could achieve more in fewer hours. They manage it in other homes."

Barbara was now mentally adding the other Empire Admin Manager colleagues to the list of those who'd betrayed her.

"Everyone's concentration slips after a full day's work. Eight hours or so. Anything past ten hours in your sort of role and you're really no use to anyone," she added dismissively.

This came as though it were a physical slap to Barbara who had already been told that she wasn't shaping up anymore as a wife. Now it seemed to her that her boss didn't appreciate all the extra work that she put in to '*her sort of role*'.

"I think you'd be surprised." She flinched, her very capacity threatened. She wasn't even convincing herself.

"And it would be impossible for you to get here to work when you can't drive."

"I've thought about that." Having considered she'd faced her demons she announced with misplaced pride. "I'm going to rent my place out and board down here, somewhere near Gramwell."

"I'm going to talk with HR about the situation, Barbara. It's my duty to do that. It's a great pity and I do feel for you. After all these years of marriage, I'm sure that it was the last thing you'd expected but there are rules and it may not work out just the way you're imagining right now. The idea that the admin and accounts of Gramwell Glade are, for a large part, in the hands of someone who has been found drunk-driving to work on a Monday morning is not the message that either Akin or the Board will want to put across."

"I shouldn't have told you!" Barbara realised with stinging remorse and accusation. "But I thought you'd be able to help."

"It would have come to my attention before very long, now, wouldn't it?" Pauline sounded supercilious to Barbara's ears. "And I'll let you know how we're going to proceed once I've spoken with HR and Akin." There was suddenly a great distance in her stance.

"But I love my job. It's what I live for!" Barbara insisted.

"I do understand that work's important to you. But it's most important to us that we project personal integrity to our community. I know that you'll understand that. If you'd like to take some time off, I'll be happy to arrange that. It would probably be the best idea in all the circumstances." Pauline straightened her laptop, moved her coffee cup and stood as though to suggest Barbara was now to leave the room.

"And do what?" Barbara looked lost. "I need my pay to survive now," she added.

"I'll let you know as soon as we've made a decision." Pauline had by now struck a palpable distance between them. Barbara, determined that they wouldn't be able to manage without her, chanced her arm. "Alright then. I will take the rest of the week off then if that's OK with you?" She imagined that she was the concessionaire. "Will that give you enough time to make up your minds? I don't know who is going to manage all the things that we're supposed to have in to Head Office this week but if that's what you want."

"That's fine, Barbara." Her boss interrupted. "If you collect your own things from your desk, I will make sure that you are paid for this week and I'll phone you at home to let you know the outcome of the decision. You will need to let us know the details when you've opened a new bank account in your own name because I don't want you to lose your pay to your husband."

"Ex-husband." Barbara flounced as she stood to leave, a little too defiantly for Pauline's liking.

"Please take care. And let me know if you hear anything about a court date? I'm sorry this has happened." Pauline spoke to Barbara's receding back. "Take care."

Tayla was engrossed, head down, in the hair appointment spreadsheet as Barbara moved quickly past her without saying a word.

The group slowly followed the Prom pathway around the point. Immediately they were hit by a stiff onshore easterly that blew hard at them. Screams of excitement and surprise and some of discomfort rose to meet the seagulls' cries.

"Oh my days!" acknowledged Brendon. "Hold on to your hats, everyone." Actually, Albert Watts was the only one who was wearing a hat today, a Homberg, and he was already pushing it down firmly on to his head with some force. A scarf threatened to leave Mollie's neck but was recovered, like the tail of a kite, by the quick-thinking of Nwaoma who was walking behind her, arm in arm with Elizabeth Hollick.

Dot had been blown slightly off-course, bumping in to David's shoulder. He extended an arm for support and she gladly reached for it so that they continued arm in arm as something of a windbreak together.

"I can hear bagpipes!" shouted Hilda Matters. "Listen!" she commanded those of the group who were struggling in her vicinity against the antagonistic wind.

"This is crazy," observed Mobo. "I reckon we goes back. It was beautiful and sheltered until we turned at the point."

Darragh nodded in agreement, steering hard to keep Marjorie's chair on a straight path.

Elizabeth Hollick piped up. "I can hear them too, Hilda. Somewhere in the distance?" she quizzed, looking out to sea. Nwaoma looked questioningly beside her.

"What's the matter, ladies?" Phoenix came up to see if she could help them.

"Bagpipes. Somewhere near here." Hilda explained. "I'd like to go to see the pipers."

"Come on, you lot," Brendon urged as he took Barney's wheelchair for a wide loop so as to backtrack the way they had come. "Let's go back. It was sheltered on the other side of the point. Let's head back?"

"We can't go now," Elizabeth protested. "We're going to see the bagpipes. And we haven't been here for long. It's not time to go home yet." She was about to stamp her foot when a gust blew hard at her side and the holes in her adjustable aluminium walking stick shrieked out a warbling tune.

Brendon parked Barney and came towards Elizabeth to steady her. He picked up her stick as he held her arm and held it up to the onshore wine whereupon it offered up a lively melody. Nwaoma gurgled with laughter.

"See, dear. Look, Hilda!" as he held the walking stick aloft it continued to play. "Not bagpipes, girls. This is your very own Whistling Willie! Who knew you were both so good at playing tunes?" He resumed his place behind Barney, unlocked the brakes and gestured to the crew that they should head back to the sheltered part of the Prom. "Come on, let's find the ice cream van!"

Brendon took his handwritten receipt for sixteen ice creams into Barbara's office for a refund from petty cash. Amity was at her desk, daintily eating supermarket sushi from its plastic bento box with chopsticks.

"Where's Barb?" he asked. It was almost never the case that he went into the Office without finding her there. The usual place for any slight absence would be out in Smokers' Corner, beside the bins. "Is she fagging on again? I didn't see her there on my way in."

"Apparently she's gone on leave. Suddenly it's beautifully quiet around here," Amity smiled; her pearl-pink fingernails juggled chopsticks as she poked at the circles of rice and salmon.

"I've just laid out over thirty quid for ice-creams and it's a week until payday. Can you do petty cash, sweetheart ?" he asked Amity.

"Only enormous cash for me, darling. Sorry, no go. I think that Pauline can do it at a pinch but Barb prefers that no one else touches it. She says that's when it all goes wrong."

"Well it's going to go tits-up for me if I don't get some money back. Things will definitely go wrong. I'll simply starve," he exaggerated the word as he closed the office door and wondered why it was that he always hammed things up around Amity. Perhaps, he thought, it was because no one really got who she was or what she did. But he did appreciate her sense of style, including calling her own shots in a setting which was otherwise dictated to the enth degree.

Out in the main Reception area, Brian was listening to Tayla's sad story about the way she'd been shouted at by Barbara. Keeping her voice as low as she could, standing behind her chair, she whispered, "She just went berserk at me. Then Mrs Graves called her in to her office and they were there for a while and I think they might have been talking about me. It was only about my timesheet but it lasted a long time. And now Mrs Fenway's gone on holiday for a week and I don't know what I have to do. Well, I know I have to answer the phone and that. See to the people at the desk. But I don't know what's happening." She was on the verge of tears. Brian went to give her a tentative hug. It was all he'd wanted to do but, when it came to it, he hadn't expected that she would feel quite so small and warm and vulnerable in his arms. He held her to him, stiffly, for as long as she felt comfortable doing that in this very public place. It seemed a long time.

And then Henry's big trolley could be heard rattling up the corridor. Tayla broke away from Brian's hold, meeting his eyes for a flashing moment. "Thanks, Bry," she said under her breath, "I needed that."

" Caught!" shouted Henry on his way past the desk, "Why are you blushing, bro?" he challenged with a laugh as he and the bain-maries crossed over the foyer to the carpeted corridor on his way to Daffodil Dining Room. "Caught in the act! I'll tell Kayleigh!" he shouted over his shoulder as he sallied into the distance. Neither Brian nor Tayla responded. She shuffled herself back onto the chair at the Reception Desk and he moved off to gaze at the security pad at the back-of-house doors. The code, something he ordinarily knew in his sleep, was now the furthest thing from his mind. Some of the older ones had told him that Alzheimer's could be catching.

Gosia was coming from serving lunch to Daphne Shaw in her room. She caught up with Brian, pressing herself between him and the keypad, as she quickly pushed the code correctly and looked back up at him questioningly. He imagined at that moment that Alzheimer's had indeed caught up with him too as he followed Gosia down the corridor.

"I love fisherman's pie," extolled Grace as she removed the rolled napkin from the glass on her table and handed the menu to Elizabeth who, with the Storricks, had joined the table. The Storricks had been later into the Dining Room than some of the others who'd returned to their rooms to put away their coats and spruce up before heading for lunch with an appetite larger than usual despite their mid-morning ice cream.

"Would any of youse like some wine with your lunch today?" Phoenix asked them in her best waitress voice. A touch of the sun was evident on most of the relaxed faces of those who were united in the afterglow of a super beachside excursion.

"I'll have a sweet sherry please, dear," Elizabeth answered straightaway. Looking for a partner in this special treat, she turned to Grace and Marie Storrick: "Won't you join me?" Grace nodded her assent.

Marie looked to her husband Ron. "Will we?" she dared.

"Thank you Phoenix," Ron replied, checking her name badge. He found it was always safe to check when so many of the young ones looked alike. Although most of them seemed to have tattoos by which he could differentiate some of them, there were a few he could never manage to tell apart and Phoenix was one of those. "Sherry for the ladies. My wife and I will have white wine," he offered before agreeing with Grace, "Fisherman's pie is just the job after a morning by seaside, isn't it?"

Dot had quickly brushed her hair and rearranged her silk scarf in her mirror before heading into lunch. This morning had triggered some odd excitement that reminded her of being in her twenties again. She knew that it wasn't just the freedom of seeing the open sea and beautiful gardens but the prickling sensation of brushing up against David's arm as they'd bumped along together in the stiff breeze past the Point.

David had been looking out for her and signalled as she came through the door to come to join his table. Hilda Matters had already taken up her place there but David was determined to have his choice of female companionship rather than take up usual discussions with Hilda. This had emboldened him to make an invitation to Dot very clear. There might have been some way of prolonging the lovely feelings that the morning had held for him and, since they hadn't finished their discussions on beach holiday destinations they'd enjoyed in the past, he felt sufficiently purposeful in asking Dot to join him. This had meant that, when the Storricks had rolled in for lunch, David's table only had one spare seat. They had been happy enough to join Grace and Elizabeth since they had all shared the beach excursion this morning.

Dot felt a little conspicuous in front of Hilda since she'd been specifically beckoned towards the table. However, there was no good reason to sit elsewhere and later regret not having taken up the invitation. "Is that alright with you, Hilda?" she asked while taking up the offered place.

"Whatever you like," answered Hilda who had never questioned her own right to any place she chose to sit. "It's Dorothy, isn't it?" she feigned not knowing Dot since she begrudged sharing David with others who, she deemed, were less likely than she to enjoy his intellect and calibre of conversational topics.

"We'll have some wine," David offered up to Phoenix. "What would you like, Dot, red or white?"

To Dot, it sounded very much as though they were in a restaurant together and David was taking care of ordering. "I'd enjoy some white wine, thank you," she smiled, settling in for a special time of it.

"And I'll have the Cottage Pie," Hilda rattled off to Phoenix as she clumsily returned the printed menu to the centre of the table.

“Henry will take your food orders in a minute, Hilda. Would you like your sherry or a wine?”

“Bristol Cream,” Hilda punched back. Turning to David and Dot she picked up a new strand of conversation to stand her ground as the purported leader of the table. “I went for a walk too,” she pointed out. “Stan takes me out every morning. Personal service, don’t you know?” she continued. “So you’re not the only ones to have fresh air today. By any means. In fact, I have it every day which is why I suppose I’ve always worked up such an appetite by lunchtime.”

David and Dot exchanged smiles. It was fine by them to allow Hilda to relish her own sense of importance and leave them less conspicuous to the attentions of others. Dot quickly looked around the Dining Room to see if anyone else was in the business of watching

Phoenix headed back from the Dining Room to the Bar in the Café to fill the drinks orders while Henry, assisted by Marigold and Darragh, saw that each of the diners was given a good serving of the meal of their choice and in the neatest possible arrangement on the plate. Pauline had been known to come into the Dining Rooms at lunch and dinner times to ensure the presentation of residents’ meals was ‘top notch’. It remained a huge challenge to Henry whose idea of a well presented plate had mostly to do with doling out large quantities. He thought it was unfair to try to make dinners look like they did in hotels when they were only working in a home. He said nothing about it, though.

“I so enjoyed our trip this morning, Dot.” David was unusually bright. The change in his tone caused Hilda to double-take. In so doing, she saw a warmth in Dot smiling towards him that alerted her, if not David and Dot, to a conspicuous change in their demeanour. Keen to demonstrate that this was a lunch in a common room and not a private assignation, Hilda meant to ensure that nothing would be putting her nose out of joint. She sipped twice at the little sherry glass before getting stuck in to the mashed potato atop Mrs Hewson’s savoury mince recipe and shovelled down some peas.

Chapter Five

HONOUR

"Will you puh-lees make sure that *this*," the woman said, indicating a paper bag in her hand, "is properly stored in the kitchen and brought to my mother each morning? I don't know what happened to the last lot. Mother tells me that she never had any of it."

Arabella Jones-Merton enunciated her demand in the direction of Tayla who was on the early shift the following Thursday morning. "My mother always has Stilton on her toast but the staff haven't been giving it to her for some reason lately."

Mrs Jones-Merton handed the smelly brown bag over the Reception counter to Tayla who managed, with effort, to keep her smile going the distance. It hadn't escaped her that there was a suggestion that some of the Team had been pinching the Stilton – or whatever it was – for themselves but seriously doubted that anyone she knew would want anything to do with something that smelt as badly as this did. She placed it on the table at the rear of the Reception desk.

"I'll make sure that it goes to the kitchen and to your mother," she replied as Mrs Jones-Merton headed to the lift and upstairs to visit her Stilton-loving mother.

Tayla looked around to check that there was no one in the foyer before ducking off to Mrs Fenway's office to see Amity who knew most of the families and might be able to help her out of this one. Amity had come in early this morning and hadn't come back out past the reception desk for coffee as yet so she was pretty sure she'd be in there.

Pushing open the door, she found Barbara Fenway's desk still empty. Amity was checking her lipstick in a compact mirror. She was in a blue trouser suit with a tangy lime-green, silk patterned shirt underneath the jacket and flowery court shoes. Enormous gold hoop earrings framed the spaces between her jet black chignon and slightly padded shoulders.

"You look beautiful, Amity," Tayla said without compunction. "You always look beautiful. But you look even more beautiful than that today. Is there something special going on?"

"One does one's best!" Amity teased, kicking one flowery heel behind the other as she leaned back in her chair. "You are sweet, Tayla. I just like to brighten up my own day in case no one else will. And I think there's a chance that Akin might drop in today to see us," she added. "Can't be sure but better to be safe than sorry."

"I'm glad you told me. No-one tells me nothing around here. I'll make sure that we tidy everything up. Is Mrs Fenway still away?" Tayla looked around. She felt that she could trust Amity although others of the younger Gramwell employees made a point of not engaging with the senior staff, just in case. Tayla had to trust her gut.

"I haven't heard from her at all," Amity sounded miffed but beastly careless, "but I think that if she were coming back, she would have done so last week. But, guess what? We're all managing without the noise and the swearing. I guess that's the main thing?" She shot Tayla a winning smile. Tayla thought she looked like a Hollywood film star but she knew better than to agree with any bad words against Mrs Fenway, just in case she turned up to make them all miserable again so she went to leave the office, wondering who was supposed to be giving her and the other Receptionists their orders if Mrs Fenway wasn't there to do that.

"Are you going to be in the Panto?" Amity called to her back, keen to snaffle as many participants as she could. "We're starting rehearsals soon."

" No, you wouldn't want me there," Tayla conceded, holding on to the door handle. "I can't sing and I haven't been on stage since I did ballet when I was little. I'm too shy for that now. Wouldn't do it in a million years," she giggled.

"Oh, we'll see about that!" Amity threatened. "We don't have too many ballerinas around here to call on."

Tayla blushed, wishing she'd never mentioned that she used to dance. There was no way she was going to do anything so embarrassing and should have known that she could be dragooned at the slightest suggestion for so many roles at Gramwell Glade other than her job description would cover. It had happened to so many of them, so often. She closed the door behind her, scolding herself for having made that disclosure before suddenly recalling what it was she had gone there for in the first place. She reopened the door. Amity immediately put down her mobile phone as though caught in some impropriety. Since she was always on the phone when anyone needed her, it wouldn't have occurred to Tayla that there was anything untoward about finding Amity mid-call.

"I forgot. I came to ask you who that posh Mrs Jones-something is related to. She brought in something for her mother and I don't know which mother it is. We don't have any Joneses, do we?"

"To keep up with?" Amity could already see that the joke had misfired. "That will be Arabella with the Stilton. It's Jones-Merton. Her mother is Millie Cloudsdale. Tulip 5."

Raising one eyebrow, Amity registered that the Reception Desk phone was ringing. Tayla flew out of the office, throwing herself behind the Reception Desk to catch it. It was Akin Akindele calling for Pauline and it had taken five rings for her to get back there. She would kick herself for that tardiness for the rest of the day if Mrs Graves didn't to do it for her. Tayla set about stacking papers into piles on the table behind the Receptionist's chair, trying to make it look neater without much success.

Pauline Graves had been going over the Month End results for October. Arranging with Olga Dean from Head Office to take over accounts payable and receivable, not to mention the timesheets, had just gone to show that centralisation was far more efficient a system. The amount of time and frustration that had been lifted from their shoulders since Barbara had been removed was a co-efficiency that she was very happy to live with, especially as it had brought some sudden changes to the bottom line. Costs were down for a start. It wasn't clear yet just how one person could have made a major difference to food costs. It might have been coincidence but bore some investigation in case questions were to be asked.

Pauline picked up the phone to summon Amity, putting it on loudspeaker so as to be able to carry on checking numbers on the reports while checking her calendar on the computer screen. They needed to go over the Waiting List together as a matter of routine: there were a few other matters to broach, too. It had been a very long week already. Pauline would have realised that the week had the better of her had she consulted a mirror. She pressed the numbers again. Amity's phone had been engaged for most of the morning. If she didn't answer in the next couple of tries, Pauline would have to get up and venture out to collect her. Suddenly the phone rang. Pauline knocked over her coffee mug in surprise. Fortunately it had been empty. She clattered with it and the pile of print-outs that littered her desk.

"You were calling me?" Amity questioned.

"I've been calling for ages," Pauline held back her exasperation with some effort.

“It’s a busy life we lead!” Amity added with gaiety. “Are you ready for our meeting? I’ll come to you.” The phone went dead.

Pauline wasn’t oblivious to the ways in which Amity took the lead so often when it wasn’t actually hers for the taking. She needed some strategies to fend off those little insurrections before they took on any further life.

Amity came in a few minutes later, coffee mug and papers in hand. She stalked like a bird in her heels to the pink settee where she settled in, arranging her mobile phone, papers and mug in front of her on the coffee table. Amity looked like spring in the middle of Pauline’s late autumn.

“Shall I get you a coffee?” Amity asked.

“Let’s turn off the mobiles?” Pauline suggested, brushing away the offer of a coffee. The cuffs of her white shirt looked a little dingy as they poked out from the sleeves of her grey mohair cardigan.

“Really? I can never be too far away from mine,” Amity pattered. “You never know when our next resident is going to appear. You’ve read the stats. We’re getting about five new enquiries each day now that it’s getting colder. The winter rush, you know.” The phone remained on following this apparently irrefutable justification.

Pauline silently coached herself that she had bigger fish to fry. Looking down at the papers on her desk in front of her she asked, “How did you get on with that visit last week? I can’t see any report in the system.”

With the suggestion that she might be missing some of her targets, Amity became a little brittle. “Are you sure? I’ve put it in under Sweetman. Nan, the mother, has been married three times. So she’s had four different names. The son who came with her is Charles Worrell. Charming people.”

Pauline pushed at the cursor on her mouse, speedily reading through the notes on the screen that she had missed.

“She’s staying with them at the moment in Colchester.” Amity summarised the notes that she knew she’d put in the system. “Lives in Belfast. Ring a bell?” she chipped. “But they’re looking for somewhere in Essex so she can be closer. Used to be an opera singer. Lovely lady. She has the tiniest hands.”

Pauline didn’t care for the tiniest details. “So when would they be ready for the move, given everything else is equal?”

“Oh more than equal,” Amity laughed, “Worrell is a record producer. Loaded, I should think. He has Nan’s Power of Attorney too and she’s not short of a few bob either.”

Both women knew that due diligence on the financial situations of families applying to Gramwell Glade was an essential part of Empire’s prerequisites. It rankled a little with Pauline. After all, people weren’t cross-examined about their liquidity when they checked in to an elite hotel. She tried to assuage her concerns knowing that the legacy for an intended resident was basically for the term of their natural life so, in that regard, signing up in the care sector was a weightier proposition than in the hospitality industry. It was annoying too to hear Amity's unending optimism. Getting them through the door seemed to be her only concern. The degree of cognitive or continence dysfunction wasn't something she needed to busy herself with on a daily basis but constituted a completely different prospect to the care staff. She merely brought them in where, at the sharp end of the stick, they became someone else's problem.

On the other hand, Amity was certain that Pauline had no understanding of the degree of difficulty in actually making a sale, especially when there were so many other homes in Essex that would prove very much more attractive when coming in at one or even a few hundred pounds cheaper on a weekly basis. That added up quickly. Nobody knew how long a piece of string was but everyone had to calculate that they could afford Gramwell fees on pretty much an indefinite period so as not to put too fine a point on mortality.

"OK. Well we don't have a vacancy for Nan in Daffodil at present. How long are they prepared to wait, do you think?"

"You said that Hilda Matters might be going to Tulip. We could move her or someone else to Tulip to create a Daffodil vacancy. I can't see Charles agreeing to Nan going anywhere other than Daffodil."

"But it's not up to Charles, is it?" Pauline asked imperiously. "We will have to see what Brad's assessment will point to. We might have another Tulip vacancy shortly, too. The hospital has told us that Meg Hardy may not be coming back to us. Bless her. She has cardiac complications and her diabetes isn't helping. It looks as though the hip was just about the final straw. So you'll have to concentrate on finding more candidates for Tulip and forget about Daffodil or double rooms, for that matter." It pleased Pauline to escalate the degree of difficulty in Amity's work. She needed to know that her staff members were working to their highest potential.

"If Brad says that Nan needs the dementia community, we'll lose them. Simple as that. She's a good prospect, Pauline." Amity insisted. "No need to make things more difficult than they need to be. They can always move her later on." There was a firmness to her tone as she called her boss out.

Amity's phone began to vibrate on the coffee table. Reading upside down, Pauline saw that the initials AA appeared on its screen. A tightening of her gut made her look at Amity to see if she could gauge her reaction. Amity reached for the phone and quickly killed the call, apparently unconcerned. It was Pauline's own inability to read Amity that caused her concern. Were these someone's initials? Surely not who she first thought of? Amity was happily married to Giles. Impossible anyway. Was it the organiser of the Armchair Aerobics calling in? Was Amity a member of Alcoholics Anonymous? Really? Not another one with an alcohol problem, she pondered.

Amity toyed with the phone as she looked up with a smile. "Well, I'll leave Nan in Brad's court. He'll need to see her in the next couple of weeks, before she goes back to Belfast. But I know they will appreciate an answer sooner rather than later. Gramwell is currently on top of their list despite the cost. It's not one I think we should miss."

"I'll let him know." Pauline moved some papers to the top of the pile. "How are the plans for the Panto going?"

"It's not only up to me, is it? I thought the whole Senior Team were on this one?"

"With Barbara's leaving, the others have to carry quite a bit more responsibility now. I think we can safely say that it's over to you for the Panto."

Amity put her head down. "I'm not sure about that, Pauline. I'll get back to you." She switched her weight, re-crossing her legs, the gaily patterned shoes making a statement in the air.

"Well I am sure, Amity, that we'll all chip in where we can. I need you to take this over because we're running out of time."

"I've already got a lot more to deal with. The door is constantly opening and closing and when people see that Barbara's not there they interrupt me all the time asking about pay and petty cash and the like. Where am I supposed to send people who are asking about uniforms?"

"Send them to me," Pauline snapped back.

"They won't go to –"

Pauline held her hand up to indicate that Amity shouldn't state the obvious." If they won't go then they won't get, will they?"

Amity remained unimpressed. "Is there anything else?"

"Yes, apparently Akin might drop in this afternoon. Head Office have let me know that he's in the area on his way back from visiting some of the homes in the North and he might drop by for a cup of tea around three." Pauline looked at Amity. It was clear to see that she needed no further preparation: her appearance was flawless. Pauline, on the other hand, thought she might have a quick word with Chantelle to see if she could be squeezed in for a shampoo and blow-dry after lunch in order to look her best for when her boss arrived. It was one of the most exciting things she could think of under the weight of the usual considerations. Perhaps he would notice that she had now lost almost half a stone. He was bound to.

Kayleigh Longbottom walked slowly and deliberately past Tayla at the Reception desk. Kayleigh was on her way out the back of the kitchen for a cigarette break. She'd arranged to meet up with Brian Petty. Most people thought she was a timid creature but today she had solemn intentions of putting him through the third degree since she'd heard from Henry that he'd seen Brian cosying up to Tayla at the front desk. She shot Tayla a look as though she were a bad smell. Tayla turned away and picked up the phone, pretending that she was ordering a taxi to collect one of the morning's visitors.

Some of the ladies were in the café, laughing over a session of Mr Potato Head, while others were sitting around waiting for comments on their newly coiffed hairdos. Naomi Page was in with them playing Frank Sinatra tunes and calling for various plastic pieces to be pushed into the potatoes she'd commandeered from the kitchen.

In the Staff Tearoom, beyond the back-of-house security keypad, there were three groups of two around the small café tables on their break. Brian Petty was washing up at the sink, avoiding what he knew to be the come-uppance that he was dreading.

"You're a good man, Bri," Ronnie Chan shouted over to Brian. "Everyone leaves their dirty dishes in the sink and then waits for a good man to come along and wash them all."

"A good man?' Rosie Rowson, the oldest of the housekeepers, shouted back in Ronnie's direction. "I ain't never seen a man wash up at my place, more's the pity." Rosie was taking a break from the laundry with Frank Goninon, another of the housekeepers, who'd been cleaning residents' rooms upstairs all morning. She looked over the top of her doorstep cheese sandwich and quietly asked Frank across the table, " So what happened to Barb Fenway then? Have you heard anything?"

"You know the score. They never say nothing. I don't think she's coming back though. Mrs Graves told me to clean her desk out."

Rosie nodded reverently and took another bite.

"Haven't you seen me cleaning, Rosie?" Frank asked in a louder voice, intended for all to hear.

"Well that's stating the blooming obvious, isn't it?" Rosie replied in equivalent volume so that no one could presume that they were talking about those who were gone and definitely forgotten. "You're a cleaner. But does you do it at home?" she asked. "That's as I'd like to know."

"Does he do *it* at home?" Marigold guffawed into her Coke bottle.

Kayleigh's head appeared around the staff room door.

“Now you’s in trouble,” Rosie warned Brian, “ Don’t you go taking him away just yet, Kayles. We don’t often get any of the men doing their duty here at the sink.”

Brian blushed as Kayleigh sternly put to him, “Thought you was coming outside for a smoke?”

“Just a bit busy here at the moment.” He replied sheepishly.

“That’s right! You tell her, love. Why go outside for a smoke when you can chain yourself to the kitchen sink?” Phoenix chipped in.

Kayleigh slammed the door behind her.

“Oh boy. You’s in big trouble now,” Rosie predicted.

“Leave the man alone!” Frank came in to bat for his friend. “We don’t need a running commentary. Just be glad the dishes are being done for once,” he protested. There were few places in this moment where Brian could imagine himself feeling comfortable. He ran water to chase the last of the bubbles down the plughole, squeezed water from the dish cloth and headed back to Tulip Community to search out some anonymity.

David Jack was alone in his room. On the small occasional table at the window beside his armchair a silver framed photograph of his late wife Celia presided over today’s crossword, folded from a page of newspaper, his reading glasses leaning out of their case and an enamelled ballpoint pen. The wall held a watercolour painting of a Suffolk scene. They had chosen the painting together in the early years of their marriage. It had always held pride of place in their sitting room. A few other ornaments from the marital home sat on the window ledge. Beyond the glass, the bird feeder that he had set up was a constant destination for some of the robins and finches that decorated the trees at the edge of Gramwell Glade’s manicured gardens. If he didn’t keep his eye out, the fat-balls and seeds he refilled daily were won by the hordes of squirrels that also shared the sanctuary. A tap on the window sent the fluffy dynamos to one or other of his neighbours: they were happily aware that there was a strip of other feeders along the length of the residential wings of this building. Most residents were delighted to see wildlife of any description and had no compunction as to which took the offerings, just as long as there were a smattering of distracting visitors to watch during the many hours each spent gazing from the window of their room.

David Jack had spent time after lunch looking from the photo to the grounds beyond. Most other days he would have taken himself to Daffodil Lounge for the afternoon to browse through some of the other newspapers of the day or to work on one of the seemingly endless number of jigsaw puzzles. On Thursdays, the knitting group met there at two-thirty. Rather than get started and have to leave when they showed up, he gave the colour and chat of those get-togethers a miss, leaving the knitters to themselves which now brought him back to his own company.

Fortunately he enjoyed his own company. It came as a welcome contrast to the casts of thousands that had seen him through forty-odd years as a schoolmaster. Heaven knows, even Celia had trouble in coaxing him away from the solace of his study at home. He'd asked himself if he were depressed these days because he seemed increasingly to be eschewing company. The answer had come back a firm 'no'. He knew that he was something of an introvert who needed to be alone in order to refuel his sociability stores or when, as happened today, he needed to look into a particular dilemma. Silence and solitude were prerequisites when tapping in to his own counsel.

In those keen last hours when Celia's breathing had come with such difficulty and they were able to bare all their thoughts and feelings one to the other in the hospital, Celia had told David to be sure not to stay on his own. She knew that he would be happier if he found someone to love and care for him when she'd gone. He'd asked her not to talk about not being there when she'd squeezed his hand as tightly as she could manage and repeated to him that she really did mean it and that he was to remember what she'd said. Those words had come to his mind so frequently in the year since she'd gone, mainly because they were among the last moments they'd together had so, in fact, they had become the parting memory he had of her. Maybe she'd meant it that way, he thought. That was certainly the way he remembered her, his companion from their first teaching days, the partner who'd travelled with him in school holidays, the person who, with him, was told that they were unable to have children of their own. Such an irony couldn't have been imagined. Between them they tended hundreds of other people's children but were never to have their own. But then Sarah made her way into the world to prove the doctors were wrong. Dear Sarah. And now she was married with a family of her own. The years had flown by.

David rapped quickly again at the window sending two younger squirrels flying next door to pick away at the feeding table that Mildred Absolom's son had set up outside her window. It was the neighbour on the other side, Dorothy Baker, who had brought some of these current considerations to mind. Dorothy, a neat, quiet woman, was a complete contrast to the outgoing Celia who had been able to take and keep charge of large groups of children or Women's Institute colleagues and call all the shots. Dot seemed so unassuming that she was almost capable of disappearing in the middle of a crowded room. Perhaps this was how come he hadn't really noticed her for the time that they had already been here at Gramwell together, he wondered.

But she wasn't sheepish or obsequious. Just quiet and considered. She had no tertiary education but had worked in retail for her entire career. Why was it that Dot never married, he asked himself? She was an attractive person. Her petite and ordered features were assembled in a pleasing way and, although she didn't always have a great deal to say, what she did say was really quite endearing. Was this what Celia meant? Should he find someone who was easy to be with, who made a sweet difference to the everyday? Celia so often had understood the world far better than he did, especially in affairs of the heart. She had known when Sarah first brought Colin home that he was going to be their son-in-law. Maybe this was exactly what she had meant. His thoughts were racing.

He decided that the distraction of a crowd might be just what was needed to quieten the discomforting narrative that bombarded him. He was fighting a battle which he supposed did not need to be fought. He put the glasses case into his jacket pocket and made an unusual beeline for the café to see what was happening there.

Along the Daffodil corridor David Jack took the unusual step of looking in to the rooms of those residents who had left their doors open. A number of residents in the corridor closer to the main facilities were bed-ridden. His eyes deflected immediately from entertaining any gaze with those who were looking back at the passers-by; these people were not on their deathbeds yet but fairly certainly lying on the beds where they would eventually die. They would be making vows of love to their dear ones as they left on that journey, leaving the rest to clear out the cell in which they had spent their last years so that a newcomer would start the pageant all over again. David vowed to himself to properly hear what Celia had been so concerned for him to understand, to listen and to honour her dying wishes.

As he headed from the corridor through the Reception foyer, David observed a commanding young African man come through from the car park on the other side of the folly walls and head through the automatic glass doors towards the Reception desk where he appeared to cause a fluster with the young receptionist. The sartorial elegance and tonal complexion of this man posed a compete contrast with just about anyone else in Gramwell Glade. David stood a little more upright, patted his jacket pocket to check that his glasses were with him and headed to the coffee machine to begin a new daily habit.

"I'm Akin Akindele, here to see Pauline," his deep voice commanded Tayla. "Is she in her office?"

"I'll just check, Mr Akin," Tayla complied, picking up the phone and put it straight down before dialling. "Actually, I think she's in the hairdresser's. I think I saw her go in there half an hour ago."

"The hairdresser's?" Akin appeared to be surprised.

"I'll call there," Tayla fumbled for the phone again, "to tell her you're here, Mr Akin."

"Don't worry," he glanced at her name badge. "Don't worry, Team Member. Unusual name?" he laughed. His shining white teeth flashed.

Tayla looked down at her chest. "Oh, sorry. Yes. I lost mine and we have to wear one. I found this one in the drawer."

"Of course we have to wear one. Look!" he laughed again as he pulled his own gold name badge from the top pocket of his tailored suit and placed it gently on the outside. It seemed to stick by way of a magnet. Tayla was fascinated that his badge looked as though it was made of real gold. *How rich was he?* she wondered.

"Something smells around here!" His nose was twitching as he left her. Tayla answered the phone, thinking that he was very smart but he was very rude too.

Akin Akindele swung through the large entrance to Ye Olde Tea Shoppe, smiling as he glanced around the room. Some of the ladies playing dominoes at the table near the Salon stopped and stared back at him, nudging their neighbours to take a look at this chap, right down to his violet socks. David Jack picked up on their clucking interest and smiled over the top of the colour supplement that he had appropriated from the paper stand on the wall.

As the door opened, Pauline could see in the mirror in front of her that she had been sprung.

"Well, hello, Mrs Graves!" Akin boomed across the salon. Chantelle stood, hairdryer now blowing hair cuttings around the floor, struck by the sheer presence of the man. She had seen his photo around the place and in the monthly Empire magazine but she'd never seen him in the flesh, as it were.

"Ah, Akin. It's not what it looks like,' Pauline protested as she fumbled to undo the cape ties at the back of her neck.

"It looks to me as though you've been enjoying the benefits of life at Gramwell Glade and that you look all the better for that." He gave away no inkling of annoyance, if that was what Pauline had expected. She grabbed her bunch of keys from the ledge in front of her and stood, her bob swishing against her jaw, as she gathered herself together.

"Thank you, Chantelle, I'll pay you later." She edged her way to the door and shook Akin Akindele's hand as he leant down to cursorily kiss both her cheeks in greeting.

"Paying customer indeed." Looking towards Chantelle who remained frozen to the spot, he observed with a wide smile, "If no one else wants their hair done at this time of day, then why not?" Pauline remembered at the last second to undo the other ties of her cape which she hastily left on the back of the chair.

Almost ready to fall backwards, embarrassment shortened her spine while infatuation curdled her stomach. Pauline willed her spine to hold her rigid for the sake of her career as she led Akin to her office on the other side of the foyer. She closed the door behind them as quickly as she could manage.

"Would you like a tea or coffee?" She wasn't able to convince herself that she wasn't flustered, "I thought you were coming later in the afternoon." Her voice trailed off as she betrayed herself.

"Which is why I am here now," he smiled at her. "Got to keep you all on your toes!" He only added to her disgrace. She could feel herself blushing. "I was up in Newcastle yesterday. Saw your mother there. They tell me that she's doing well."

"She is." Pauline took a deep breath. "I know that they take wonderful care of her at Jesmond Lodge. It was easier for me, of course, when I worked there to keep an eye on her all the time but they do well. They really do." She heard her own voice gushing.

"They actually manage without you?" he appeared to tease. "You can trust Empire Homes, you know, to 'exceed your expectations'." Akin revelled in the feeling of being lord of all he surveyed.

"Of course. We go through the Empire Promise at all our staff meetings here at Gramwell too. I make sure that it's top of mind for the whole team." Pauline landed in her chair, feeling a little stronger with the barrier of her desk between her and whoever was visiting her office for whatever purpose. Her leather upholstered office chair let out a puff of air as her bones rested on it. She still could kick herself for having been caught out in the hairdresser's – on the first and only time she'd ever used Chantelle's services.

"You look different, Pauline," he looked at her face. "Could it be the new hairdo?" he questioned.

'*Could it be the weight loss?*' she hoped. He had been top and back of mind at her every moment of deprivation as she had cut out eating carbs for the past two months. It was torture but it was worth it if he noticed.

"Occupancy?" he moved on, settling back into the feathered upholstery of the pink sofa.

"Yes," she complied, the discipline of work kicking in, "a couple of vacancies in Tulip, as you know, that we've had for a month now. Amity has a good waiting list but they are mostly able, mostly wanting a room in

Daffodil. And there's quite a demand for double rooms. Maybe we could think about refurbishing to create one or two more double spaces? I'm sure we'd get a good response if we did that work."

"No refurb on the agenda. I want those vacancies filled by the end of the month, Pauline I'm going to give you three weeks to work that out. We're currently working towards an internal audit at the beginning of November so that we can go to market at a moment's notice if need be." Akin's right foot tapped slowly on the carpet.

"You're selling?" Pauline was shocked. She knew that a mere lapse at the hairdressing salon would not warrant these drastic steps. Something else must be afoot. Surely they wouldn't sell just one home from the portfolio? What if they were to sell them all? What would happen to her mother if Jesmond Lodge were to change hands? Or to the residents of Gramwell, come to think of it? Her heart was beating ten to the dozen.

Pushing at something imaginary in mid-air, Akin gestured with his handsome, large hands that the pressure should be brought down. "Calm down, lady!" he laughed again. Akin was almost always smiling or laughing: it was one of his traits that she found so magnetic. "No need to press panic buttons yet," he went on. "We just want to take the *exact temperature* of Empire, know the lay of the land, know where we stand." His modulations were so tuneful to her ears that she thought it almost as though he was singing or rapping when he talked.

"OK. I trust you," Pauline forced a smile. "Can we get you something to drink?"

"I'd like a macchiato, thank you. And then I will hit the road, head back to London. Beat that traffic, you know." His long fingers beat out a tune on the arm of the sofa. He gave the appearance of being extremely pleased with himself. Pauline never felt with anyone else the simultaneous quivering of almost all of her bodily organs: he had a disarming effect on her that jeopardised her ability to think straight.

Pauline phoned Tayla to bring in the coffees. She wanted him to stay for as long as possible but, when the hairdressing incident came to mind, she wanted him to go. Maybe she wished he'd never come at all. *Akin Akindele will be my undoing*, she thought to herself.

Pauline waved from the window as Akin waved back, driving his car away from the Gramwell castle wall and out of the visitors' car park. Alex Durwyn flew through the automatic doors to the signing in book. "Tayla, sorry I'm late," she rushed. "Did you see that car? I think it's a Ferrari. Looks like the *Batmobile*!" Alex unwound the home-knitted scarf from her neck, dropping her bag beside the Reception desk as she unzipped her coat. "What's that smell?"

"That was Akin. He came to see Mrs Graves and she was in the hairdresser's," Tayla reported the most exciting event of the day. "He said there was a smell too. I thought he meant me!"

"It's around here somewhere," Alex indicated the table behind them.

"I tried to tidy it a bit but it's been so busy."

"What's new?" Alex and Tayla always told each other that they'd been ridiculously busy each time they had a handover. Mostly that was true. There was seldom a quiet moment at Reception, unless it was the weekend when it could be so quiet that they would be bored rigid watching the clock make slow progress as they recorded the times that residents were going in and out on their family outings.

"Here, it's here." Alex indicated a paper bag underneath the Continence Reports that had been printed for the Carers. "What's this *shit*?" she winced, holding up the bag with shiny, damp patches seeping through it.

"Oh my God!" Tayla wailed. "It's Mrs Jones-Whatsit's Stilton for her mother. She brought it this morning. I was supposed to take it to the kitchen but things were too busy. And then I forgot it was there when I tidied up."

"It smells dead, whatever it is." Alex assessed. "What should we do with it?"

"Take it to the kitchen?" Tayla suggested sheepishly.

"I reckon Mrs Hewson would scalp us if we took this into her kitchen. But we can't leave it here. It's stinking the place out."

"I can't tell them that I forgot it." Tayla realised. "How about I take it out to the bins before I head off?"

"I don't care what you do with it except it's not going to sit there beside me all afternoon and evening, even if it's just about ready to walk out by itself. Just get rid of it!" she ordered as she took up her place at the desk. Tayla threw on her parka, grabbed the bag after signing out and headed for the bins where she found Brian Petty, smoking alone and looking completely crestfallen.

"Just putting you through, Dr Dunwoody," Alex punched at the keypad and looked up to find Amity standing in her scarlet swing coat, having left a memory stick on the desk.

"Can you please print forty copies of this, Alex? It's the script for the Panto. Forty should cover it, I think."

Pauline Graves came over to join them. "Are you leaving already?" she asked of Amity.

“Meeting in Colchester. It’ll probably take the rest of the afternoon so I’ll see you tomorrow.” She left no room for discussion.

Pauline sighed deeply. “You’d better put your thinking cap on then,” she edged. “Poor Meg Hardy has passed away. Evelyn just let me know that the hospital are issuing the death certificate today. We need to contact the family to see when they’re going to collect her things and to see if they want to have the Wake here at Gramwell.” She started to walk through a long list of tasks that followed the passing of residents. “And we now have another Tulip vacancy so we need to talk,” she pressed, looking back at Amity as she retreated to the solitude of her office.

“Tomorrow morning, then. It’ll probably take you until then to print out the Panto scripts, Alex, won’t it? Such sad news for the Hardys.” Amity signed out, leaving both women surprised at her determination and the skip in her step.

Chapter Six

OBEY

"Sluice the slurry!" Barney Perry urged Lavinia as she neatly juggled a blunt syringe into the hairy shell that was his left ear. Lavinia Marin was one of the few staff members that Barney Perry didn't send packing from his room which was precisely why Brad had asked her to do this job that most of the others would have balked at. She'd known plenty of grumpy old men in her time and wasn't about to let Barney avoid the extra ablutions that were now called for in preparing him for the upcoming Armistice Day celebrations. Barney Perry had been called to do his duty, to bring honour to Gramwell Glade.

"Who is 'Slootha Surrey'? Keep still now!" Lavinia turned her head to ensure she was inserting the syringe properly until her own head was practically upside down. "Do as you're told, Barney!'"

"Sluice the slurry. Sluice the slurry. Try saying that three times quickly," he taunted before hearing his ear pop, making him sit bolt upright in his chair.

"What have you done?" he asked in amazement.

"Look here!" The collection of quite so much ear wax in the syringe fascinated Lavinia as it would many of her fellow nurses who always seemed interested in human extrusions. "Sluice the slurry? Is that it? " she asked, returning the disposable syringe into a kidney dish on the table beside Barney's armchair.

"No need to shout!" he retorted. "It's what they used to say on the farm after milking. 'Sluice the slurry.' And I says, 'No need. There'll always be more tomorrow.'"

"Let's hope that the ears stay clean for longer than that. The television people are coming to meet you on Monday, Barney. For the war story. We need to make sure that you scrub up well." Lavinia rubbed the little piece of red plastic that was his hearing aid clean on a sterilised wipe before neatly popping it back in for him.

Barney snorted down his nose. He hadn't noticed before that Lavinia had a strong accent."Where do you come from then?"

"You know where I come from Barney. Romania. I've told you a hundred times before. And then you tell me –"

"Rum lot, the Romanians," he continued.

"That's it! And then I tell you that we don't drink rum in Romania. We have *tuica* but it's hard to find it here."

"Two cars?" he asked as she put a paper towel on top of the kidney dish before placing her hands on both arms of his chair and looking Barney straight in the eye. With her right hand she ruffled his hair back into the makings of a side parting.

"I'm going to check with Chantelle to see when she can fit you in. Get rid of some of those whiskers and neaten up this mop, ready for your television show."

Lavinia bustled out of the room with her trophies as Barney shouted behind her, "Sluice the slurry!" As she left, a changing of the guard immediately took place with Amity knocking on his door and walking straight in.

"Morning, Barney!" she offered cheerfully, dressed in yellow and smelling of roses.

"No need to shout!" he protested. "Can't a man get a minute's peace around here?"

"Well that's good news, isn't it? You can hear again! We won't have any trouble understanding the interviewer when they come to see you, then?"

"Who is 'the interviewer'?" Barney seemed surprised.

"The television news crew. I don't know who it will be but you'll be on the news. Has your daughter brought in your medals yet?"

"Haven't seen either of them," Barney grunted. It displeased him that his family had taken charge of his belongings. When he was at home he'd been able to decide what went where but these days it seemed that his daughters were in charge. And it wasn't easy to know which of them was the bossier. Freda and Joan had bickered ever since they were little girls and now that they were in their sixties, none of the rivalry had waned. As it was, they arranged to visit Barney on different days so as not to bump in to one another. "I don't know which one has the medals. They should leave them here," he grunted. "They belong to me."

"Indeed they do," Amity acknowledged. "I'll have a word. Perhaps they took them home to polish them for you?" She assured him, knowing that she'd pressed the point with Freda who had agreed to do as required so as not to allow Joan a chance to outdo her. "Now, we need to make sure you know what you want to say in the interview. You were proud to serve your country, weren't you?"

Although she was trying to help Barney frame his piece-to-camera, he felt pretty sure that she was only stating the bloody obvious. It would be helpful, he thought, to give people a flavour of what serving in Europe had meant all those years ago with his mates, so many of whom had fallen.

"And so were those who were lost," he added sympathetically.

"Of course. Armistice Day is to celebrate their contribution too. Lest we Forget. But I'm pretty sure they want to hear what it meant to you and how proud you are that you served your country so well."

Malgosia knocked at the open door and came straight in with Barney's lunch tray, a silver cloche in pride of place. "Lunch!" Barney broke a smile as Malgosia set the tray on the table beside his chair. "Quiche today!" she explained cheerfully as she removed the cloche from the dinner plate with a flourish.

"Quiche? I wanted bacon and egg pie!" he moaned.

"Sorry, I meant bacon and egg pie," she began to retreat, sharing a smile with Amity as she backed towards the door.

"Do you come from Romania?" he quizzed as she retreated.

"No. Poland," Malgosia said by way of leaving.

Barney looked towards his quiche and then to Amity. "We saved their bacon. So many of them here now, I wonder who's left in Europe?" He stabbed his fork at the food on the plate.

"I'll leave you then, Barney, and wish you luck for Monday. Enjoy it. They are here to celebrate all that you did for your country." She turned to leave before remembering to ask, "Would you like to think about being in our Christmas Pantomime?" No sooner were the words out of her mouth when the answer became apparent and she continued on her way.

"Sluice the slurry," called Barney after her.

Gramwell Glade's Senior Managers sat in the Tulip Dining Room for their Friday meeting, the aim of which was to discuss the events of the week and the plans of the one to follow. Pauline regarded it as the *Owners' time*, an opportunity to put across the messages and requirements that set Empire apart from other care homes and a vehicle to ensure that she met all the 'key performance indicators' on which her performance, as well as theirs, would be assessed.

Brad was sitting at the end of the dining table that faced the French doors to the garden and opposite their Chairwoman, when she finally got there. He was about the only one who didn't mind sitting straight opposite Pauline, to get the full thrust of her volleys, throughout the meetings that generally went on for over the prescribed hour and sometimes closer to two.

Brendon sat on the side closest to Brad, his chair a little further back from the table so that he could look at the back of Brad's neatly cut hairline and breathe in the various but classy aftershave perfumes he wore. Amity, beside Brendon, was wearing the tight green Capri pants of her silk suit without the jacket she'd left in her office. The Senior meetings in Tulip were always stoked at least by the full twenty degrees of the central heating but often with an added boost of streaming afternoon sunshine, so that, despite the season, it could get up to almost forty in that room. The meetings usually became a rather beastly hothouse of orders, ideas and perspiration. None of them looked forward to Friday afternoons.

"Have you got fake tan on, Ams?" asked Brendon, looking down at her shapely ankle and aqua patent court shoes that matched her silk blouse.

"That's the real thing, Brendon, from Capri. We were in Capri a couple of weekends ago."

"I can't keep up with you and Giles," Brendon sighed. "So that's where you were when Brad and I were slaving here as Duty Managers three weekends ago?"

"When Hilda walked out in the middle of the night," Brad chimed in. "And we had to deal with her family the next morning. What do you think, Brendon? A police interrogation in Essex or poolside in Capri: which would you choose?" he asked with a giggle.

"Hmm, let's see…" Brendon put a finger to his chin and his head to the side. "Anywhere with you, babe," he teased.

Brad immediately blushed, uncharacteristically letting his professional guard down for a second. "Well, I know where I would rather have been!" he insisted, breaking off Brendon's reverie in an instant.

"Where is she?" Bessie Roberts asked, doodling in the corner of her notepad. "I don't want this to go on all afternoon. I've got much more important things to be going on with."

"Like the Panto," Amity pushed a large pile of paperwork to the centre of the dining table. "It's time to say who you'd like to be in the Panto, before we open auditions to the residents. We need some strong leads," she insisted.

"Are you doing the Panto?" Brendon asked in amazement. "I thought it was going to be a joint venture with all of us in charge."

Amity pushed the pile of scripts to Brendon. "Fill your boots!" she laughed. "I didn't want to be doing it. Pauline said that it was up to me. I can use all the help you can give. It's got to be ready by Christmas and I'm going on holiday in a fortnight."

"*Another one*?" Brad asked in surprise. "How come I'm chained to Gramwell every day that God sends and you're away every other week?"

"Maybe because I've been with Empire for years and you've only been *chained* to the place for the four years since we opened here?" They laughed together as Peter Spence, dressed in his deep red Empire overalls, came in to join them, apologising for being late.

"Don't worry, Pete," Amity assured him, "you're not late. The boss isn't here yet but I need to talk to you about building the Panto sets."

Peter pretended to make a beeline from the meeting when they all called him back in. The Friday meeting was one of the few times that the Handyman sat with the Seniors. They enjoyed his droll humour and his unusually informative slant on the whys and wherefores of Gramwell which he seemed to pick up around the traps in ways that were not available to them.

"What is the Panto this year?" Brendon asked. It was clear that he was showing more interest than the others.

"Because you want to be the leading lady?" Brad joked.

"Depends on which one it is," Brendon admitted. "I don't want to be Dick Whittington or Aladdin. But if it's Goldilocks or Cinderella, you can count me in."

"Typical," observed Peter. He'd learned to join in now with the camp jokes that, only four months ago when Brendon arrived at Gramwell Glade, made him feel desperately uncomfortable.

"Well, it's Sleeping Beauty!" Amity announced, hoping to muster some enthusiasm.

"I'll be Sleeping Beauty!" Brendon called in a falsetto voice.

"Or the Bad Fairy?" Amity offered with expectation in her tone as she looked at him along her nose.

"Now there's a dilemma," Brad acknowledged.

"Can I get back to you, Amity?" Brendon was taking the matter very seriously.

"Monday morning at the latest," Amity acknowledged. "I really thought you'd go for the part of the Bad Fairy but OK, have a think about it and we'll touch base first thing Monday."

"Glad to see that you're working without me," Pauline noted as she entered the room and, with her, a shot of cooler air. "I'm sorry I'm late. The

Hardys were here to let us know about the arrangements for Meg's funeral." Opening her Agenda, a myriad of coloured Post-It notes marked out the business of the day so that all thoughts of pleasurable activities were put aside. "The Wake will be here, two weeks today. I'll let Peggy know about the catering. Brad," she continued without a breath," would you tell us the Empire Mission Statement today, just to put us in mind of the context of our meeting and our work?

Alex Durwyn was trying to captain the Reception Desk through a session of Gerry and Harry's singing. Every second Friday, Gerry and Harry set up their backing tapes and microphone stands in Ye Olde Tea Shoppe, picked up their guitars and thrummed out the same old favourites of the 'thirties, 'forties and 'fifties to a captive audience who were encouraged to join in. The amplified efforts of both Gerry and Harry held sway over those of their fans but the confluence of sound waves would wash over the Reception Desk and for distances beyond so that the largest part of Gramwell Glade was both inundated and soothed with the same old songs.

Barney Perry had been taken to the hairdresser in a wheelchair earlier in the afternoon. A neat trim of his hair and a smooth shave later, his chair was parked in Ye Olde Tea Shoppe waiting to go back to his room when the setting up for Gerry and Harry had started, so the mission to send him back to his room had apparently been overlooked. Marjorie Simmonds' chair had been parked up beside him as the Care Team scattered to bring as many residents as they could to the afternoon's concert, giving them a chance to dash away and catch up on entering their notes into the system to record the eating, sleeping and excretions of each and every resident.

Alex answered the phone and had to ask the caller to repeat themselves. "I'm so sorry. There's a concert going on here and I can't hear you very well."

Olga Dean shouted from Head Office that they needed to have the timesheets in early this week and could they be done by four pm.

"Mrs Fenway's not here," Alex shouted back from her end.

"I know that!" Olga shouted back. "Pauline needs to get them done. Is she there?"

"Mrs Graves is in the Seniors' meeting. I can leave her a message about it and give it to her as soon as she comes out."

Gerry and Harry had sung 'Blue Moon' a thousand times before but never with as many mistakes as they were now managing. Harry stopped the song half way through, pushing the buttons on the tape recorder before Gerry had finished "... saw you standing alone" without the benefit of the backing tape until he realised that Harry had pulled the plug. The audience clapped and laughed as Harry rejigged the tape so they could start again. "Starting to forget!" Harry confessed into his microphone with a shrug of his shoulder as the intro sounded out for the second time.

Alex took advantage of the rare break in transmission to assure Olga Dean that she would get the message to Mrs Graves as soon as possible before the musical accompaniment started up again.

"Is that tune called 'Starting to Forget'?" Barney shouted through the noise to Marjorie.

"Yes, dear. I think I am," she admitted.

Alex looked up to see Pauline stalking through the foyer towards her office.

"Mrs Graves!" she called, putting down the phone receiver. Pauline appeared not to hear her through the broadcast of 'Everybody Loves Somebody Sometime' so Alex got up from her chair, walked around the desk with the phone message slip she'd completed some time ago and followed her, knocking at the open door as Pauline slumped into her office chair. Both she and the chair gave a deep sigh before she startled when she saw Alex in the doorway.

"So sorry to disturb you. Olga Dean's been trying to reach you about a deadline for today so I thought I'd better let you know. She sounds very cross or very impatient. Maybe both?"

"That's fine, thanks Alex," Pauline reached across her desk and took the slip that Alex was stretching to get rid of, quickly returning to her bottom to the chair. The phone had been ringing again but was drowned in the relentless sounds of Gerry and Harry who were warning "that sometime is now".

It was the last thing she felt like doing on a Friday afternoon, particularly after a steep Seniors' meeting. Pauline was pleased that she'd had the last word but had given the Team little choice since she'd left straight after delivering that word. This was one tactic that never failed. She had just told it to them straight and it was now up to them to make it work.

"Hi, Olga." She tried desperately to put a smile into her tone but really was aware that she'd merely come across high in the saddle of the exhaustion that rode her. "I've been with the Seniors. A lot to deal with today," she pressed on.

It became clear very quickly that there was a lot on at Head Office too. After speaking with Olga, she found herself back at square one with enough work to last a week even though they were at the end of a hard week already.

"Yes, I understand," she laboured. "You know how difficult it's been with Barbara not being here."

"Yes, I do appreciate that you're doing the lion's share of the work but…"

All of Pauline's efforts seemed to go unacknowledged while the list of demands just grew and grew. "OK," she conceded." I'll bring Donna Herbert in on a temporary full-time basis to get things rolling again at this end and we will ask HR to get an advertisement rolling to recruit. Of course they take some time with their processes but that will be the best I can do. The cost of Donna won't jeopardise the budget because, of course, Barbara's not drawing wages anymore but are still included in the budget figures. So is it all right if we get those timesheets to you on Monday as usual, but you give us an extension on the staff records because…"

Olga Dean had conceded the proposed schedule with no grace, just as Pauline had expected. The phone had been hung up in her ear and she was left wondering how it had come about that there was really no one in whom she could confide. She had been a celebrated appointee only a few months after having started at Jesmond Lodge before being ricocheted into the General Manager role at Gramwell when Empire needed to register a new leader there in a hurry.

In those days, ten short months ago, no one could do enough for her. Now the Seniors were obviously unhappy with the dictates she'd had to pass down the line, Barbara had crashed and burned so now there was no one to perform even the most basic financial or performance reporting. Akin, the only man who'd fired her interest in a very long time, now seemed to have his mind on things other than her just when she'd made a deliberate decision to make him part of her personal objectives. She wondered if he even noticed her anymore and, while there was very little to tempt her on the coming weekend other than complete rest, it now looked like being just another weekend locked in 'the castle'. Pauline picked up the phone during a short break following a rollicking version of 'Knees Up Mother Brown' to set her latest plan in place.

"Alex, can you get me Donna Herbert's home phone number and print me out a new Staff List with *all* their contact details?" She slammed the phone back on its cradle and looked out to the car park, the trees surrounding the grounds now almost completely denuded of leaves.

In the lounge, a few of the Seniors were still left reeling. Brad had called Lavinia Marin in to join them when he'd seen her bustling past the glass door and began to explain the dilemma to her, a trusted nurse.

"We've been handed the *Sword of Damocles*," Brad looked hollow around the eyes of his fellow managers.

"If I knew what that was, I might be able to join the fight," Brendon chipped in, "but as it is, I'm more worried about what's going to happen to our lovely ladies and gentlemen."

"You don't look too concerned, Amity," Brad accused. "I suppose it doesn't matter to you since it all boils down to more new residents?"

"Hold up!" Amity stood up straight and made for the couch near the window, her heels clacking on the laminated floorboards. "It's a fact of life in the care sector, isn't it Brad? We have to move with the times and, no doubt, Pauline has her reasons."

"Her orders, more like," Brendon chipped in. " Surely not even Pauline could come up with this on her own?"

"I think I'll leave you chaps to it," Peter apologised as he went to leave the room. "Got to put the chickens to bed and finish up the painting of the empty room in Tulip before I knock off today."

"It's easier for those who don't have to pick up the pieces, is all." Brad reasoned. "I mean, how can we choose which one should be sent to Tulip when they are all doing so well in Daffodil?"

"And does this mean that Maisie has to stay in Tulip when she's doing so well?" Lavinia's face creased with concern.

"Well, yes, that's what it has to mean if we have to move two to Tulip. And in a week!" Brendon's voice found a new, higher register that reflected his concern.

Bessie Roberts, in trying to hold a management line, had not contributed to the ghastly prospect that befell them all. To choose two Daffodil residents and move them to the higher security of Tulip Community meant that two new Daffodil vacancies would be created and they all knew that those were the ones that were more easily filled. Even families who knew the full extent of their loved one's dementia would baulk at consigning that loved one to a full dementia community. Minimising the condition had become their stock in trade outside the home. On the other hand, at home, their hearts were often broken with the sheer devastation that the disease brought to previously active and caring brains. What's more, they had promised there would be no care home – ever – for the future of their partner or parent, never mind sending them to *Bedlam.*

"What about Barney?" Lavinia suggested.

"Oh, don't even go there!" Amity raised her blocking hand from the couch. "We'd lose the family. Neither Freda nor Joan would stand for that and, for once, they'd stand united. Barney would dig his heels in. We'd lose them for sure. It's just not an option."

"Brad, please don't even consider moving Elsie to Tulip?" Bessie pleaded. "She's been doing well despite some escalation in her dementia. She would be broken if we put her somewhere where she couldn't have her mobility scooter."

"She'd probably never smile again," agreed Brendon.

"Hey, guys," Brad pleaded. "It's not *me* that wants this! We wouldn't even be having this conversation if the order hadn't been made. I don't want to move anyone any more than you do. The disruption to them in getting used to a new room, new neighbours and a much different regime when it comes to everyday life, it's not what I want at all."

Brendon patted Brad's hand. They were in safe company all under the same pressure together. He was so relieved to see that even Brad would not be happy to toe the line. They were aligned. This was a cruelty they had not imagined.

Since Gramwell Glade had only been in existence for four years, none of them had seen this particular configuration of the 'numbers game' before. In the beginning the place had to be filled. Amity worked tirelessly with all comers; perhaps some of the first takers they might not have selected themselves, but at that time at least no one was dancing on anyone else's grave. Then there were the natural ebbs and flows when, sadly, some of the residents passed away as a result of whichever infirmity they had come in with or, less frequently, just as a result of old age. There was no doubting that the residents all had the very best of care at Gramwell which had become their cosseting hearth and home, their port in any storm. But now, it seemed, they had reached a point where consumer demand meant that some of the less able had to be relocated from their known room to another, still under the one strong Gramwell roof, however one that was new and more damning because it was to point them out as needing more acute care and attention.

"It's a fact of life," Amity continued. "They'll still have the same friends and the same friendly staff. Some may not notice," her glance took in the faces of Bessie, Lavinia, Brendon and Brad, "too much anyway. We can make sure that as little as possible changes for them. And we will do up the rooms for them before they move in. Meg Hardy's room has already been painted and re-carpeted. Peter's just finishing off the last touches there." This did not seem to have appeased her audience in any degree. "We've got our marching orders, guys, It's time to take action. It's only a very short window that we've been given." Amity knew that the others all knew that she was in line for commission payments on all new admissions but money wasn't her only motivator. Amity knew about keeping the bosses happy. As did Brad, but sometimes it hurt.

"So it looks as though Mildred Absolom will have to move from Daffodil 4?" Brad asked, wishing that someone would come up with a miracle or at least a less painful solution to the problem.

Lavinia slapped her hand on the dining table around which they all sat. "Well, I agree with Bessie. We can't move Elsie. She'd be a broken woman. She knows enough to know that would be a diagnosis she couldn't take on. And she's harmless. Leaving Maisie in Tulip is almost as bad. She's been so good lately and fully understands that she could be joining all her Daffodil friends before long."

"Or a lot longer than that. But it's not as bad to leave someone where they are as it is to move them, is it?" Brad was becoming exasperated with the tension of the decree that left no apparent room for their humanity. "So, if it's not Elsie and if we agree that, because of these new orders, we have to leave Maisie where she is, then it will have to be Elizabeth Hollick? She'll have to leave Daffodil 3 and her friends, the Storricks?"

Each of them looked to the other around the table. Amity had taken herself off to the relative comfort of the couch near the window: she was well entrenched with the future propositions; they seemed to cause her no discomfort at all as she looked from the window to the squirrels racing on top of the fence.

"Oh God. Then it's Mildred and Elizabeth. I feel like an executioner," Brad confessed. "I'll arrange family meetings for next week. " No need to delay the agony." He picked up his notebooks and stood at the side of the table, head bowed. "Thanks for your support," he offered in a smaller voice. "I couldn't do this without all of you. There's no doubting that, you're always there when it gets tough."

Brendon squeezed Brad's hand. An electric line pierced their connection in Brendon's arm. His every mission was to support Brad to the limit. He loved that his support was recognised. They could make this work. He just had to find a way to make sure he was always going to be Brad's protector.

Both Freda Thorpe and Joan Payne had visited Barney over the weekend. Somehow they seemed to know when the other would be in since neither wanted to spend time with the other although, on occasions of celebration, such as the coming Monday, they would have to grin and bear it. Well, bear it in any case.

On Saturday, Freda had miraculously produced Barney's medals, all polished up. With a flourish she greeted him with the opened case as though she were the officer first presenting them. It was never easy to move him but Barney had been pleased to see the medals again. Freda then took him for a brisk walk in his wheelchair around the garden all wrapped up in hat, scarf, coat and gloves. Hearing was now far less of a problem for Barney but his sight was letting him down. Although it was a dull early November day, everything seemed so bright to him and almost blurred. Freda had pointed out some birds and a squirrel as they made their way around the long path but Barney hadn't been quite quick enough to pick them up. When they had come around the final bend to the fenced off Visitors' Car Park, Barney had gasped as a wide beam of sunshine lit up the castle wall of Gramwell's façade.

"Where are we?" Barney asked in amazement.

Freda momentarily pulled herself up. Was her father now forgetting even where he lived, she wondered. "It's Gramwell Glade, Daddy. Where you live!"

"I don't live in a Castle!" he chided. "I live in a bloody dungeon, locked away from the rest of the world," he grunted.

"Come on now. You love it here. It's very comfortable." She bent down to speak into his hearing aid as she held on to the wheelchair handles. "It's the old Senerwell Folly. Don't you remember? We used to come here to collect you after you played golf when we were little? It was a castle built by the Earl of Essex, except it wasn't finished. And this tower wall is all that he managed before he ran out of funds."

Freda wasn't sure that she was able to jog his memory. This was making her feel uncomfortably uncertain. Unknown to her, that very feeling was a constant companion to her father. She rattled on in a quest to override the uncertainty,

"It was left unfinished in the woods and then, years later, the Golf Club bought it and then they decided to sell it off because the Council were demanding that the Folly Wall be maintained under a Heritage order or something like that". It appeared to be of no use. There didn't seem to be a flicker of recognition on her father's face.

Freda straightened up and put her back into it to push the chair back in the direction they'd come when Barney piped up, "Bloody Council! They're always telling us what to do," he shouted, "and that's when Empire bought the land and wall from the golf club and built Gramwell Glade."

His rhetorical recognition came as a wave of relief to Barney's daughter who happily pushed him into the foyer and signed him back in with a nod to Reception, arriving back to the room that, in a process unbeknown to them, and thanks to Amity's pleas, would remain his own.

"I'll see you on Monday then, Daddy." Freda went to leave having restored him to the warmth of his room, his hat and coat hanging on the back of his door.

“Why? What’s on Monday?” Barney demanded to know.

“The television people are coming to record an interview with you in the afternoon. For the Remembrance Day broadcast, remember? That’s why I brought you the medals. See you then,” she offered in the brightest way she could manage, knowing that both she and her sister were going to have to make some temporary kind of peace if Barney was going to have any sort of fond memories of the day.

When Joan visited Barney on Sunday she had been completely taken up with the business of dressing her father for the big event. It seemed he now lived in tracksuit pants and old woollen jumpers or, worse, windcheaters. She had left clothes for best but it seemed that the carers and the laundry staff preferred the easy-access, easy-wash garments that made her father look no better than a slob. In fact, Barney also preferred the softer fabrics and the ease of getting elastic-waisted pants down or up as he needed.

Joan had brought one of his old suits with her. She’d sewn up the fraying in the backside as best she could. Since he’d be in the wheelchair, the TV camera wouldn’t pick up that they’d been mended. It seemed a silly idea to buy him a new suit at this stage especially as he only wore it once a year at most. Joan had called the TV station to see if they wanted Barney to be resplendent in his old uniform for the interview and was relieved when they said he should just wear what he normally wears to be comfortable. She’d had no doubt that he’d grown beyond the dimensions of any piece of uniform which she’d held on to through the years. His time at Gramwell Glade had marked an expansion of his waistline if not his tolerance levels.

Phoenix had popped her head around the door to ask if either Joan or Barney would like a tea or coffee. Joan had been pleased for the excuse to have something to focus on other than themselves as she *played mother*. Communication had become more stiff and difficult, while the only progress Barney seemed to make was towards dementia and deafness with progressive loss of both sight and temper. Neither did she think much of the way he slurped his tea but coached herself that they may not have a long time together so they needed to make the most of what they had.

“So your suit’s mended, Dad, and I’ve put it in the wardrobe. I see that Freda has managed to bring your medals back to you. Now you’re all set!” she patted his arm. “If there’s anything else you need, just give me a ring. The Carers will bring you a portable phone if you want to call.”

In all the time that her father had been at Gramwell, he had not phoned her once so this was a bit of a ‘furphy’, he thought, but he was pleased that she still came to see him. Freda looked so much like her mother had done that it comforted him to see her face but, for the rest, it seemed so much of an effort to think of anything to say so he, too, kept to their signature script. It gave them both comfort to go through the same motions each week. "I will, girl. You just look after yourself and your family. I'll be just fine here." They exchanged kisses on each other's cheek and said goodbye until tomorrow when Barney would be on his mettle.

After a relatively quiet weekend, it was *all stations go* first thing on Monday. The housekeepers had already been through. Diverted from their regular Monday laundry duties, they'd been told to have vacuumed all the corridors and washed the hard floors. Special attention had been paid to Pauline's office long before she'd arrived. This task had been at the top of the list she'd given them, with a note that the television people would be using her office as their base all morning.

Pauline was in early enough to see that the planned seven am start for Reception had somehow been delayed. She had taken up position at Barbara's old desk by the window so as to leave her office available to the television people for their shoot. Amity wasn't in yet but that was no surprise. It was rare that she would arrive before nine each morning. Pauline checked through the rota on the whiteboard. Alex Durwyn was supposed to be on Reception but that had been crossed out and Donna's name had been substituted. This just wasn't working. She had told Donna to come in from nine until five now that she was virtually taking up Barbara's load. So who, she wondered while spitting chips, had decided that Alex would leave her post, thereby leaving Reception unattended and on a Monday morning of all shifts?

A knock on the door preceded the appearance of Evelyn Dunwoody's head.

"Ah, they said you were in here!" the doctor chortled. "There was no one at the Reception desk and the cleaners are in your room. I didn't know where to find you!"

"Don't even go there," Pauline gestured with a swish of her arm that all had gone behind. "It's going to be one of those days, I can tell."

"I wanted a word about Barney Perry. His blood pressure is really high this morning." Dr Dunwoody could see in the worn glaze of Pauline's eyes that this information was not registering. "Shall I call Brad when he comes in?" she suggested. "It looks as though you've really got a lot on?"

"Too much!" Pauline opined. "The television people are expected shortly to do the interview with Barney and apparently we've got no one on Reception until nine."

"OK. I'll speak to Brad." The doctor began to move her adequate behind backwards into the corridor.

"Will Barney be OK to go ahead?" Pauline shouted as an after-thought.

"I think it would be a bigger problem if we told him it was off the agenda. He's really pumped about it. Likely the reading will be much lower later today when the excitement is over. Take care!" she added before disappearing from view.

So if it's about the excitement of the interview, why did she bother me about it anyway? Pauline wondered to herself. There were concerns enough without inventing problems. Pauline often thought that the medicos and clinical team beat up unnecessary alarm. If it wasn't an emergency, it was very often true to think that things would sort themselves out but, no, they always wanted to make a case and then case notes. No wonder this business was so heavily labour-intensive.

The door opened again and Amity appeared in perfect glamour. It was as though she'd already been to the hairdresser. Nothing was out of place. Even Pauline had to admit that she looked sensational in her shocking pink dress as she hung her red coat on a hanger on the back of the door. High pink court shoes were the perfect match for the dress. A green jade pendant set off the pink and green silk scarf which was poised across her shoulders. For Pauline, this was completely over the top. She had made sure that she was looking at her best in a blue pinstriped skirt suit and plain navy courts but, it had to be conceded, that all eyes would be on Amity and, of course, Pauline realised that this was Amity's intention.

"So you're at Barbara's desk today?" Amity asked, nonplussed and a little out of sorts. She'd grown used to having the office to herself: that had been an unusual treat in the time since Barbara had disappeared.

"Yes, I've cleared out of my office so that the crew can set up in there for the interview with Barney," she explained.

"Don't worry, Pauline. That won't be necessary," Amity was quick to point out. "I've been in touch with them. We've decided that the interview will be in Ye Olde Tea Shoppe. They said they want it to show the typical life of the home with others enjoying themselves in the background while they sit with him. It's all arranged."

"Is it? Arranged?" Pauline responded, hardly knowing what to say next. "I wasn't aware that you were the liaison person for Gramwell?" Her tone was curt.

"I wanted to save you extra work." Amity thought to assuage the perceived damage. " However, I have to tell you that they asked for me when they came by last week. Head Office arranged the visit. I've shown them around and introduced them to Barney." It was starting to annoy her that so many of her efforts could go unnoticed. "And I've been keeping Freda and Joan in the loop."

"Freda and Joan?" Pauline asked absentmindedly. They had no staff by those names that she could recall.

"Barney's daughters. They've arranged his wardrobe for today. And I arranged for his haircut and shave. A lot of work has gone into this, Pauline," she laboured.

"So I can go back to my room then?"

"Indeed you can," Amity tried to keep any sting from her voice as she took her mobile from her bag and, reaching over her desk with her back to Pauline, started up her desktop computer.

Pauline didn't see Amity again until, later in the morning, when she ushered a man and a woman into her office while chatting to them and blatantly making no effort to knock before bringing them in.

"And this is Pauline Graves, Gramwell Glade's General Manager," she pointed out to the petite blonde girl and a good-looking forty-something man wearing jeans and a leather jacket.

"Hello there, Pauline," Ben Thompson offered his hand across Pauline's desk. "I'm Ben. I'll be organising the shoot today. And this is Rebecca." Rebecca Grant offered a tiny, flaccid hand across the desk while Pauline reciprocated their greetings as she remained half-seated, her rear raised from her chair by only the few inches required to reach the intruders, just to underline that she wasn't going to go out of her way today to accommodate them.

"I'm sure Amity will take good care of you. I hope you enjoy your time at Gramwell Glade. By all means come back to me if you have any questions about us. Barney Perry will be a trooper, I have no doubt. When will you be showing the piece on the television?" she asked.

"Amity's been looking after us beautifully, thanks Pauline," Ben flashed his winning grin in Amity's direction and saw it mirrored back in Rebecca's fixed, coquettish smile. "I'm sure it will go beautifully. We're going to set up in the café there and it'll probably be shown on Wednesday along with the other Remembrance Day news. And, if we get time, we might just do a few shots of the swimming pool if that's OK? Show off all you have to offer here at Gramwell Glade. All good!" Ben turned to Amity to indicate that they were now ready to get to going on an advertisement that was going to put her sales' efforts streets ahead of the opposition. "The crew are just setting up now. Hopefully there won't be a lot of disruption for the old folks," he flashed his whitened teeth again and followed Amity and Rebecca across the foyer into the café. Pauline finally unseated herself and moved across the room to close the door behind them when she saw Donna setting up at Reception.

She walked over to the desk wondering how best to frame the concerns that were flooding her brain.

"Hi, Pauline," Donna smiled up at her as she sat and began to arrange the things she needed on the desk in front of her. "You're looking so smart today!"

"One has to make an effort," Pauline brushed at the lapels of her suit jacket while adjusting her name badge. "Besides, we've got the Channel Six people here today for that interview with Barney."

Before she could start to list the tasks she was about to delegate, Donna chimed in. "It's so exciting, isn't it? I bet Barney's family are thrilled. It's good for him too, isn't it, to have some recognition for his war efforts?"

"If he lasts the day out." Pauline snapped.

"Is Barney poorly?" Donna looked horrified.

"No, fit as a fiddle. Forget I said anything." Pauline knew that her ironic barbs never went down well in this setting and had tried to curb them more than once. "No, look, what happened with the rota? I thought that Alex was in this morning?"

"She was but she has a hospital appointment and she asked me to swap but then you told me to come in at nine and work a full day so it got confused and it turned out that there was no one on the early shift."

"That's not what I intended. Donna, I want you to look at the rota and make sure that it's going to work properly. We can't have this happen again. What's wrong with Alex?"

"I don't rightly know. She hasn't said much. I think she's had gynae problems. We haven't really talked about it."

"And look through that list of reports that have to be at Head Office. Some are due before lunch and others before close of business, which means five o'clock to them even if I'm here until ten-thirty. Just make sure that everything Barbara used to cover is now seen to by you. And can you get Peter to check that everything is ship-shape in the pool room? Apparently they've taken it on themselves to film in there too."

"I'm not sure I know everything that Barbara did." Donna was capable and had, indeed, given Barbara a great deal of help when that had been needed but she hadn't put herself up for the position when it first came up and she wasn't going to apply for it now that it was being advertised again. It seemed more than a little unfair that she would be asked to take on the full load, especially when there was no reflection of that in her pay rate.

"The list of reports is there with their deliverables." Pauline left the pages on the Reception Desk for Donna to tackle. "Any questions, call Olga Dean at Head Office." Pauline turned on her heel and headed for her office but was immediately waylaid by a glare of lights in the café. The television crew had set up one of the settees near the French doors with floodlights and fluffy microphones. It seemed that white light was filling the entire space. Pauline doubted that many of the residents would be interested in visiting the café this morning in all this chaos but shut her door against it, lest it would interfere with the mountain of reporting that awaited her as it did every Monday morning. There was too much to be done before the usual eleven o'clock catch up with the Senior Team. She had some two hours to herself and time was precious.

Freda Thorpe had pushed her father's chair to Ye Olde Tea Shoppe following the argument she and her sister had had about his suit. Joan had already been in and pinned his medals to a blue windcheater. It was the newest and most respectable of his tops. The suit, it seemed, had been rejected by both Barney and Joan as unsuitable for the occasion and, while Freda thought that medals looked ridiculous on a windcheater, it couldn't look any more downmarket than the beret atop his balding pate. Nevertheless, she had taken up the handles of the chair and despatched him to the café where the crew was waiting for him.

Barney's filmy eyes watered against the floodlighting. A number of residents had gathered, intrigued by the goings-on and hopeful of some diversionary excitement. Rebecca was busily arranging them on chairs that would form the backdrop to the interview. A small table was placed beside Barney. Phoenix and Marigold had been instructed to make him a coffee which was duly placed on the table, only to be ignored by Barney who, feeling the weight of the situation, began to register some of the butterflies of stage fright in his stomach. It hadn't occurred to him that he might be at all nervous about being interviewed or, worse, filmed. His mouth felt dry. He looked to the frothy coffee on the table. He'd never liked that stuff. Fortunately, Freda had asked if he would like a glass of water and he held on to it for grim death as last-minute rearrangements of the lights were made by the crew who then asked him to say something so they could check sound levels.

"Barney Perry reporting for duty, Sir," he quipped, to the delight of the assembled ladies.

Amity fluttered near Rebecca. It had taken her quite some effort to arrange this publicity. Empire would certainly regard this as a feather in her cap. A few minutes, even on regional news, were worth a hundred newspaper articles when it came to publicising the brand.

"Oh I love your heels! Spendy, yah?" Rebecca noted Amity's pink high heels. "Is that a Choo shoe?"

"Bless you!" offered Grace Garrett, trying to muscle in on the conversation. "What's going on today, dear?"

Rebecca looked at Amity, trying to hide her giggles. She hadn't had a great deal to do with senior citizens and was a little afraid that people so much reduced in size and covered in deep wrinkles might not understand modern-day conversation. "We're setting up a shoot," she explained.

"*Oh my days*! Is that why Barney's wearing his army clothes? Will we be safe? Maybe I should go back to my room?" she asked Amity.

"Everything is fine, Grace." Amity assured her. "There's no need to worry at all. They are going to make a film of Barney and it will be on the news. We can make sure that it's shown on the big television in here and you can all come and see it."

"That sounds lovely, dear," Grace climbed down from her panic. "He looks so handsome in his medals, doesn't he?" Grace sat back down between Marie Storrick and Marjorie Simmonds.

"Barney is an absolute hero," Amity trilled.

At this point, Ben announced in a louder voice across the café, "We're ready for a take now. Can you make sure that everyone stays relatively still but let them carry on with their own conversations as normally as possible?"

Many of the residents who had assembled in the café by now had no real need of the warning since they were already absorbed in their own conversations or hidden behind newspapers, rereading what they had already read. The setting was just what Ben had asked for.

"And Take One," he announced. "We're here with Barney Perry, who has served his country and whom we honour on this Armistice Day. Hello Barney, how are you?" he asked as a boom mike sailed above his head. Barney looked up to check that it wasn't about to fall on him.

"We do our best," Barney answered dutifully, his shoulders hunched.

"And you were in France?" Ben went on to set up the piece.

"Yes. And my comrades. Very few of us came home."

"That's right, Barney. They were very tough times, and that's why we all recognise that you are a hero for all that you did for your country."

"It was tough. It was horrible but we showed Gerry who was boss alright. Even when supplies were blocked." Proffering a small, blood-coloured lump in the palm of his hand, Barney asked Ben Thomson. "Can you put an ear in?" The cameraman deftly swung to Ben as Malgosia poked Barney's hearing aid back into place.

"And yet you all continued to fight for freedom?" Ben was high on his horse, his patriotic fervour flowing freely.

Barney wasn't sure what he should say about fighting for freedom. He thought that might have been a different war, maybe in Spain. In a flash his limelight was perfectly dissected by Elsie. She shuffled her bottom in between Barney and Ben on the settee smiling all the while directly at the camera. Elsie looked radiant. It was not a surprise that she could still fit in to her wartime overalls since she had become quite birdlike in her eighties. Her beret sat jauntily on the side of her head.

"I used to fix the engines and I was a driver! Just like the Queen did." Elsie was thrilled with her contribution.

Ben looked to Rebecca who looked to Amity who indicated, with a shrug of her shoulders, that maybe they should just carry on, try their luck and see what might pan out.

"And you are?" Ben asked by way of eliciting an introduction that might be included but could well be edited out of the footage.

"I'm Elsie Lister and I served with the women of our country. We made very important contributions when the men were away. We kept the war effort moving. It would be a very different country now if not for the efforts of the women."

"And we were in the trenches," Barney had realised that his thunder was being stolen, right under his nose. "All the service men were brave and they were all heroes and when the supplies didn't come through." he insisted.

Elsie smiled directly at the camera as though she had worked in media all of her life.

"And we had to eat rats!" Barney snapped.

Freda moved quickly into shot. She knew that her father had reached his limit and the only recourse was to take him back to the safety of his room. She helped him onto his chair while the cameras continued to roll and Elsie obliged with her practised word-pictures about her war contribution as the camera narrowed focus to her animated face.

Freda swiftly pushed Barney in his chair. He shouted "We did eat rats!" as they left the café with Joan following quickly behind.

A full post-mortem of the Channel 6 news team visit was offered up by Amity at the eleven o'clock meeting. Those present, particularly those who knew Barney well, were not surprised in the slightest. They appreciated that he had been feeling pressured, both by the weight of the occasion as much as by having been slighted by Elsie when she stole his thunder. Brad was first to come in to bat for Barney, pointing out that the carers would need to keep a special eye on him as remorse was one of his fairly constant companions.

"So they went on to film the pool but there was so much condensation, it fogged up the camera pretty quickly apparently so it's unlikely that will be included in the feature," Pauline retold what had been explained to her when the television people had come back to disturb her work only about twenty minutes after they'd started.

"It's scheduled to be shown on the ten to six local news on Wednesday evening," Amity explained,

"So can some of the carers, on Wednesday evening, bring some of the residents to the café and set up the big television so that they can see Barney's interview?"

"Make a note of that," Pauline nodded in the direction of Brendon. "And see that Barney's there to bathe in the glory that might be salvaged with some good editing? Now, while I was mentioning the pool, Brad, can you please encourage the carers to start taking residents for some aqua therapy? The pool lies there doing nothing day after day and it's costing a fortune to keep it going. We really must make use of it."

"If I may," Brad interrupted, "I think we'd be inundated, pardon the pun, by families' complaints if we tried to have their loved ones strip off and put on a bathing costume at this time of year. It's a lovely facility in the summer but it's really not going to work coming in to the coldest months now."

"We're under instruction to use it, Brad." Pauline looked around the room. "If you keep that in mind, I'm sure you'll find that it will be a useful therapy for some of our more sprightly ladies and gentlemen at least. See what you can do."

Brendon looked around the room to gauge reactions. His colleagues, who had been under Pauline's orders for longer than the four months he'd been at Gramwell, knew not to engage in any telling glances. They had developed their own way of staring into the distance or closely examining the notes in front of them rather than letting slip their position on some of the frequent but querulous dictates that came their way.

In the same way, both Elizabeth Hollick and Mildred Absolom had been relocated to Tulip community to make way for the newcomers. Millie had been back on numerous occasions when able to get through the security doors. Often this had happened by following the food or laundry trolleys through to Daffodil when staff were still used to her being in Daffodil. She'd turned up one afternoon in the doorway of Daffodil 4 to let it be known that this was her room. Happily ensconced was Nan Sweetman listening to a tape recording of Delibes' 'Flower Song' from *Lakme* which Millie knew was the music for instant coffee and aeroplanes.

Turning from her reverie and bathed in sunshine, Nan asked, "Hello dear. Are you alright?"

Millie was drawn into the serenity and pleasure of the comfortable room that now did not look familiar. "I used to live here," she remarked in a hollow way, as though her soul had been misplaced.

"I used to live here," she repeated. It was difficult for Millie to make out if she even believed it herself as she took in the paintings of snow-covered scenes in the Alps, the sweet harmonies of the duet and the tiny lady who perched elegantly on a new brocade recliner armchair as though she were on a throne.

"I'm Nan," Nan offered. "Why don't you come in?"

"I'm Millie. I used to live here. I'm friends with Elizabeth. She used to live next door. Now we live in Tulip and I don't see much of Bert or my friends anymore."

To Nan, this seemed the familiar strain of those who had been relocated from their homes to live in the sheltered bosom of Gramwell Glade or other homes around the country, although she wasn't having any truck with separation anxiety. Many of them seemed very old to her and some of them a bit mad. "It's like living in a hotel, isn't it dear? I've only been here for a short time but already it feels marvellous. We're so lucky! There's always someone around to help out if needed and the meals. I haven't eaten like this since I used to travel with my last husband, Albert."

"Bert's my friend. You make sure you don't see him anymore, you hear!" Millie's voice was strained with the hurt that came with being told that Albert Watts might be 'seeing' this jumped-up newcomer who was the cuckoo in her nest.

"No, dear, my last husband was Albert. He's passed away now," Nan was feeling uncomfortable with this stranger shouting in her doorway. Phoenix had heard the commotion from the Nurses' Station nearby and come to assist, realising that Millie was visiting her old stamping ground. She swiftly put an arm around Millie to turn her back towards the corridor that led to Tulip community.

"You've got lost, Millie. Sorry, Nan," she nodded as she walked slowly with Millie. "Let's go back to yours, shall we? They'll be serving afternoon tea shortly. You won't want to miss out, will you? And there might be some nice cake." Millie trailed along, gripping on to the side rails of the corridor with a sense that a great deal was now missing while Nan rewound the tape to try a second take on the perfection of the song she loved more than any other.

On Wednesday evening after tea, the diners in Daffodil had been encouraged to relocate to the café to watch the local news with the promise that Barney's interview would be featured. Dot Baker and David Jack made their way from the dining room to the circle of chairs that had been lined up in front of the large TV on the wall. Having set up the room, Darragh and Marigold were fiddling with the remote to bring up the television channels. Channel 6 had been located and muted until the big reveal. Nan Sweetman had been taken in hand by Hilda Matters. Ron and Marie Storrick had obediently joined the others along with Elsie Lister who had brought along newcomer John Nicholls, a retired dentist from London who had, just this week, moved into Elizabeth Hollick's old room, Daffodil 3. Elsie was dressed to the nines in a calf-length black dress with black sequins decorating the décolletage. Her smile was beaming. John had taken particular note that her teeth were very well preserved. There were so few people of his age who had taken such care with their dentition.

A frisson built amongst the audience. After-tea activities were uncommon and came with the excitement previously held for dinner dances or cinema visits in their old lives on the 'outside'.

Amadia Stokes brought up the rear which consisted of Barney in his wheelchair and sporting his medals which she'd encouraged him to give another outing in order to improve his mood, given it had been severely deflated since the interview with the television crowd on Monday.

"Here is our hero," she braved as she positioned Barney's chair in the centre of the back row. A small round of applause followed: they all felt that they should somehow acknowledge what was being built up as an occasion of merit.

Darragh stood in front of the television. "Ladies and Gentlemen, thank you for coming this evening. This is a special screening of the South East news tonight as it will feature our very own Mr Barney Perry." He paused for another tilt to applause. "We're expecting that to start in just a few minutes from now and thank you for finishing your tea that little bit early so that we can join Barney here and perhaps see some of you who were also here in the café on Monday morning when the interview took place.

"Before we start, Amity has asked me to see if any of you have ever been in a choir because –" Darragh paused as a number of hands had shown, if only tentatively. "Well, that's better than we could have expected. The thing is that we're going to put on a pantomime for Christmas."

This announcement was greeted with genuine applause. “Great!” Darragh acknowledged. “Because we are looking to form a residents’ choir to do some songs for the show.” At this point almost all the audience had shown their hand. “I’ll let Amity to know that you’re rearing to go then. And we’d better not take up any more time.” Darragh increased the volume as the news belted out its signature beats. He sat back beside Marigold at the bar and waited as the regular information on crime and weather had set the pace.

Ben Thomson’s face appeared beside the presenter at the news desk to some gasps among the group.

“I know him!” Elsie’s voice was full of excitement. “He’s the one who was here and he gave me a kiss!”

Barney sat motionless in his wheelchair at the back of the circle.

“So now, Ben,” noted the newscaster. “I believe that you have been out and about, talking with some of our wartime heroes?”

“That’s right, Charles. Earlier in the week, I took the time to visit with a couple of the many Essex residents who played their part so well, going to war for their country, for us and, remarkably, we have often overlooked the fantastic contribution made by our womenfolk who had to stay at home, to keep the home fires burning, the engines turning, to make the arms and ammunition and, of course, to feed the children who are now reaping the legacy of the efforts made by all of them. One, in particular, will impress us all, I think…” His voice trailed off to signify a cross to the featured interview. Barney’s fingers gripped the arms of his wheelchair. Elise bounced on her chair and quickly grabbed John Nicholl’s hand in excitement.

The large screen filled with a close up of Elsie’s face and winning smile. There was both dismay and elation in the crowd. This was not what they had been expecting. Elsie was triumphant and vivacious as she parried question and answer with Ben Thomson. From time to time, the camera opened to a wider shot where those now assembled recognised themselves sitting in virtually the same places as was shown on the television. Enthusiastic calls of recognition rocked the room. A brief glimpse of Barney coincided with the moment just prior to his announcement about eating rats. Joan’s shoulder featured as she scooped up his wheelchair with a flourish and the camera immediately focused back on Elsie’s face and her articulate account of the contribution that women had made before the television screen showed Ben back in the studio with Charles, the newsreader.

“That was Mrs Elsie Lister of Essex,” Ben concluded, “a really bright and happy octogenarian who is still filled with national fervour and vigour.”

"Indeed she is!" agreed Charles, neatening up the papers in front of him. "Let's hope that we all look as well as Elsie does when we reach that grand old age."

Elsie clapped her hands together as the others looked to her with pride. She had done a good job. No one had the first idea as to what should be said to Barney. Fortunately, Darragh stood up to fill the gap while Marigold turned off the television. Barney had been many things in his long life but this was his first role as the *elephant in the room*.

"Barney," Darragh asked as Amadia was taking the brakes off his chair in order to wheel him away, "have you ever been in a choir? We were checking to see who might form a new choir for our Panto."

Barney's hand swept away Darragh's question and the whole mess of humiliation. They needn't have polished his medals. What would be the point of having medals anyway? None of them understood anymore, he muttered to himself as they made a speedy journey down the corridor.

Amadia left his room after she had put on his television to the programme about bailiffs taking away people's possessions if they couldn't pay their debts, settled him into his recliner chair and put his medals back in their silk-lined box, which Barney threw into the wastepaper basket the minute she left him.

Chapter Seven

ONCE UPON A DREAM

A blanket of thick fog surrounded the castle wall of Gramwell Glade on a late November Tuesday. Few staff had been able to get in. Others braved the country roads to ensure that their ladies and gentlemen would not go without. Peggy Hewson, let down by deliveries of fresh milk, bread, fish or meat, found sufficient in the pantry and freezer to *make and make do*. The aroma of baking bread and doubled batches of scones had accompanied the usual breakfast wafts of sizzling bacon and sausages. Peter Spence leant against the warm oven, cradling a warm mug of coffee in his hands and talking to Peggy's back as she continued stirring, peeking into the oven, wiping her hands on her apron and throwing utensils on to the chrome trolley beside her for Henry to take to the washing up station when he came back from delivering the Tulip breakfasts. Peggy and Peter were the two functionaries at Gramwell Glade who, like a husband and wife, ensured the running of the household.

"So Eric's just checking the boilers. I've put a load of torches in the store cupboard just there in the hall if you're looking for them."

"Don't even mention that the power might go out, Pete. The gas tanks are OK, aren't they?" If her ovens went down, Peggy would be stymied.

"You'll be fine, girl. We've got you covered. And it looks like you've got us covered too," Peter looked enviously at the batch of scones that Peggy was whisking from the oven. "Later, you leave them be for now!" she scolded.

"And we're leaving the chickens in. A fox could sneak up on them no trouble and they wouldn't see what hit them!" he laughed. "Poor old girls."

"Don't you 'old girl' me, Peter Spence. Now get out of my kitchen. There's enough to do without skirting around you all morning!"

"Thanks for the cuppa then, old girl!" Peter jumped to the door as Peggy tried to flick him with the tea towel she had tucked into her apron pocket.

"And don't come back today!" she shouted behind him.

Pauline moved into the kitchen as Peter passed her in the doorway, shouting, "What about me scone?"

"Do you welcome all your visitors like that?"

Peggy didn't know whether or not Pauline was joking. It was never easy to tell and she thought it best to err on the side of 'not'. "Sorry, Mrs Graves. I didn't mean you," she broke off.

"I should hope not but perhaps it's not the best greeting for anyone? I just came to see if you're alright here in the kitchen because I know that today's deliveries didn't get through yet."

"We're fine. There's always enough in store to cope for a day or two. And Henry, bless him, rode his bicycle in all the way from Senerwell to make sure I had the help we need when we're having to do the bread ourselves and change the menu to use what we're able to find in the freezer."

Henry pulled the door partly open behind Pauline before wheeling out the bain-marie that held breakfast for the Tulip residents.

"Well done, Henry. That's the kind of dedication that makes Gramwell the best in its class!" Pauline enthused.

"Couldn't leave Mrs Hewson to do all the extra and have no one to serve, could I?" He pushed the ungainly trolley out of the door while Pauline watched. Peggy took another batch of scones and two loaves from the large oven, pushing back the white cap on her head.

"You won't get cold in here today," Pauline noted as she began to head for the door. "I can't stay. All your beautiful baking would be far too tempting if I did."

"I thought you'd lost some weight," Peggy wished that she hadn't made what could be construed as quite the bold comment to her boss.

"It's hard work," Pauline said by way of leaving, " but I'm getting there." Pleased that finally someone seemed to have noticed, she was gone.

"'ard work!" Peggy said out loud to herself, doubting that anyone would feel quite as pressed as she today.

By lunchtime it was clear that the fog was not going to lift. All the windows and doors of Gramwell Glade presented a flat, white, glowing wall to the world within. Mildred Absolom and Elizabeth Hollick had met up while wandering in the corridors of Tulip community. Since they'd both been relocated there on the same day, they each saw that there might be someone with whom they could share something in common, even if it was the dislocation that haunted them both. Mildred had been completely confused in her new room, which was designed as the mirror image of the one she'd known so well. Eric had come along and put up her pictures in the corresponding places to where they'd hung in Daffodil 4 but this only added to the confusion. She'd now been *caught short* on a couple of occasions when mistaking the bathroom door for the one that lead to the corridor. Notes had duly recorded her lapses in bladder control, reinforcing the decision to have made the move to more intensive care. She had been coached to wear nappy pants to avoid further mistakes and encouraged to use a wheelchair as her walking was becoming increasingly unsteady.

Mildred and Elizabeth had tried a few of the tables in Tulip Dining Room. Few of the other residents seemed to notice them or have much conversation at all so, when they found Maisie talking away by herself alone at a table for four, they thought to take their chances. At the very least, Maisie was able to speak.

"Do you mind if we sit here?" Elizabeth pulled a chair back so as to sit opposite Maisie. "I'm Elizabeth and this is Millie." Millie clumsily tried to guide her new wheelchair to sit at the other side of the table.

"I'm Maisie and this is John," Maisie indicated the doll on her lap. "Well, it's not really John, is it, but it's as good as I've got and it beats spending the days without him," she laughed. "See, John, we've got some new friends."

Elizabeth looked at Mildred sideways. They had both thought it best to find someone who would at least acknowledge them and this was what they had come up with.

"Foggy today, isn't it?" Elizabeth asked looking over the blank, white window.

"It's usually very nice out of that window," Maisie was glad to have their company, it was obvious. "You can see the trees and birds and squirrels most days. Reminds me and John of living on our farm, doesn't it, John? We lived at Dedham, just outside."

"I lived in Coventry," offered Mildred, "but my son wanted me to come here because he lives in Chelmsford."

"I lived in Senerwell," rallied Elizabeth. "I know Dedham. I've been there!" she said, delighting in the unfamiliar sensation of recognition.

"Lots has been to Dedham. People went there in droves in the summer. They'd stop their cars if they saw us and ask if we could tell them where John Constable's house was, didn't they, John? And John would say, 'You're here. I'm John Dunstable!' and then we'd laugh, didn't we, John? Haven't I seen you before?" Maisie asked Mildred.

“Could be. I’ve moved. We’ve both moved. We used to live in Daffodil, didn’t we, Elizabeth?” They both nodded dolefully. “Only they said we had to move to here and we haven’t met anyone really yet to talk to.”

“John used to say to people, ‘Don’t you worry about a thing, when you move, I’ll help you carry your money,’ didn’t you, John! And we’d laugh.”

“I’ve seen you in Daffodil, too.” Elizabeth had worked out the puzzle that had been pressing her.

“That’s right. That’s where I saw youse both before. I go to Daffodil most afternoons.”

“How do you get there?” Mildred asked keenly. “We’ve tried but they keep bringing us back again. To here.”

“You can come with us this afternoon. We always join in the knitting club on Tuesdays, don’t we, John?”

“And do you reckon we can go too?” Elizabeth challenged, temptation testing her patience.

“My word, yes. You come with us and I will bring you back home again here when we’re done. There’s a lot of them there who are bits of snobs and don’t want us around.”

“There’s no menu today, ladies, but Mrs Hewson has made some lovely treats.” Kayleigh placed bowls of homemade soup and cheese scones on the table with the help of Rosie Rowson who had finished cleaning Tulip and been roped in to give some extra help due to the staff shortages.

Having put all hands to the wheel, the Staff room was lively with a crowd gathering to grab a bite to eat and take the weight of their feet. Frank Goninon and Brian Petty had set up at one of the café tables while Darragh and Naomi had flopped on the couch at the other end of the room, having supervised the Tulip lunch and before heading off to do the Daffodil dining room. They were deep in thrall to their mobile phones.

Frank had been eager to cause some mischief by way of letting off steam. The cleaning duties had been doubly difficult through the morning with only half the team on. He’d even been dragooned into helping in the laundry which he regarded as *women’s work* and where he’d built up that head of steam in double quick time.

“So, fellow,” his tone suggested he was about to charge his companion with an offence, “ is it Kayleigh or Tayla? I hear you’ve been seeing quite a bit of female company of late.”

“Bit of both actually,” Brian boasted.

“In your dreams, Petty!” Naomi called from the other side of the room. “None, more like!”

“You wouldn’t know,” he shot back.

"If I was a betting man, I reckon I'd be backing Naomi on that one!" Frank teased, looking around the room for an audience.

"And *you* wouldn't know either," Brian's nose was a little out of joint.

Marigold burst through the door, holding a pile of towels. She sank into the settee beside Darragh and threw her head down into the towels, screaming, "Oh my God! Oh God."

As she sank her head in the towels, Naomi reached across to hold Marigold's arm and shake it. "What's up? Are you hurt?"

"I'm never bloody going there again!" Marigold protested.

"Where? What's happened?" Darragh was now getting concerned too.

Frank and Brian exchanged glances as though to commiserate on the topic of female hysterics.

Naomi had moved Darragh to her seat so she could put an arm around the girl who was still buried in towelling.

"I went in to the Storricks. Rosie told me to take the fresh towels to them when the dryer was finished because she had to go help out in Tulip."

"So what happened?" urged Naomi. "Are you OK?"

"I'll never be OK. I never want to see that again," Marigold lifted her head putting her hands over her eyes. "I knocked on the door and no one said anything so I thought they'd probably gone on down to Daffodil dining for lunch. I went in."

"For Christ sake, what happened?" shouted Frank, tiring of the suspense.

"They were *doing it*!" Marigold blurted.

"Doing *the business*?" Frank guffawed and the room erupted with laughter."Naughty old Ronnie. I thought he'd had a bit of a twinkle in his eye these past few weeks."

"Who was on top?" laughed Brian.

"Oh shut it, Perry!" Naomi looked back at Marigold. "I guess that must have been a bit of a shock alright," she consoled.

The men were still laughing as Naomi tried to soothe Marigold. "You stay here, have a cup of tea I'll take the towels down later and you can go help with the Knitting Club in Daffodil Lounge when you're feeling a bit better, OK. Were the Storricks OK about it, do you think?"

"They didn't seem too bothered," Marigold explained while handing over the towels, as though they had been responsible for the whole mess she'd been in. "Mr Storrick said, 'Is there anything you want?' to me."

"Like a *threesome*!" joked Frank. The room erupted in laughter.

"What's all the noise, then?" Brendon came in to the room carrying a plate of sandwiches that Peggy had prepared for the staff since they wouldn't be able to drive out to the shops today to bring any of their usual junk food back with them.

"Marigold's had a bit of a shock," Naomi patted Marigold's shoulder.

"What's wrong?" Brendon asked with concern.

"She saw the Storricks doing some horizontal folk dancing!" quipped Brian.

"Ronnie was giving it to Marie and Marigold walked in on them," Frank was delighted with the whole idea of it.

"Good for them!" Brendon surprised them all.

"But I've never seen that before," Marigold mitigated.

"Only with your boyfriends anyway," Brian teased.

"Shut up, Brian!" Brendon had seldom been so blunt. Brian was immediately silenced. "It's all part of the human condition, Marigold. You probably hadn't seen anyone defecate before coming here either but it's all part and parcel of this *rich tapestry of life*, working in the care sector. Although, I grant you, it's not something we come across that every day."

This set the males off again. Even Darragh found it hard to resist the *double entendre*.

"SO childish!" Brendon noted, turning back to Marigold. "You're OK now, right?" She nodded and left to head for the Knitting Club, hoping that there wasn't going to be any funny business there.

David Jack and Dot Baker had enjoyed a light lunch together amid the din of Daffodil Dining Room. With nothing but white glare at the French doors and windows, all attentions were confined to the room, its clashing and tinkling and the aroma of home-made soup and a fish pie that Peggy Hewson and her co-opted team had whipped up from the contents of the pantry and freezer. Under this white siege there was a hint of festivity in the air, a foreshadowing of the Christmas that was to come, for some their first at Gramwell Glade. This was the case for David, the first in this new home and the first without his wife.

After eating, a torpor was settling in for most, their stomachs full of warm, easily digested food that was somehow more satisfying than the usual menu. Barney was wheeled back to his quarters. The Storricks, with mellow smiles, were taking things in their stride, Marie having dotted the corners of her mouth coyly with her napkin before standing to massage Ron's neck proprietarily as they said their goodbyes to John Nicholls and Elsie Lister who had joined their table today.

"I'm off to practise my Scrabble, David. Are you going to join me?" Hilda demanded as she scraped her chair back on the hard, laminated flooring.

"I think I'll just take a little rest this afternoon," David addressed his reply to Dot, leaving Hilda feeling doubly annoyed with his demeanour today.

"We've got to keep our hand in," she urged, "otherwise they'll get the better of us if we don't hone our prowess." It then occurred to her. "Perhaps some time on your own would do you good."

David smiled at Dot, who was pleased to be counting in his thinking. "You're having your hair done this afternoon, aren't you, Dot?"

"Oh, well. If you can't be persuaded."

"Another time, Hilda. I feel like having a bit of quiet time for now."

"You go ahead and rest, David." Dot patted his hand. "You said you hadn't slept well last night."

"I'm not surprised," said Hilda, pivoting directly into the Storricks as they were leaving the room.

"After you," Ron beckoned to Hilda to go first through the door and took advantage of his sweeping gesture to tap his wife gently on the bottom with its return sweep.

"She's becoming quite a nuisance," David confided to Dot.

" Marie Storrick?"

"No, Hilda. She seems to have a never-ending list of things devised for me to do," he grimaced.

"That's because she's keen on you," Dot smiled. "Most of them here are keen on you."

"And you? Are you on the list?" David surprised himself. He seldom let his guard down. He'd been feeling so tired with much on his mind but now relaxed in Dot's company. He could immediately see that he'd pushed the usual boundary of their polite chatter because Dot's cheeks blushed a little: her vulnerability made her even more endearing.

"Oh, I'm so sorry. Please forget it."

"No, it's fine. It's nice, actually. Of course I'm keen on you. Just like the others." Dot began to back down a little as she felt her cheeks glow. "I'm not used to spending time with a man – someone as easy to talk to, at least."

"That makes two of us then. The talking part." David placed his hand on top of Dot's little hand that had been patting his.

She placed her other hand on top of his. "Do you remember this childhood game?"

David put his left hand onto the pile and removed his right from the bottom. "One potato, two potato?"

"Three potato." Dot added to the pile.

"Four!" They both sat back in their chairs, laughing as David firmly grasped Dot's hand in the accumulated pile.

“Can I get you another tea or coffee?” Darragh asked. “What’s all this laughter then? I could do with a good joke.”

“Nothing more, thank you,” David held his hands up in surrender. “I think you can safely say it was one of those *had to be there* efforts.”

“Well, let me know next time,” said Darragh, “and I’ll make sure I am *there*.”

David stood behind Dot’s chair and helped her from her seat. Her neat frame and perfect posture appealed to him no end. Just like Celia, Dot was a woman who took great care with her appearance.

“You don’t need to go to the hairdresser’s,” he flattered, “but I shall look forward to seeing the elegant results.”

Dot wished that she could control her tell-tale blushes but was delighted to have this promise to go on with. She walked with David to the door of his room.

“Later then,” David looked down into her green eyes. Kayleigh Longbottom swept purposefully passed them, down the corridor, with Brian Petty in firm pursuit behind her.

“I shall look forward to seeing you later then.” Dot hadn’t realised before that David was a good head taller than she and, even though now, she was wearing a three-inch heel.

David walked into his room, closing the door slowly behind him. The stark white at the window stared back at him, threatening that he may have somehow reached the end of a line. The amaryllis that Sarah had given him was near the heater on the chest of drawers opposite his armchair. It had already produced two thick stems in these cosseted confines. He looked to the framed photo of Celia and smiled. There were no indiscretions, only harmony to be shared with her. The room was almost cloyingly warm even though the world outside was speedily turning colder.

David chose Elgar’s Concerto for Cello on his iPod and, putting on his earphones, sank into the armchair on the brink of slipping into a silky afternoon nap. The first crescendo of the Adagio came quickly. Every time the cello moved downscale, like an augur into deep, fertile soil, it filled him with longing. The expectations of the notes soaring always made his heart quicken and his entire body tingle. He took off his glasses and laid back into the highest notes. Looking to the window, he imagined himself to be in a plane, flying high in the clouds. He closed his eyes and remembered the stark elegance of Helsinki, Elgar’s city, when Celia and he had flown there on an Easter break. Years ago now. He closed his eyes and waited for the next crescendo, some seven minutes into the piece. Life could be wonderful, he reflected, hearing his breathing deepen and take him into the pleasure that is an afternoon snooze.

When he opened his eyes, David's gaze was fixed on the spearheads of the phallic amaryllis. They were both waving. Ever so slightly but they were vibrating. He checked the room. Nothing else appeared to be moving. Music played in his earphones. He sat completely still, eyes fixed firmly on the plant in its bulbous glass vase, rooted in pebbles. The shorter of the two stems moved more than the larger where the bud had now started to part: the faintest stripe of pink was showing through. From side to side, both spears shuddered as though in time with the Concerto, the resonance of the rich cello tones were only audible to him but seemed to dictate the pace of this odd dance.

A soft knock at the door an hour later heralded the beautifully coiffed Dot Baker. "I just thought I'd look in and see how you're doing," she excused her intrusion.

David lifted the earphones from his head. "Come in! My, don't you look glamorous!" he greeted, moving slowly up from his chair. "Here, come and sit down. I've got something to show you!"

Dot sat in the warmed cocoon of the comfortable armchair and looked to him quizzically. The TV wasn't on. Nothing could be seen through the fog at the window. She wasn't sure what she was supposed to be looking at.

David perched on the edge of his bed beside her and pointed to the amaryllis on the chest of drawers. "The plant. Do you notice anything?"

Dot fixed her gaze. "It's got two buds. The big one is coming into flower." This didn't seem enough to warrant David's obvious excitement.

"Just keep watching for a minute," he instructed as he sat quietly beside her, fully focused on the plant. He started to worry that it wasn't moving quite as much now as it had been but it was still moving, regardless.

"I'm not sure," she began, "not certain, but, is it moving?" she asked falteringly.

"Yes! You see it too! I've been watching this for over an hour, with perhaps a little snooze in the middle, but it's been dancing!" he gushed. "It's actually shaking itself into bloom."

Dot looked back at the amaryllis. "Yes, I can see it. And the shorter one is pushing even faster – to help it?"

"That's what I thought too!" David grabbed her hands. "It's extraordinary, don't you think? I've had these before. My daughter gives me one for my birthday each year. Because I once said I liked them, and because she says that they're foolproof." His eyes indicated what his narrowed lips were preparing to sugar-coat. "Be careful what you wish for is the message there, I suppose." He laughed. "But, do you know, I've never seen this before. And I'm so glad you've seen it here with me. Not just to prove that I'm not going completely mad, locked in here!"

"Far from it!" she assured. "You're definitely not imagining it and I'm so pleased you showed me."

"It also goes to show that there are always new things, new joys to had, my dear. I've been thinking that I'd really like to take you to dinner somewhere, some place where Hilda and the others won't be chiming in all the time. It'd give me something to look forward to. I'm not sure how we'd go about arranging that but I'm going to try to find out. In the meantime, would you like to join me for coffee in the Ye Olde Tea Shoppe? That's about as far as we'll get in this *pea-souper*."

"Are you sure you want to leave the amaryllis dance?" Dot felt a little uncertain about *'stepping out'* with David. What on earth would Hilda do if she saw them together? Setting up any kind of target for gossip would be the last thing she wanted to deal with.

"I've got to take you somewhere while you're looking so glam. Who knows? The plant might still be doing it for a while yet. Time will tell."

"Or it might be flowering when we get back?" Dot suggested as David put on his jacket, pocketed his reading glasses and led the way out of the room, ushering Dot to take his arm.

Chapter Eight

A PLACE FOR US

"What are you doing at Reception?" Pauline asked Donna as she passed by on her back-of-house inspection which had been postponed after a frantically busy morning.

"Alex was supposed to be on the later shift today but, because she did both shifts yesterday, because of the fog, she rang in exhausted and she has pretty much lost her voice."

"We all worked double hours yesterday, though. When *needs must* and all that."

"She wouldn't have been able for it, Pauline. She was really croaky on the phone. So I said I'd step in. Give her a chance to catch up today and on her day off tomorrow and then she'll be right as rain."

"But not fit for fog apparently? Well, I'm sorry to have to ask you to do this, Donna, when I know you're already doing the timesheets, but we need this notice typed up for the noticeboards. Evelyn Dunwoody has agreed to take the choir for the Panto songs and I want us to be quick to get it together, before she might change her mind. And have I given you the interview list?"

"I've got three appointments on this list here. For Barbara's job?"

"It's not Barbara's, is it? For the new Office Manager, yes. Can you offer them a tea or coffee when they come in and ask them to wait in the café? I've allowed forty minutes for each interview and twenty in between for me to write my notes."

"Will do, Pauline. I really hope that there's someone really good today so I can go back to my usual hours. My boys are missing me at home. James is home from uni this week and I've hardly seen him."

"We don't get much home life, do we, in this work?" Pauline looked musingly distant before landing squarely back with matters at hand. "And we're back on the proper menu rotations now that Peggy's had her deliveries, so can you get the menus for today and tomorrow done and distributed to the dining rooms before you do anything else?"

Pauline walked off quickly. Donna knew that she wouldn't broach being asked to relieve for a quick toilet break: Pauline would not take up Reception duties, even for the briefest moment. Although she said it was because residents and family members would be confused to see her at the front desk, the Receptionists were fully in agreement that she would not be able to manage the pace and diversity of requests that came constantly to the one visible person who sat in the heart of the home.

Donna kept an eye out for the visitors between answering the phone and dealing with the timesheets. Andrea Wallace had been visiting her mother Mildred Absolom, now of Tulip Community, and had her grandson Archie in tow. As Andrea went to sign out of the Visitors' Book, Archie made a beeline for Donna as was his habit since he knew that she had brought some animal stamps from home to reward young visitors with a 'tattoo'.

"Can I have a tattoo, Donna?" She was surprised that he had remembered her name.

"And what do you say when you ask?"

"*Please* can I have a tattoo?"

"Of course you can." Donna reached into the drawer under the desk return to find the ink pad and stamps as Andrea joined them with a relieved smile.

"Thanks Donna. Half-term headaches, don't you know?"

"Long gone for me, I'm afraid," Donna acknowledged as she opened the box of stamps.

"Don't be too keen to call it a day. I thought those days were over too."

"A giraffe?" Donna asked Archie who nodded his head violently as though head-banging to music.

"What have you been up to today, Archie?" Donna asked as he admired her handiwork on his forearm.

"Visiting Gran's mum again. It's all we do here."

"And get stamps of course," Donna put away the stamp pad and box.

"Only really when you're here," Andrea pointed out. "The others all seem too busy. Thank you for making the time," she acknowledged. "Come on Archie, time for home now." She took Archie's hand as they said goodbye to Donna and waited briefly for the automatic doors to register before heading out into the carpark.

"Will your Mum be lonely when you go away?" Archie asked, looking up at his grandmother.

"Look how many people there are in there, Archie. How could she possibly be lonely? Let's go home and get some lunch."

Brad's Senior Team Meeting was relocated to the Daffodil Dining Room since a company had booked the Lounge to show residents and their families a new product which *every family would need* to preserve their memories. That special offering, a glossy coffee table book collating all the family memories, was designed to *'celebrate the life of special people'*, a gift for the elderly to bring back all their happy memories; in truth, a memoir for the grieving once the *special person* had passed, before it was too late to put all the random source materials together. The process involved one of the franchisee consultants spending hours with *the chosen one* to record their memories and write up notes appropriate to the gathered photos. The *memories*, as generally delivered in a sea of confusion, may well be disputable. The cost would more certainly be more than customers might have expected but who could argue, asked the presenter, when memories, however dubious, are *priceless*?

A percentage of takings would be payable to Gramwell Glade. After checking with Head Office, Pauline was delighted to find that there was another potential source of income permitted to at least fractionally offset the growing overheads. So the whole project, she urged at the eleven o'clock catch up that morning, must be wholeheartedly supported by the Gramwell team. What was more, the afternoon tea provided today by Peggy Hewson was also charged out to Fulsome Memories Pty which would mean a little bit more. It all counted. Pauline had wondered if the company actually realised that 'fulsome' means 'nauseating' even though in popular parlance people seemed to think it meant 'whole-hearted'. Memories could be so fickle.

"Brendon said he will have to be a bit late today," Brad explained. He's having a word with Elizabeth Hollick's family about emerging continence issues. But he shouldn't be much longer now. Thank you all for coming. We have a shorter time this afternoon because I've had to agree to let Amity join us in half an hour. Even though we're nearing the end of November, nothing's actually been done about the Panto yet, so she's coming to see which roles we will take. The Residents will get a real kick out of seeing their carers and nurses making fools of ourselves, so we have first dibs on the roles apparently. So this meeting will be your chance to hit the Gramwell *casting couch*."

"It's behind you!" teased Ronnie Chan. Those assembled at the table craned to see what was behind Brad.

"Oh no it's not" replied Brad.

"Oh yes it is," grinned Nwaoma, indicating Brendon in the corridor with his body spread-eagled against the glass door. He had been sticking out his tongue and crossing his eyes, all of which started to hurt since it had taken Brad the longest time to pick up on what was going on. Brendon's pose also concerned Grace Garrett who had slowly been wheeling her frame along the corridor behind him. She had contemplated calling the nurses' button that hung around her neck when she saw the man splattered against the door.

Pushing at the door and staggering in, Brendon feigned exhaustion. "I thought you were never going to notice me!" he panted, flopping into the seat across the table form Brad. The Nursing and Senior Carers' Meeting was now ready to begin.

"Of course I noticed you, playing the clown as always. And we wouldn't think of starting without you," Brad went on while Brendon smiled broadly, "because you're taking the Minutes today."

The others laughed as they moved wine glasses, napkins and cutlery from the tables they'd joined together with others behind them in order to make room for their notebooks and tablets. Amid the smells of recently departed gravy and custard, those residents most in need of attention were discussed and records taken of the Hollicks' agreement to Elizabeth's new continence plan, a general agreement that Mildred Absolom's relocation was going well, particularly since she'd made friends with Maisie, and that she and Elizabeth could join in Daffodil activities in the afternoons.

Grace Garrett pushed the door open with her walking frame and looked around the group of staff members sitting at the dining table. She thought this was a strange time to be eating but put forward her concern. "Have you seen the mad man?" she asked them. "He was trying to get in here. I think he might be injured. He was stuck on the door."

Nwoma helped Grace turn her walking frame to leave the room and showed her into the Lounge next door. "We don't have any madmen around here, do we, Grace?" she coaxed, concerned that Grace might be inventing bad dreams.

"He was there alright," Grace assured her. "He looked a lot like Brendon," she added, which tickled Nwoma as she thought about it, returning to the meeting with the giggles.

"Actually," she announced, "Grace was right. She saw you spread-eagled against the door, Brendon. So who's the mad one now?" she laughed.

Brad sliced the air with a grim twist of his lip as he let Brendon know with one glance how seriously his messing around had messed up. He continued the meeting in sombre tone to underscore that point.

The Storrick incident was noted. Visits to their room would require waiting after knocking, rather than the usual walking straight in.

Betty Harrison in Tulip 15 had had a fall, the ambulance had taken her to hospital but she was sent back the same day. The records had been duly filed and she was being monitored closely.

The new residents seemed to be settling in well and their families were very pleasant: a large box of chocolates had been presented to the staff by Charles Worrell, Nan Sweetman's son; he knew on which side his bread was buttered. The box was in in the Daffodil Nursing Station but the chocolates were going quickly if anyone was interested.

Both Stan and Gosia had been taking some time out to talk to Dorotka Grzyzyna. She'd become very angry of late and was swearing at some of the younger carers. Kayleigh Longbottom, in particular, had copped a mouthful. But, now that they'd been speaking to her in her native Polish, she seemed more at ease with things and certainly around bathing and cleaning routines.

People were getting more used to entering notes into the system more easily although there were still some Luddites who were writing them on scraps of paper – or worse, on their arms and hands – and typing them up later.

"We risk confidentiality if anyone's details are written on an arm and then you're called quickly to another room, to state the bleeding obvious. No more writing on hands or arms, understood?"

"Thank you for that, Brendon." Brad continued. "If you have any other concerns, please see me immediately. As we always say, it's better to be safe than sorry."

Amity pushed open the double doors to the Dining Room and took up a chair at the corner of the table beside Brad. "Thank you for letting me disturb your meeting but, as you know, we're in a dreadful hurry now to get this Panto on the road."

All the other women assembled were in their burgundy Empire uniforms, the nurses in full dress, the carers with tabards over black trousers. Amity's radiant orange dress appeared like a ray of sunshine in the dull afternoon.

"Who died in here?" she asked, her nose twitching.

"It's dead lunch. Steak and kidney doesn't smell the best when it's on the table, never mind two hours later," observed Amadia. "I've never understood why anyone would eat steak and kidney and neither has anyone who's worked with elderly gentlemen."

"You say the sweetest things," Brad shut her down.

"I'm just saying," Amadia observed.

"Yes, we get it!" Brad insisted. "I don't think I'll ever enjoy steak and kidney ever again now you've said that. And it was one of my favourites," he added with a sense of loss.

"So you'll be fine when you're an old man," Amadia encouraged cheekily.

"Enough! Puh-lease!" Amity pulled some printed sheets from her folder. "I've got the Panto parts here and I thought you'd like to have the first choices."

"Or are we being told?" Brendon asked.

"Well, you were very keen when we spoke about it before."

"I *am*! I'm only teasing," Brendon looked at the list she had prepared. "Where's the ugly Stepmother?"

"Are you thinking of Cinderella? The scary woman in Sleeping Beauty is the Wicked Fairy who curses her when she's a baby."

"A fairy!" Brendon's voice reached falsetto excitement. "Put me down for that one!"

"And she comes back as the nasty old lady spinning. When Sleeping Beauty's finger is pricked."

"More time on stage!" Brendon trilled.

"And a lot more lines to learn than some of the other parts." Amity explained.

"No problems. I'm just the fairy for the job." Brendon grabbed the list to register his name on the Wicked Fairy line only to find that it was already there. He gave Amity a sweet smile for her trouble.

"Now we've got that out of the way, what other parts are there?" Brad smiled towards Amity, looking for something more distinguished and weighty.

"Just the thing for you, Brad. Sleeping Beauty's father, the King."

"Is there a Queen?" Brendon appeared to be changing his mind.

"Brad's wife, yes, but she's quiet and obedient and has almost nothing to say."

"Put me down for that then!" Amadia threw her hand in the air.

"I was hoping that you would be one of the good fairies who wished lovely things for Sleeping Beauty. I thought actually the very first one who grants her Beauty. And you would be dressed beautifully, of course."

"Oh that sounds really good," Amadia snuggled back into her chair, thinking about a time when her residents could see her as a beautiful creature.

"Great," Amity rustled the list back to her keeping. "Shall I tell you who I thought for some of the others roles?"

Realising that this was a *done deal*, the others sat back as Amity read through the cast list. What did they think about Gosia playing Sleeping Beauty? She could wear her long blonde hair loose and she probably had the most petite figure of any. Then it became obvious that Stan would need to be the Prince who eventually wakes her since they were good friends, he had a great physique and might not object to a stage kiss. Amity read through the list of good fairies to accompany Amadia before making it known that she had cast herself as Queen to Brad's King.

The most difficult to swallow was that a number of animals were needed. "But they can be cute animals like in a Disney film," Amity encouraged.

"A pig is a pig in any language," Bessie noted when she and Nwaoma were listed.

"But think how much fun the residents will have when they see some of their nurses as little farmyard animals!" Amity encouraged.

Brad's exchanged glance with them belied their confidence in the proposition.

"How's it all going?" Pauline came into the room. "Did anyone think of airing this room after lunch? It really smells as though there's still food lying around."

"Just us," Amity relayed. "We're all sorted now. I'm going to see those who aren't here and then we'll put the cast list up in the Staff Room. I've already told Peter that he and Eric will be building the most incredible Hedge of Thorns to cover their flowery castle wall," she added.

"Shame about the season, really. We could have used the real castle wall if it wasn't going to be at this time of the year." Pauline mused.

"But Panto's always at Christmas," Brendon blurted.

"And have you told them that everyone will be responsible for their own costumes due to time and budget restriction?"

"Not so far," Amity conceded. "Perhaps they know now?" she offered.

"Where do I get a pigging pig costume?" Nwaoma moaned.

"We can probably help with some hired costumes for the animals. And I gather that you're going to be the Wicked Fairy?" Pauline smiled at Brendon.

"How come I'm always the last to know?" Brendon flashed at Amity.

"You were the obvious choice, darling. We'd all be so disappointed if you didn't have the starring role."

"I'm not the Princess!" Brendon pretended to sulk as he banged his fist on the table, setting a couple of teaspoons flying.

"And would a Princess behave like that?" Brad winked at him. "We'll all look forward to you as the leading male. Does that work for you?"

"I'll be your lead male any day!" Brendon teased but both he and Brad knew that this was more than a tease since they'd recently had a discussion of sorts along those lines and decided, at Brad's bidding, to wait until the New Year to see what might develop.

In Ye Old Tea Shoppe Dr Evelyn Dunwoody stood beside an electronic keyboard that she'd brought from her home along with her husband Harold who sat with it in silence as the café filled with those brought to muster by their Carers. They looked at him with expectation. He wished now that he'd placed the keyboard facing the wall. The list had been compiled by Amity and Bessie who were both just guessing as to who might have a passable singing voice. Evelyn had told them that she wasn't expecting miracles so they would reserve judgement as to whether they might find a tune among them. All, of course, except Nan Sweetman who had been an opera singer in her youth and David Jack who had listed his interests as being part of a male choir for over twenty years on his Admission form.

Amity had approached them earlier to ascertain if they would agree to sing some solo parts among the list of songs that had been chosen for the Panto this year. David Jack had gone along reluctantly, while newcomer Nan Sweetman was grateful for an opportunity to show her new neighbours what she was made of, since she had appeared to rise to stardom so quickly in her time at Gramwell Glade.

Molly Tipple, Joan Fairs, Marie and Ron Storrick, Dot Baker and Marie Taylor had been mustered, along with *new boy* John Nicholls who had been told by Elsie Lister that he was needed. Delphine Thomas was one who regularly joined in the sing-song sessions that Edith Holmes conducted in Tulip community at the old piano there and Delphine had also been heard joining in with Gerry and Harry on their Friday afternoon visits. Maisie Dunstable and Elizabeth Hollick, seeing a trick, also had a valid reason to be revisiting Daffodil community and were duly gathered up to boost choir numbers. Both Marjorie Simmonds and Albert Watts had been pushed in to make up the back row. So often had they found themselves as wheelchair neighbours that they had now become used to spending time together. Neither saw themselves as any great Caruso or Sutherland but had never refused an offer for distraction and so found themselves, once again, going along for the ride.

"Not all of you know me," announced the Doctor by way of introduction, raising her voice over the gathering chatter. "My name is Dr Evelyn Dunwoody. Some of you will have seen me around Gramwell because I'm one of the GPs who comes here and, of course, some of you are my lovely patients. So I'd like to welcome you here today for the first of our rehearsal sessions for this year's Panto, *Sleeping Beauty*. I say 'this year's' but actually this is the first time we've ever tried something quite as ambitious, so you are the inaugural Gramwell Glade Choir."

Some applause quietly broke through. "And this is my husband, Harold, who has conceded that one way to spend a bit more time with his wife might be to act as our accompanist here." Harold nodded briefly as the onlookers managed another attempt at clapping.

"We've chosen some songs we hope that you will enjoy singing to go with the story line of *Sleeping Beauty* and we're very fortunate to have Nan and David here to take some solo parts we need. They have both sung previously. I believe, Nan, you sang professionally once upon a time?"

All eyes searched the room for someone who may not be as familiar a face as the others who were fully established as part of the furniture. Nan's perfectly permed white hair and sparkling eyes stood out as she gave a little, royal wave, delighted to have her debut so appropriately acknowledged.

"Nan and David will sing 'True Love'." A little gasp rattled in the room. This clearly was a popular choice. "And I'm sure they will give a super rendition of a song you obviously know and love. Together we will sing the choruses to 'Some Day My Prince Will Come'. We're going to learn 'There's a Place for Us', which you'll no doubt remember, and 'Once Upon A Dream'. I don't know if you remember Billy Fury?"

Excitement built as neighbours rattled their approval to one another. Even if they couldn't immediately bring to mind the actual songs, something about those titles seemed to trigger pleasant sensations. All in all, it seemed a very creditable project; however, David Jack was feeling slightly tremulous at the thought of standing out from the crowd in a solo with Nan which would completely dwarf his previous, more anonymous, choral experiences.

"What's this?" Maisie Dunstable asked her neighbour Elizabeth Hollick as papers were passed along the row.

"I think it's the words."

"It looks like words."

"Words for the song we have to sing. Look, it says 'There's a Place for Us' at the top."

The pages continued to be passed down the line until everyone was contemplating where the place was.

"And for this first one, we'll all just sing along together!" Evelyn Dunwoody gave a deal of zest to perk up the choir's energy levels on the basis that these first impressions of fun and achievement were going to set the tone. Harold played an elaborate introduction while his wife waited, forearms poised, for a suitable place to lead the assembly into song, whereupon her arms shot forwards as though she were about to dive into water. The noise began. In the midst of some great confusion, Marjorie looked askance as Albert belted out a credible 'hold my hand and I'll take you there' – and in the correct place too.

At the Reception desk, Donna knew that the afternoon's efforts in the café were highly likely to impinge on her productivity binge. She had completed the distributed both the menus and timesheets. She had shepherded three candidates for the Office Manager position with as much goodwill as she could muster, having counselled herself that an appointment would mean huge relief, since weeks of her caretaking the role were impacting sorely on both her family life and peace of mind.

Pauline had given her a list of the candidates. It was likely that any one of the three who had presented at Reception that afternoon would make a fine Office Manager. Derek Simmonds seemed a pleasant, middle-aged Essex man. A Nigerian entrant in the competition would certainly set the cat among the pigeons. He seemed to have come from further afield since he'd mentioned to her, when asking for the lavatory, that he'd been driving for four hours to arrive at Gramwell. The plump, early-twenty-something Gloria Barton seemed more familiar. Maybe she had visited a few weeks ago and asked if she could look around. Donna had been on the front desk when an enquiry along those lines had led her to refer the enquirer to Amity: it might have been this one, scouting around. Anyway, Pauline would surely have some choice. With luck, an appointment could be made swiftly. It would depend on how much notice the successful candidate would have to give their current employer.

"'Time together, with time to spare'," belted from Dr Dunwoody who was standing with her back to the café's windows, facing the 'choir'.

"Sounds like us," Marjorie was leaning over on to the arm of Albert's wheelchair.

"How so?" Albert was focused on the singing and not on any notions of romance. Marjorie's supposition rather jangled him.

"Time together and time to spare. All day every day," she explained with a resolute grimace.

"Really belt it out!" Dr Dunwoody urged. "I want to hear all of you in full voice now."

She nodded at Harold to take his accompaniment back to the start of the line and perhaps to pump up the volume.

Donna answered the phone with the usual greeting through the insistence of the choir trying the same line over and over again until Dr Dunwoody was satisfied.

"Excellent. Let's keep up that pace then and try it from the top."

"Where's the top?" Elsie Lister asked John Nicholls. Of late she would try to think of all sorts of reasons to chat with him. John pointed in some disbelief to top of his page while she smiled at him enthusiastically.

"I thought it might be," she smiled and they began again with as much of an improved version of the song as they could muster.

"That's a lovely greeting, Donna. I wish the others would be as attentive to the script when they answered the phone."

"Well I knew it was you, didn't I?" Donna replied with a smile in her voice. "Your number came up on the phone display."

"Even so, they don't always look." Pauline explained. "Now, I've got some reference-checking to do so I don't want to be disturbed. Can you stop putting calls through please?"

"Will do," Donna was relieved to hear that an appointment might be in the offing. "Any clues?"

She didn't think it likely that Pauline would divulge any information at this stage but her curiosity had spurred her on.

"I don't think that we can have a man in the Office Manager role is all I'll say at this stage. Does that help?"

"OK. It might indicate something about Ms Barton in that case. I thought she looked a bit familiar, actually."

"Oh she's done her homework all right. She came and checked us out, apparently, a few weeks ago. And she's done a lot of research on us. She even knows some of the families who have residents here."

Donna wasn't convinced that these points were necessarily the best prerequisites for the job. "But she's going to be an experienced Office Manager, isn't she, because that's what counts?"

"She's worked in offices, yes, of course." Pauline went on. "How long are the choir going to be making this racket, do you know?"

"Dr Dunwoody has booked the café until four. So they're likely to be there for another hour or so. It's making things quite difficult out here. I can hardly hear the phone ring over the singing."

"If Gloria is successful after reference-checking, I'm going to ask you to sit with her and show her the ropes since you have all the knowledge that Barbara passed on."

Donna squirmed in her seat and held her hand over the mouthpiece as the choir's efforts became increasingly confident. "Ah, I think it would be really important for the successful candidate to train at Head Office. Barbara had learned on the job without proper training and she'd developed all sorts of little ways of remembering how to do things. I still have to think of her Uncle

Charlie when I am working out the order in which we enter data on the timesheets. It's not something I'd be confident in passing on."

"Uncle Charlie?"

"Yes, early every morning, late each afternoon. Apparently he was something of a workaholic but that's how she remembered a way to put overtime in the system. I don't really understand it either. So we really don't have a lot to show Gloria here and there are probably lots of other things that Head Office know about when we don't. But, if she's managed offices before, she won't take too long to learn the systems we use," Donna offered hopefully."Are you sure – how can I put this? – sure you aren't just trying to get out of training the new manager?" Having stretched to every call beyond her duty in the past weeks, Donna now felt under-rewarded both in terms of remuneration and recognition. "No, Pauline. I truly believe that she should learn properly from the source and then she will be in a position to train others."

"It's not like you to put your foot down like that. I'll keep your idea in mind."

"Just before you go," Donna realised that there had been pressing business at hand, "who do I refer new enquiries to? We've had a few calls today from people looking for places for family members. Apparently a home in Colchester has been closed down. There seems to be a bit of a rush on. Should I tell them to call back when Amity's back from her holiday?"

"I suppose you'd better put them through to me, then. But not at the moment, I need you to hold my calls while I sort out this business about the new Office Manager."

Donna hung up the phone, realising that Pauline's view of her was that she was completely biddable and easy to take for granted, a thought that didn't sit comfortably with her.

Pauline had been steeling herself in her office. For some time she'd been working on an idea to bring Akin back to Gramwell Glade. It was not only her pride in the home that motivated the call once she'd heard from Olga Dean at Head Office that Akin's Personal Assistant was away sick today.

With a deep breath, she picked up the phone and dialled the number for his PA. "Oh Akin, Hello. It's Pauline Graves calling from Gramwell Glade. Hi. How are you? I was a little surprised. I thought Lydia would be on the other end. It's nice to speak with you personally, though. I've been thinking it would be nice to see you here and have some time together."

Her eyes closed briefly as she listened to his mellifluous voice. "Yes, Kalu Tinubu. He was one of three that I interviewed this afternoon. Well, not exactly, no. You see. Yes, I will be in touch with HR. Actually, that's not why I was ringing you." She bit her lip as she listened. "As it happens, I've offered the position to another candidate who may not have Kalu's qualifications as such but I believe that she will be a better fit for the Team and she lives close by. Kalu told me that he came from London and it had taken him four hours to drive here in the traffic today. No, he didn't tell me that he would be moving when he got the position. That might have been a little presumptuous?" She tried to supress a laugh but a something had already gripped her stomach. This is not what she had expected of the call that she had been planning for some time.

"You see, I wanted to ask you to come to our Panto. We're putting on a production next month of *Sleeping Beauty*, involving the Residents as the choir. I'd like to invite you to be our Guest of Honour. It will be in the late afternoon so I can arrange a hotel for you for the night. That way you don't have to go back late in the evening, after we've had dinner and that would give us a chance to catch up?"

Pauline felt in her gut that she was not hearing the sorts of responses she'd rehearsed. She took a deep breath to stem the stammer she felt rising in her throat. "You'll be overseas? Oh, I'm sorry to hear that. Sorry for us. The Residents really put a lot of stock in having you visit us here. Yes I see. But I've already offered Gloria Barton the position, Akin. I can't go back on that offer, can I? I'm sorry that I didn't clear it with you first. I had no idea that you would be interested in the appointment of our Office Manager, knowing how busy you are. Okay. I'll speak with HR. And there's really no chance that you can be with us on the twentieth? I'm so sorry to hear. Well, I wish you safe travels. Yes, the same to you. I suppose this means that we won't see each other now until next year? All right. Thank you. Bye."

Pauline put the phone down and stood up from her chair. She walked over to the window of her office and looked out on to the car park, to the space where she'd last seen Akin's car, where he waved to her before heading off after his last visit. All her plans had been dashed – introducing him to the residents and families, sitting beside him during the Panto, standing beside him as they shook hands with family members, heading off together to the country hotel she'd had in mind for dinner and for his stay. A stay which would ideally might have included her. She inhaled deeply with the realisation that these wonderful plans were now only a figment of her imagination. For the time being. She desperately wanted to see him before next year. So much work and effort had to be dealt with between now and then with no comfort at all to brighten her winter.

And now she had to work out how to engage HR with the dilemma that sat in an ugly pile on her desk. Although she hadn't in fact actually offered

Gloria the position of Office Manager, it had seemed best to tell Akin that white lie because there was no way that Kalu was going to be the right person for the job even though now she realised that he was a friend of Akin's. It might be the worst possible outcome for Gramwell.

She couldn't bring herself to broach with Akin the inherent scepticism if not actual racism that some of her elderly residents held when it came to African staff members. With Akin it was different. He was the prosperous, prepossessing owner of Empire Homes. The wariness of the older generation was mostly due to inexperience. People of colour were not thick on the ground in rural Essex in years gone by. Many of the residents and even their families had not met many African people at all. Some had met none before coming to Gramwell Glade. It hadn't been easy to have these older folks feel confident about Nigerian nurses working with them. But somehow those women were better able to be jovial and competent, to gain the confidence of their patients than were the men. Mobo, on the other hand, was a genuine favourite among all the residents who enjoyed going out on the bus with him.

As she looked to the naked trees and navy sky beyond, Pauline now wondered whether it was just she who thought that appointing Kalu wouldn't work. Apparently he was prepared to move, to live nearby so as to avoid the London traffic. If he was somehow close with Akin, would it mean that Akin might visit more often? Pauline sat at her desk, elbows on the table, her hands on her cheeks as she pondered the dilemma of how to do without her first choice for the position.

"'Somehow, someday, somewhere'," ricocheted from Ye Olde Tea Shoppe into her thinking.

Dr Dunwoody was busy collecting the song sheets that had been left around the room as Maisie, Elizabeth and shuffled off with their Zimmer frames, followed by Millie in her wheelchair, to head back to Tulip. Harold was balancing the electronic keyboard at the end of a table while he opened the case to pack it away. Elsie Lister came smiling towards the Doctor with dainty steps.

"Hello, Doctor." It was clear in her that there was a request coming.

"Hello, Elsie. I really enjoyed watching you sing today. You give the impression that you really enjoy singing."

"I wanted to ask you, Doctor, if I can be Sleeping Beauty in the pantomime?" Elsie's expectations were certainly exceeding any possibility that Dr Dunwoody had dreamt of.

"Oh, Elsie. You've come to the wrong person, I'm afraid. I'm doing the choir part of the presentation but the staff are dealing with the acting parts."

"So who will I ask?" Elsie was determined to take her demands to the top if need be. In her mind it was a foregone conclusion that she would play the lead.

"I suppose you could ask Mrs Graves but really, Elsie, I think you'll find that the staff are playing the roles because there are a lot of lines to be learned and not a lot of time in which to learn them."

Elsie felt certain that she would be able to learn any amount of lines, especially as the part of a princess would come so naturally to her. Besides, she already knew the story.

"Thank you Doctor. I'll see Mrs Graves, then." She started to head off to the Manager's Office door before turning back. "Did you see my new friend John?" she asked.

"I did see that you have a new friend. I'm sure that I will meet him in time. He looks a very nice man."

"Oh he is," Elsie assured her. She went to head off again but had forgotten her mission to knock on Mrs Graves' door. She needed to find John Nicholls. He seemed to have gone off without her.

"Why do they always leave us until last?" Albert asked Marjorie. She was getting used to his northern accent but slowly. When she'd first heard Albert speak, she could barely understand anything he said. Her straightforward prejudice was to imagine that all northerners were working class but it had turned out that they had a great deal in common. Albert was eighty-five and Marjorie eighty-four when they'd first moved in; however, growing up in Grimsby and Brighton respectively had made them two very different kettles of fish. Marjorie hadn't been inclined to give Albert a great deal of time because it had been so difficult to understand him. Over time she had heard him converse readily with others as they shared tables in Daffodil Dining Room. Her ear had become more attuned to his intonations as much as to his accent. When Marjorie, whose husband had been an army captain, had discovered that Albert had had a long career as an engineer, she realised that her prejudice might have been misplaced. He was an educated man after all, even if he didn't sound it to her ear. Besides, they had come to live in Gramwell in the very same week all those three years ago after a number of the original residents had perished in a rotten winter of severe flu outbreaks. They were two old boats bobbing on the same tide.

"Maybe we've become invisible in our old age?" Marjorie returned laconically.

"They're always eager to get us here and then they forget to take us back. Time was when I was able to take charge of not only me but a load of others. People took notice of Albert Watts, they did."

"I'm sure they did, Albert. I still take notice of you. All's not lost!" Marjorie urged. "But why haven't we ever thought of rowing our own canoes? Do you know how to drive these things?" she asked, looking down at her foot rests.

"Well, there are brakes. I think you just pull that lever upwards," he explained, leaning over the side of his chair to demonstrate. "Watch out, girl! I think I can get yours from here."

"Well, that's not very safe, is it," she asked, "if any Tom, Dick or Harry can come along and let my brakes off?"

"We're both on the loose now but here's the question," Albert puffed as he hauled his arms forwards on the wheels of his chair. "I think I can just wiggle out this way. They've put us so close together that it's hard to steer a path." He pushed backwards and forwards by tiny strokes until his chair backed into the side of Marjorie's.

"We're not in the dodgems, Bert!" Marjorie rocked forward with laughter, her chair following her until they were both facing opposite directions.

"A fine mess we have here," Albert panted with laughter and effort. "Swing around this way if you can and I'll race you down the corridor!" he dared. Both of them were making very slow progress in their new venture but whipping up a great deal of laughter as they headed with stops and starts into the foyer where their good humour was noticed by Donna who waved to them from the Reception desk as they inched their way towards the Daffodil corridor.

Pauline had pulled herself together. There were days, like today, when she felt such a tyro in this business that she wondered if she shouldn't simply go back to working in hotels. They were far more logical, in her experience; but then again, there was never the depth of relationships possible that the care sector had afforded her and, more importantly, Gramwell Glade would flourish under her management. She had a great deal to give so it was imperative that she continue with her hard-won efforts. And she possibly had a great deal to win too. Dialling Olga Dean's number, she girded her loins for a confession.

"Hello Olga. It's good to hear your voice. I've got a bit of a situation here and I wondered if I could ask your advice?"

Olga jumped in quickly, "I hear that Kalu is going to be starting with you shortly when he's finished his training here?"

"Where did that news come from?" Pauline was astonished.

"It's well known here because he's been in training. Kalu is Akin's cousin, well, second cousin, I gather. It's been on the cards for a while that an

Office Manager position would be set up for him. Yours is the first available, so to speak."

"So why was I the last to know if it was all arranged then? Is it the Nigerian Mafia at work?"

"Sorry?"

"You know, *looking after family*." Pauline felt as though she was tying herself up in knots and had to find a way to back pedal, quickly.

"I think all families look after each other, don't you, Pauline? Can't pin that on any one race as far as I know. Best to steer clear of race in any event, don't you think?"

"Maybe, but was this arranged already? This is the problem that I wanted your advice on. I've sort of offered another candidate the position, you see."

"You're kidding."

"Well, she seemed the best fit and I guess I've led her to believe so."

"Did she do any practical exercise for you? Show you any of her work?"

"No. It's just that she came across as a team player. She'd done her research and, in my judgement, will fit in better than the other candidates."

"Well, you will have to find a way to change your mind pretty quick smart, won't you? I tell you what, you call her and tell her that we have to have her complete an Empire practical test as such. I'll set up something on the computer that will simulate our Pay program and set up some timesheets with a few of the usual problems in them. I'll email the exercise you to in a zip attachment tomorrow. You arrange for her to come in and do it before the end of the week. Then, I think, we will have solved your problem."

"Thank you so much, Olga, I'm really grateful to you. I'll get on to her straightaway. I can't thank you enough."

"Just make sure you check with HR and follow the procedure next time," Olga warned.

"If I even knew what the procedure was." As soon as the words had left her mouth Pauline knew not to follow that line. She'd been offered a lifeline and she was about to grab it with both hands. "Talk soon," she said with some warmth and some regret in her voice. Putting down the phone she wondered when she would be permitted to make her own choices and when Empire might acknowledge that she was an experienced manager who could get things done her own way, given half a chance.

Chapter Nine

TÊTE-À-TÊTE

Tayla had only just thrown herself into her work chair before the phone rang. This was going to be an especially busy day. The morning shift was always a struggle for her in terms of punctuality, or even being properly awake, but at least she was not going to be here when the masses turned up for the quarterly Family Matters meeting at six this evening. There would be the cacophony of *AA* to deal with later in the morning; for now, the phone was on its fourth peal and she hadn't managed to pull the phone message notepad from the top drawer. She grabbed at the receiver which slipped from her grasp, landing in the drawer between the stapler and the hole punch. Tayla's quickest thinking took her to press the bits on the phone that would cancel the call in order to stop ringing as she collected the things she needed from the drawer and retrieve an earring that had flown across the desk. Brian Petty walked by on his way to the kitchen. His contribution was to point and laugh as the phone started to ring again. Tayla stuck out her tongue at him before trotting out the obligatory: "Good Morning, Gramwell Glade. This is Tayla speaking. How can I help you?"

Pauline Graves answered immediately, "For one thing you can keep hold of the phone and not drop it in the caller's ear."

"Sorry, Mrs Graves. It flew out of my hand as I was setting up the desk. How are you today?"

"Fine, thank you. Can you please get today's menus distributed? Yesterday's are still on the board. And, when Kalu Tinubu arrives, can you bring him straight to my office? Thank you."

The call was over almost as soon as it had begun. Tayla looked into the receiver as if it might make sense of the directives she'd been given if she just held on for a few seconds longer. Nothing was forthcoming. She wrote down the word that she thought was the best interpretation of what Pauline Graves had told her and switched on the computer to crank up a busy morning ahead.

It was not until after the eleven o'clock catch-up meeting had finished that a statuesque man came into the foyer and introduced himself in dulcet tones over the flurry of *AA* noises spilling from the café that she realised the elusive word had in fact been two words and was actually the name of the new Office Manager. She took him to Pauline's room and couldn't wait to tell some of the others as they passed by during the lunch period about this discovery. The new Office Manager was a tall, fit, black man. Yes, he was younger than the other managers and so different. He was *hot*! Who would be the first to offer to be measured by him for a uniform order? Rosie Rowson made a few extra trips to and from the laundry with the tall trolley hung with residents' clothes to see if she could get a gander but Mr Kalu Tinubu remained in the Manager's Office for the whole morning. Henry Pratt took some sandwiches in with a coffee pot some time later. Tayla frantically beckoned him over to her desk on his way back.

"What's he like?"

"The man in with Mrs Graves?" Henry scratched the back of his head. "Dunno. Looks a bit like that guy who owns Empire. Really dressed up. Being very polite to Mrs Graves. Said 'hello' to me which I did *not* expect. Nice guy, I'd say."

"He's the new Office Manager!" Tayla tried to hold back her excitement. "He's my new boss, I suppose. Will he be a good boss, do you think?"

"Don't ask me!" Henry laughed. "How would I know? All's I know is that I wouldn't want to be your boss."

"And I wouldn't want you to be either!" Tayla swung around on her chair to take some pages from the printer as she called behind him in louder tones, "Laters Henry. Let me know if you hear anything else?"

Henry headed off, slowly pressing the code into the keypad on his return to the kitchen to give Peggy Hewson the news of the day as they got on with the next extra order of sandwiches and cakes for the Family meeting. "Why oh why," Peggy asked, "do they not think about us trying to get out the residents' teas when they decide on a six o'clock meeting for the families? You'd think it would only be sensible to have them at a different time."

"Maybe so as they don't keep us late?" Henry offered in his attempt to answer her rhetorical question. Work was always easier when Mrs Hewson was in a good mood. Extra food orders always met with her sounding off but there was almost never a time when the kitchen didn't turn up trumps for all the daft orders that were made, even those at the shortest notice. The hardest of these were last-minute calls for things like pancake demonstrations that he had to put on in the café wearing a chef's hat. Then there were cooking 'classes' when they might be suddenly told that a group of residents, with their carers in tow, was going to invade the kitchen to try to bake and ice cupcakes or biscuits.

"Long as they don't get in our hair, I suppose," Peggy Hewson grumbled as she handed Henry a large packet of smoked salmon from the fridge. "Here, let's show off a bit."

Brad and Brendon had set up the Daffodil Lounge with all the chairs and sofas in a semblance of a circle with the side tables lined up at the French doors for the catering.

"It wasn't helpful that Pauline brought Kalu into our meeting," Brendon observed as he plumped up some of the cushions that had been flattened or thrown to the floor.

"I had to tell her that she could," Brad agreed. "We would have looked too precious or closed off if we'd refused, as though we had something to hide. But we did have more to discuss. We could have used that time to prepare for this evening, for sure. I can see that there will be a few noses out of joint about the moves we had to make and I don't blame them really. We could have done with that extra time to prepare the others for what's to come."

"For sure. We'll just have to wing it, babe," Brendon said mechanically as he put the magazines into a pile on one of the coffee tables. "Will I leave David's jigsaw here on this table?"

"Of course" Brad retorted. "What would he think if we just junked it?"

"It looks a bit untidy."

"It looks as though the residents are gainfully occupied. Don't forget, it's –"

"It's *their home*. Yes, I know, but the ones paying the fees, they think it's their business."

"It's the old argument – it would be a great place without residents and especially without their families. But these are our 'customers' and we're in the business of 'customer service' as well as nursing care."

"And you're preaching to the converted, dear heart." Brendon bent down to pick some biscuit crumbs from between tufts in the carpet. "Hasn't Frank been in here to clean today?"

"I know that you know." Brad remained fixed on the business of exceeding families' expectations or even the prospect of meeting them. "I'm just a bit apprehensive about the evening. We can hope that they're going to be contained, that Pauline will hold her own and that they see what we do for them and their loved ones, not just what they think we aren't doing."

“You look so sweet when you’re worried. I feel like giving you a huge cuddle. Come here?”

“Not at work! What would any of them think if they came in here and found us cuddling?”

“That we love our work?” Brendon giggled as he dodged a cushion that came flying his way. “Stop it!” he laughed as he sent it back just as Henry came in with a tray of sandwiches.

“Where do you want these then?”

“On the tables over there, thank you Henry.” Brad quickly composed himself.

Brendon cleared the way for Henry to bring the tray through to the tables at the window. “Is that smoked salmon I see?” he asked as he made to snaffle a sandwich.

“Good luck with that then,” warned Henry “There’s about five layers of cling wrap around that tray and it’s not coming off until the people get here. Mrs Hewson’s orders.”

“The ‘people’?” mocked Brendon. “They’re our families, our bread and butter.”

“I’ll get the cakes and then bring a tea and coffee trolley up for you after I’ve done the Daffodil dinners.” Henry was tired after a long day’s work and never felt entirely comfortable with Brendon. He made his exit as quickly as he could manage after putting down the sandwich platter.

“No rest for the wicked!” Brendon called after him.

“And especially not for you,” warned Brad. “Come on, have you got your tablet here? We’ve got to finish the notes from our meeting this afternoon before there’ll be more from the session at six o’clock. No rest for any of us. And I want to talk to you about something else too when we’ve cleared the decks with all of this.”

Andrea Wallace was one of the first family members to arrive. She had quickly touched based with her mother Mildred who was off for her tea in Tulip Dining Room. She then headed for the Daffodil Lounge so as not to miss the meeting. Brendon had made her a perfectly welcome cup of tea and she sat on the sofa before being joined by Marie Taylor’s son, Andy. Andy was a large man in his fifties. He had been a bricklayer for thirty years before retiring hurt with a bad back some three years ago, about the same time as his mother had had to come into the Home. He had sold her house under her Power of Attorney and was now watching his inheritance very quickly disappear in return for huge monthly invoices from Empire Homes.

"Thought I might be running late," he said by way of introduction, "but had a good run. Good to be here first, perhaps? We might get extra points for being early."

"It feels just like a parent-teacher meeting to me. And I should know, I've just come from one," Andrea explained, adding, "And you don't expect to be doing parent-teacher meetings at this age, now, do you?"

"How come?"

"My grandson, Archie, he's eight. My daughter and her husband split up. She moved out to France with her new partner. His father lives here but Archie refuses to live with either of them – says he hates both their partners and acted up really bad. But he's fine when he's with me and my hubby."

"Not the sort of thing you expect to be doing at this time of life, I expect?" Andy parroted back to her. He was trying to contemplate what it might be like if something similar happened to him and his wife.

"You're right. It was the last thing I thought of. Don't get me wrong, we love Archie and he's no real bother. Tiring, yes, bother, not really. It's just that your life isn't your own, is it? We'd already reared our children and now we're back in the same business. We can't go haring off to sunny foreign beaches in the winter term time like our friends do."

"And expensive, I suppose?" Andy was reflecting on those steep monthly bills that he was paying out of his mother's savings for her care.

"Kids these days! The things they need and, worse, the things they want. *SO* expensive and then there's Mum here. But I was at the school this afternoon for Archie's parent-teacher and now I'm here for Mum's" she laughed.

"Oh well, at least we get a free sandwich and a comfy chair here," he laughed.

"I'm not so sure that makes up for it but, yes, it will be quite nice just to sit down and try to find out what's going on here. At least I'm not held responsible for any of Mum's bad behaviour, where anything Archie does out of turn is immediately thrown back – not at his parents but mostly at us."

As the corridor rattled with bain-maries being taken back to the kitchen from the Dining Room, Pauline came into the room with Kalu and began introducing him to some of the family members that she knew. Both staff members were wearing business suits, Kalu's startlingly white shirt standing out amid all the duller colours of winter clothing assembled. Having been here for only a few months, Pauline was surprised at just how many faces she recognised; these were the '*squeakiest wheels*', the usual suspects. However it did no harm to be able to take Kalu around to make personal introductions: this also deflected from any prospective *bees in bonnets* that people had come to set free. It was all very polite. Many of those gathered had come straight from work. Six o'clock had been settled on as the time that they'd favoured in previous discussions when the topic of poor attendance had been canvassed. Coming straight from work was very often what they did anyway as a matter of routine. For many, it was an opportunity to help with the business of feeding their frail older relative while on their way to their own homes for their own dinner.

The smoked salmon sandwiches had gone very quickly. There were some egg mayonnaise ones left and a pile of biscuits which were unlikely to appeal to those who were *en route* to an evening meal. Brendon stood by the urn to help dispense cups of tea and coffee. A few of those gathered were talking amongst themselves. This was potentially a dangerous situation where people might find strength in feeling that they shared problems. It was always better to keep them talking with a staff member, preferably one who worked with and knew their parent well. Nigel Storrick was in a group discussion with Bob and Deidre Shaw, looking from time to time at the Managers who were on duty in the room. Brad gave Bessie a knowing glance to send her in the direction of Barney's daughter Joan who was closing in on Millie Cloudsdale's daughter Arabella Jones-Merton, one of Gramwell Glade's most squeaky wheels. No one needed that noise to rub off onto Joan.

Pauline's voice streamed over the gathering as she tapped a teacup with a spoon. "Ladies and Gentlemen! Welcome to our Family Matters meeting this evening." The assembled groups put down their cups on the side tables as they watched Pauline. Some took to the seats closest. "Would you mind all taking a seat so that we can begin our meeting?"

Arabella Jones-Merton had met up with Charles Worrell. They had introduced themselves, coming together with some sort of immediate recognition of boarding school accents, like two peas in a pod. Charles pulled out one of the dining chairs that formed part of the circle of seats in the middle of the room. Arabella smiled up at him as he went to sit beside her.

"Thank you," said Pauline from the sofa where she sat with Kalu beside Maisie Dunstable's daughter-in-law, Maureen. "Are there enough seats?" she asked as Brad and Brendon came through the door bringing chairs recently surrendered from the Daffodil Dining Room. "Thank you, Brad," Pauline noted. "There are some extra seats there now," she indicated rather redundantly as Brendon arranged a chair for the Storricks' son, Nigel.

"Okay," Pauline rallied. "I think we're all here now and seated. Thank you all for coming to our Family Matters meeting. This is my second as such at Gramwell Glade so you possibly know each other better than I do but I – all of the Team – really value the opportunity we have to get together and talk about the things that we've been doing here with your family members, and ours," she smiled to underscore the meaning she hoped to bring to elucidate. "On my left you will see a new face," the attention of the group pointed, past Maureen Dunstable, to the obviously different face at the other end of the red sofa which gave a winning smile of white teeth. " This is Mr Kalu Tinubu who has joined us at Gramwell just today, although he's been training at Empire Head Office in London for some time." Kalu nodded as some the group gave a little laugh at his expression which indicated with a grimace on cue that he'd been undergoing hard labour in London.

"Kalu is our new Office Manager so he is the '*go to'* person if you have any questions about invoices or fees. We hope you'll give him a warm, Gramwell welcome." Andy Taylor and Andrea Wallace clapped by way of response while Kalu nodded in apparent appreciation.

"Well then, let's get on with the Family Matters at hand. I haven't printed out an Agenda for this evening so we could keep it all fairly informal, but we wanted a chance to tell you a bit more about the new electronic records system that has caused a great deal of work but is now up and running with all the residents' records entered into a computerised system." She indicated the tablet on her lap as being the source of the solution. "This will be a boon when it comes to retrieving information and especially when we are inspected. And we'll be streets ahead of some of the smaller or, shall we say, less well organised homes." Pauline broke off to look at the list of things that she'd brought to discuss. "Oh yes, then there's the Panto. We're looking forward to telling you about that and having you make sure it's in your diaries. And we'll let you know about some of the bus trips we're planning for next year. And one shopping one, I think, in December, Brad?" Brad nodded back to affirm that they had mentioned this in passing at their last Seniors' Meeting.

Charles Worrell raised his hand. "Excuse me, Mrs Graves, will there be an opportunity to discuss the things that are on our minds?"

"Certainly, Charles. We will be asking for discussion items too. This is definitely your opportunity to bring up anything that you would like to discuss," she went on, looking, one by one, at the faces around the room. It seemed that there were might be a few burning issues to be sprung upon them. It was her sincere wish to contain the meeting as far as possible while, of course, allowing the visitors to feel that they were being heard. Kalu was watching her at the closest of quarters while she was trying to look relaxed on the sofa, at the same time making sure that Maureen Dunstable had the lion's share of the seating.

"Shall we start with the electronic record-keeping first, go to the news about the Panto and then hear from the floor about the things that you wish to discuss? You'll have noticed that Donna is sitting over there busily typing up the notes of the meeting so that we'll have an accurate record of what's been said and decided."

Donna looked up briefly from her keyboard to smile at the assembly.

"That will work well," noted Charles Worrell in a formal manner, having become something of a spokesperson for the whole gathering. "Actually, one of the things that I want to raise is that new records system. Not that my mother has been here very long." He looked around some of the more blank faces in the group and realised that he could explain further. "My mother, Nan Sweetman, has been at Gramwell Glade for only a few weeks and she's settling in well; however, I haven't had any information or feedback of any kind on her progress as, it seems, there are no notes available to families."

Having taken steps in the elusive pursuit of self-awareness, Pauline consciously aimed for her face in repose to appear curiously interested: the effect, true to nature, could, however, take on the shroud of boredom or, more likely to her subordinates, resemble a critical parent.

Immediately Arabella Jones-Merton had chipped in, "I was able to read the notes about my mother when they were handwritten. I could check on what she'd been doing or how much she'd eaten or drunk or when her medicines were given. But now there's nothing."

Brad leant forward from his seat as much to save his boss's skin as to justify the huge amount of work that had been undertaken. "If you don't mind, Pauline, I would like to answer this question."

"Perfect," acknowledged Pauline as Brad continued.

"There are so many aspects of the lives of our ladies and gentlemen that have to be accurately recorded in order to satisfy the authorities. We have been through an enormous exercise of setting up each one of our residents on the system. Now that's been achieved, it's almost instantaneous that every dose of medicine, fluid ounces of drink and all matters relating to their health is recorded. You will find that the record-keeping much more accurate."

"But invisible. That's not improving service, is it?" announced Arabella Jones-Merton. "I've brought things in for my mother and they haven't even reached her."

A murmur of discontent issued from some of the ladies gathered nearby as though in solidarity. Arabella's authority centred on her self-confidence and association with the other wealthier-looking person who'd introduced himself as Nan Sweetman's son.

Brad went in to bat. "We were sorry to hear about the Stilton, Arabella, and hope that will never be repeated. However, the bringing of goods in to Reception is not something that would ordinarily be recorded in the system. Perhaps if you had given it to a Carer in Tulip, it could have been noted?"

He looked to the wider group. "The system is designed to chart every aspect of the care of each individual resident. It will also include notes on the activities they're involved in, every time they are signed out of the Home on outings with you or with the group bus."

"But how is it of any use to us?" Maureen Dunstable asked. "When my mother-in-law first came here we could read the notes that had been written. Now there's nothing to read. And we were told that Maisie would be moved here to Daffodil but she's still in Tulip." It was clear that Maureen and Don had been bottling up this issue for a while. Why she'd chosen to air it in a group meeting was baffling Brad.

"We can talk about Maisie's situation *offline,* Maureen. I'd love to see you and Don and we can look at the reasons why Maisie hasn't been moved. When it comes to the notes, each one of you can have a password to the individual notes for your resident on a *Read Only* basis."

"Which means that we can't add anything to them?" Charles Worrell threw in.

"Certainly we can include comments and observations made by families where that is helpful," Brad conceded. He had bitten off more than he'd wanted to chew. Brendon kept up his smile but hoped that Pauline would rescue Brad from the firing line. His glance in her direction had somehow triggered the right result.

"So we'll issue you with *Read Only* passwords, those of you who are interested, and that way you can tune in to see what's been going on. Will that work for you?" she asked to the rumbling assembly.

No objection was raised within a few seconds so she gratefully changed the subject.

"Ah, the Pantomime," she said, looking back to the framework of the list on her lap with a hope that little or nothing could go wrong with so benign a subject. "As you know, we've decided to amuse the residents with a Panto this year."

She looked around to find a gaze with which she could engage. The first and only animated face she saw was that of Nurse Bessie Roberts who had been pleased to dodge the issues raised about the new records system since she'd already had to labour through so many teething problems when nurses and carers had told her that it was the bane of their lives. She didn't need that again from another potential user group. Bessie's glance had therefore been somewhat dispiriting; Pauline saw that Brendon, as ever, was engaged and apparently enthusiastic.

"You're going to see our Brendon as you've never seen him before," she promised as Brendon puffed himself up with exaggerated gestures, crossing and uncrossing his legs to relieve the tension that had been set up by the 'us against them' flavour of the previous discussion. The group laughed at his antics. "And I'm not sure how much we really want to see but we know that the residents will be thrilled to see him in the lead role as the Wicked Fairy."

Maureen Dunstable laughed out loud with Kalu, on the other side of Pauline, joining in.

"Most importantly, we've formed a choir and I can see a number of you whose parents will be part of the choir. Charles' mother will be a soloist and will also sing a duet with one of our lovely gentlemen so we're really looking forward to that. Dr Dunwoody has kindly agreed to take the choir through their paces and they're already underway with their first practice sessions. Singing, as you know, is a wonderful release of creative energy for the elderly and particularly for those living with dementia. We're actually hoping that we might be able to keep a choir going after the Panto. It will be a terrific addition to our activities here. So please note the times for the Panto. We have one performance on a Wednesday afternoon, the twentieth, and a second on the Saturday, the twenty-third, for those of you who are working. Having two performances means that you will most likely be able to make one of them and it will also allow the staff to come along when they're not working."

"How did it come about that the residents weren't considered for the acting roles?" Charles Worrell asked. A few nods and murmurs from around the circle seemed to support his query. Brendon looked to Pauline in asking permission to go into bat.

"There are a lot of lines to learn," he explained, "even with the very much shorter version of the story that we're doing. Amity wrote up the script to keep it short and simple. Even I am having trouble trying to remember it all." He feigned wiping his forehead of sweat which won a few giggles. "And then there are mobility issues. We have to fit in very small spaces at either side of the stage. There are some dance moves too. It would all be too much for our residents really. So we thought we'd be the ones to make fools of ourselves and they could enjoy laughing at us while relaxing in their chairs rather than be stressed with learning lines and moves. But they are really enjoying the singing," he added.

This appeared to appease the group. Pauline looked to her list. She had covered most of the things she planned to talk about – the new Office

Manager, the new records system and the Panto. Lots of positive new steps for Gramwell Glade. And the bus trips. However, she had undertaken to give the visitors a chance to air their concerns. "Is there anything else anyone would like to bring up before I go through my last item – the outings?" she looked around the circle. "I know it's hard for you to find time to come out to meet here like this but we really appreciate the chance to meet face to face and let you know of developments here."

"Hello Pauline. My name is Andrea Wallace. Mildred Absolom is my mother. I don't think we've had a proper chance to meet yet." Pauline nodded sagely, putting in a supreme effort to indicate that she was listening. "I'd like to ask why my mother has been moved to Tulip when she was so happy here in Daffodil. Brad and Brendon have tried to explain it to us but it's been hard for her to get used to the new surroundings, even though it's not far away from her old room. For an older person with dementia, it's not an easy thing to adjust to and it seems to have resulted in her going downhill very quickly."

Brad shot a look to Pauline who nodded her permission, pleased not to have to defend what had, in fact, been an order they had dared not refuse. To have Brad explain it in clinical terms would be the very best outcome she reckoned; besides, he was the one who'd dealt with the family some weeks ago.

"If it's OK with you, Andrea, it would be best for us to meet *offline.*" He looked around to address the whole group. "With any of these matters that relate only to your resident, it's always best if we meet face to face to talk about things. There are confidential and personal issues that are best not aired in a whole group session like this. And we'd love to talk though Mildred's progress with you, so shall we meet to find a time that suits us both?"

Andrea nodded in agreement while Trevor Hollick brusquely offered up: "I suppose that goes for me too because I want to know why my mother was moved." His expression was unmoved.

"Absolutely, Trevor. We are due to have a catch-up about Elizabeth so let's be sure to schedule something before you leave this evening?" Brad fielded.

A couple seated on the blue sofa closest to the door and not in the circle had been latecomers. Bob Shaw and his wife Deirdre had come straight from work and had missed the earlier refreshments. Both gave the impression that they were unlikely to be easily appeased. Pauline mustered a smile while making a note to herself those Family Matters evenings should not be held when Amity was on holidays. Having been at Gramwell since the planning stage, and with her easy manner, she had built a rapport with just about all the significant family members of the residents. It was she who was perfectly cut out for heading off problems before they might grow into real difficulties with her upbeat, marketing chat lines and interesting clothes.

Bob Shaw stabbed the air as he put up his hand, commanding the attention of the entire gathering. He looked as though he meant business.

"My mother, Daphne Shaw, is in Tulip too. She's been there since she moved in. She gets on well considering that she's not *with it* for most of the time but she's happy enough until recently when she tells us that the staff speak to the residents in the Lounge in a foreign language and it's annoying the daylights out of Mum." Bob Shaw put his arm back down by his side and watched Pauline's face to see how she might react.

She wasn't sure. Brendon piped up to rescue her. The group had instantly shown some concern to match Bob's even though what he was saying didn't make much sense.

"Hello Bob," Brendon pulled Bob and Deidre's focus to his side of the circle. "Hi, yes. There has been some Polish spoken in Tulip lately. Without going into too many confidential details, I can tell you why. We have a lovely Polish lady, Dorotka Gzyzyna who lives in Tulip 13. You may not have seen much of her before because she used to stay in her room. She doesn't have much family – her daughter lives in London and can't get here very often. She had become isolated so we talked about this with our carers Malgosia and Stan and they agreed to work with Dorotka to bring her out of her shell, so to speak. So now she has formed relationships with them. They've been managing to get her out of her room and into the Lounge. And it's because they all speak Polish together, that's how they *broke through* that barrier. So it's been a really happy story for us."

Deidre Shaw had not been as swayed as Brendon and some of the others. "Well, Bob's Mum doesn't want to hear foreign languages in her home. It drives her crazy." Bob put his hand on Deidre's forearm to bring her to a halt. "No, Bob, you know that it's all we hear about when we come to visit these days." Bob nodded in agreement but didn't seem to want her to force the issue as though it was up to him to go into battle for his mother.

"We can have a chat about this then," Brendon offered. " We will think of something. Of course, no one resident is more important than another. It's helpful to hear what you have to say, so we can make sure we're doing our best for everyone."

"Mealy-mouthed toad." Bob whispered to his wife before opening to the group, "You see, it's not much fun when people around you are talking and you don't know what they're saying, is it? It's downright rude!"

Brendon had taken some of the wind out of the Shaws' sails somewhat, although Bob clearly wasn't relishing the prospect of spending time in conversation with an outwardly effeminate man. The Shaws looked straight ahead, their matching clenched jaws not giving any ground.

"So if that's everything, I would like to thank you again for coming and wish you safe home. We will send you a copy of the Minutes of tonight's meeting," Pauline glanced over at the clock above Donna's head. "Oh, it's been an hour and a half since we started," Pauline noted, "doesn't time fly? On the Minutes you'll see the date and time for the next meeting. Is six o'clock still your preferred time?" People looked from one to the other. No agreement came forward; neither did any dissent. "Fine. We'll see you then but, if you would like to discuss anything at any time, my door is always open or you can see Brad, Bessie or Brendon too. All the 'B's!" She smiled as she got up from the sofa. Kalu followed, shaking out his shoulders from having been cramped between Maureen Dunstable and the arm of the sofa for ninety minutes while he sat trying to remain motionless and silent but engaged.

He followed Pauline back up the corridor while Brad and Brendon stayed behind to make arrangements for meetings with Maisie, Mildred and Elizabeth's families.

"Well, what did you think of that?" Pauline turned back to ask Kalu.

"They seemed a bit steamed up, didn't they?" he asked. "Do you send out newsletters to explain some of these things?"

"We do. But sometimes you get the feeling that they don't take any notice because the same things tend to crop up in the meetings. That was my second one. The first one was probably more difficult because I didn't know any of them and they wanted to know why my predecessor left."

"And did you tell them?" he asked as they smiled at Hilda Matters who was passing by, heading back to her room having done her daily exercise of making three lengths of the corridor without a walking stick.

"I didn't really know many of the details. Best kept that way, I suspect, and I got the distinct feeling that it was perhaps best to plead ignorance anyway."

"I know that Akin sets a lot of store in these Family meetings. *Stakeholder management* it's called."

"You will tell him that we're doing it well, I hope?" Pauline was keen to be reminded that there was a new lifeline through to Akin. It was going to be important to develop that connection. "I think we did well tonight, don't you? I feel it's important to let the Seniors all be heard, to develop their bonds with families."

“They seem to know the Seniors very well.” Kalu’s smooth tones allowed Pauline to build on the congratulations she had awarded this evening’s efforts. He reminded her so much of Akin and he was close to Akin. She reminded herself that she had a new and perhaps more direct route to the man who had formed part of her planning for as long as she had been on the staff of Empire Homes.

“They do. There’s no doubt that Gramwell Glade is the flagship of Empire – or should that be ‘flag castle’?” she asked, looking up into his face with a tentative smile.

“But don’t forget that they all want to feel that they have the ear of the General Manager. That’s the sort of thing that they believe they’re paying for.”

“Is it? But of course it is.” She laughed tentatively.” I am gradually getting to know them all – all the staff, all the residents and all of their families. There’s a huge army of people behind this castle’s battlements. I’m certain we will have stakeholder management down to a fine art before very long. I know my place, Kalu, I can assure you of that and of my continued support in your role.”

“As long as we both do it well,” he replied enigmatically as they reached the foyer and her office door.

“But of course we do,” she bravely put forward with an attempted laugh and headed in to her office.

Brad and Brendon had stacked all the used cups and saucers on to a tray on the side table and reinstated the Lounge furniture as best they could so that the room would be in reasonable order when the residents arrived in the morning. Brendon then threw himself into the deep cushions of the red sofa.

“I’m exhausted!” he whined.

“That makes two of us,” Brad agreed as he grabbed the backs of two of the chairs that had to be returned to Daffodil Dining, placing them near the door.

“I mean, I started at seven,” Brendon laboured. “Eleven o’clock catch-up meeting, our Seniors’ meeting this afternoon and now the interminable Family Matters. I feel like I spend my life in meetings when I’m actually supposed to be here to care for residents and look after the Care team.”

He looked up to find that Brad had left the room at some point during his litany. He saw the outline of his body returning to the room against the duller night lights of the corridor. “Where did you go when I was speaking to you?” he demanded playfully.

“Someone’s got to do the work,” Brad teased. “while you lounge around the place.”

Behind Brad, Brendon saw that David Jack was making his way into the Lounge. It was unusual for him to be anywhere other than his room after dinner was over.

Brad turned, sensing his presence. "Good evening, Mr Jack. Fancy seeing you here! Have you come to do some more of your jigsaw?" he guessed.

"In fact I've come to see you if that's okay?" David Jack explained sheepishly. He was finding it difficult to make eye contact with Brad. "I'd like to ask if you would have some time to have a chat with me. There's something I've been wanting to ask about."

Brad nodded towards Brendon by way of dismissing him from the room, just when Brendon had thought that there might have been a few moments that they could have enjoyed together without the constant presence of others. He gave Brad and David a tired smile as he left them, lumbering with two chairs back to the dining room.

"No time like the present, David. What can I do for you?" Brad indicated that they could sit in the two armchairs he'd placed in front of the faux fireplace near the French doors to the garden.

David sat gingerly opposite him on the edge of his chair. "Have you seen the owl who visits here?" he asked, indicating the large oak tree at the back of the garden. "My room shares this aspect. If I leave the lights off and watch carefully I can see him in the twilight in that oak." Brad looked from David to the tree. There was no owl in view although the moon was lighting up the otherwise darkened grounds.

"Face like a dinner plate," David was watching the tree carefully, as carefully as he was in avoiding Brad's eyes.

"So what is it that you'd like to talk about? The owl?" Brad prompted, adjusting his shirt cuffs fussily below his suit jacket.

"I'm not sure how to put it. Sometimes it feels as though my life is running backwards now and that I have to ask permission for things, just as when I was a child, that I have taken for granted all of my adult life."

"How so?" Brad asked, watching the puzzled furrows of David's forehead. Brad wasn't able to imagine what it was that was bothering the kindly old man.

"Well, I want to take Dorothy Baker out to dinner," David Jack blurted out in a tangle of embarrassment. "We enjoy each other's company but we can't ever have dinner here without others on the table. There are some, naming no names, who appear to delight in joining in our conversations." He slowed to take a deep breath. "I mentioned to Dot that it might be nice to go out to dinner one evening when it was just us. And I've discussed it with my daughter, Sarah. It took her a little while but she has come around to the idea that I might be *walking out* with someone since it's now two years since her mother passed away. And now I can't seem to walk anywhere with her that would give us some privacy." He had exercised his concerns and now sat back in the chair awaiting a decision on his determination. This had taken an enormous push of energy when it had been such a simple request that he wondered why he felt so disenfranchised by his own existence.

"It's so lovely to hear that you and Dot care for one another, David." Brad spoke softly, reaching a hand across to touch David's knee. "I've noticed you two spend time together. It's such a good thing to happen to you both. And I can see that there are a few problems in finding time to spend in each other's company when we're always so busy here but I wonder if you have thought about a few of the issues that might present if you were to *step out* together?"

"What would they be?" David had tried to go through the eventualities and had come up with solutions. "I know that I shouldn't drive any more. Anyway I don't have a car. Sarah uses mine now, But I could arrange a taxi for the occasion," he explained. "And arrange for them to collect us, to bring us back here. We wouldn't be out for long. I could agree to a curfew if that's what's bothering you?"

"Not that. I know that you're very responsible, David, and that you care for Dot and I think that's marvellous. There are some things that we can't mitigate, though. There could be difficulties in not having a carer around if they were needed."

"I'm not taking a carer with us!" David rose to the degree of petulance that matched the adolescent situation in which he found himself.

"No, I'm not suggesting that, not for a minute. The thing is that you said Sarah is fine with you taking Dorothy out one evening, but I'm not so sure that we would have the same degree of agreement from Dot's niece. Without breaching confidentiality, since you are close with Dorothy, you will know some of the reasons why her niece came to place her here at Gramwell Glade?"

"Not really, I suppose. We don't talk about that. Other than that we're both in our later years and perhaps aren't best left to live alone at this stage of life? My angina is under control now, though."

Brendon's head appeared through the door. With expectant raised eyebrows he hoped to relieve Brad of his duties, having decided that it was time they both left after a thirteen-hour workday. Brad shook his head, signalling that Brendon should leave. Clearly this conversation was not yet concluded. Brendon duly retreated.

"It's perhaps a good idea that you speak with Dorothy about what might happen if you were to leave the premises and be out and about in the community at night time?"

"Because?" David was becoming aggravated that the matter was not going the way he'd expected. It had taken such courage to bring the subject up. The embarrassment caused was not the only detriment that he had imagined would ensue bit also because he was having real difficulty trying to understand what the barriers were. "What are you saying?"

"I think that I'm saying you could ask Dorothy about her dementia and how she came to live here."

"Dementia? Dot doesn't have that, does she? She always seems so perfectly in tune. I don't think that she forgets things. I've not seen that in her."

"Not that so much. It's that it could lead to panic attacks which are extremely difficult to manage and really a horrible experience for her to face. And you, if you were with her. With the smooth regime she enjoys here, there haven't been any incidents for a while now but I would not feel safe in having you both deal with that out in a strange restaurant or pub somewhere. Can you understand my concern, David?"

David retreated into the armchair, devastated with the news that had hit him like a salvo. A small voice uttered, "I had no idea,"

"Of course not. Things are well contained at present. And it's a delight that you have found friendship with one another. Can I make a suggestion?" Brad asked as he leaned forward with some enthusiasm. "Can we book the private dining room for you here at Gramwell Glade? I know that's usually for family meals but why not for a couple? You could choose something from Mrs Hewson's menus and we can arrange for you both to have a special dinner together with a nice bottle of wine and with no one disturbing you – except the carer serving the table. How about that? It could be a delightful escape from the everyday but within the bounds of the manageable, so to speak. Not perhaps so much a *big bang* event but one that's comfortable." He looked to David who didn't appear to be in any way convinced that hour or so in the Private Dining Room would in any way match the expectations of David Jack's plan.

"How to put this, David? I feel as I get older and a bit wiser that it's not all about the drama. Love isn't so much about the *big bang* theory, is it? It's to do with the day-to-day rubbing together, don't you think? Just the familiarity of having a cup of tea or working out how to navigate in the car. Well, no, not that so much. Just the being together for the ordinary things?" His intonation rose, hoping to have found some recognition. " No?"

David Jack spoke slowly and in a deeper voice than usual. "This seems like a father-son talk in reverse," he observed. "Not that I had a son but, if I had done, I imagine this is how one of the *facts of life* talks might have run."

"I don't mean to tell you how to *suck eggs*, David, really I'm sorry if it sounds like that in any way."

"What you mightn't know yet at your tender age," Brad's eyes were widening as David took the higher ground, "and I don't mean to patronise you Brad, but, when you haven't yet reached half the number of years that I've known, you're still a tender lamb."

Brad laughed a little both a little embarrassed and a little flattered. "You're not ancient, David," he protested.

"But old enough to know that all the cups of tea become the next cup of tea and all the arguments just go to put you off car trips. The things that are remembered are that late supper on the terrace in Portofino. I can still taste the Chianti. Or making love on a cliff headland in the middle of nowhere on a sunny afternoon when you realise that there is no one around for miles and you're in love."

"David! You're shocking me now! Now I know this isn't what you would tell a son of yours!"

"And why not? You need to know that there are only a few precious memories you can reasonably carry with you through life so why not *go for it*, find them out and make the most of the most important moments?

Brad shuffled in his armchair as he wondered whether this old man was giving him a lesson of value or if he'd headed further down the blurred track that would eventually swallow him in his dotage, the illness that they hadn't spoken of during their rally about life's dimming possibilities.

"Amongst other things, David, we can't forget your angina. I would never forgive myself if I gave my agreement to your going out with Dorothy and something, God forbid, happened to either one of you."

"Over a dinner?" David made it sound all so implausible.

"We can't be too careful, can we? It really is not something we can agree to while holding your best interests at the forefront."

"The *forefront*?"

"The forefront." Brad took back his authority and stood, shaking his legs and reaching to offer David a lift from his chair by taking his elbow while David looked to the oak tree.

"He's there! Look, see! He's come out tonight." He sat upright, looking at Brad eye to eye as he was bending to assist David out of the chair. David shrugged him off. "Thank you for your time. I appreciate that. I obviously have some thinking to do. If it's OK with you I might just sit here for a while."

"Come on, David. Let's take you to your room where you can be comfortable for the night and not miss out on your evening meds or a cup of cocoa if you're lucky."

He put his arm through David's crooked arm and they walked slowly out of the Lounge along the dimmed corridor until they reached his door.

"Thank you, I'm fine. I will let you know if that's what we decide to do. I'm glad you saw the owl. I wasn't just making him up."

"Have a good night, David. Enjoy watching your owl."

David walked into his room, wishing he'd never left it. He'd been in trepidation before tonight's conversation. Just now he wished for no further conversations or memories like the one when he had gone to his room, admonished by his father as a boy of ten, some seventy-odd years ago. The way he felt now was not only of that memory but of an amalgam of all of the times he'd been told *no*. The room seemed small and empty. A photo of a woman he used to know smiled out at him. He slumped in his armchair, questioning, without a shadow of doubt, how he could have been so stupid, his father's angry voice echoing in his brain.

"Oh there you are!" Brendon chirped as he swung into the nurses' station on Daffodil.

"Just writing some notes up on David Jack and his somewhat unrealistic flights of fancy of late. I might get Dr Dunwoody to take a look at him on her next rounds." He looked up from his chair at the tired face that he was beginning to know so well.

"I heard some of what you said to David. You were terrific," Brendon tried to bolster his exhausted partner. "It would have been so hard to know what to say. Where did he get the idea?"

"Where does any of us get our ideas?" Brad asked as he punched the final sentence into the desktop computer. "Come on, let's go home."

"And have a quiet cup of tea, just *rubbing together?* I like the sound of that!" Brendon smiled slowly,.

"That's not what I meant and you know it!" Brad turned off the light and locked the door behind them. "And anyway, you shouldn't be listening to private conversations."

"You'd rather I just read it in the notes?"

"I want you to be there with me," Brad vowed with solemnity. "Goodness only knows how long any of us has got. Best to take his advice and *go for* the significant moments that make memories. But, in the meantime, you have lines to learn. Miss Amity's back tomorrow for a dress rehearsal."

"Heavens, don't remind me! I'm sure I'll forget every line, all of it. And she's going to be a heartless taskmaster. Who would have thought that David Jack would be the one to teach you about the importance of *big bang theory*? Come on, let's get our coats and go home. It'll be time to come back again if we don't leave soon."

The two left the building after signing out at the unattended Reception Desk. Even Pauline had left for the evening. As they headed for Brendon's car, Brad stopped a while in the car park to look for David's owl in the oak tree. The wind was cold around them.

He threw his laptop into the backseat while Brendon waited at the wheel, the car belching condensation into the evening's darkness. "Come here, Brad. It's your turn to navigate!"

"If you don't know the way to my place by now, there's no hope!" Brad laughed as he buckled his seat belt.

"I've decided! I'm going to bleach my hair for the Panto." Brendon's threat pierced the quiet night.

"You are not!" his partner insisted.

"I am so! You just watch me. Anyway, I'm sure that Sleeping Beauty has blonde hair."

"You seem to forget," Brad pontificated, "Gosia is Sleeping Beauty. You're the old hag who caused all the trouble. She wouldn't have had long blonde locks. Then again, she wouldn't have been razor cut around the sides." He rubbed his hand at the back of Brendon's neck, a gesture in their relationship that they both enjoyed. "Surely you can wear a wig and keep your own hair reasonably presentable?"

"You say that as though it's not always immaculate," Brendon protested as he turned at the junction, instinctively heading to his own flat.

"You're going the wrong way!" Brad protested.

Brendon grabbed at the wheel to force a tight three-point U-turn on the narrow country road in silence and the car headed on with the moon lighting empty fields on either side.

"I'd like to thank everyone who attended the Family Matters meeting last night," Pauline addressed those standing around her room and the early birds who had snaffled the pink sofa. "I think we put on a credible show of professional care, don't you, Kalu?" She smiled at Kalu who was seated on an office chair on the other side of her desk.

"It was an interesting meeting. I learned a lot about Gramwell." He smiled at each of the participants around the room as he spoke. "Your residents have a few concerns and, of course, we must keep on top of those," he added, taking up some kind of new authority in his post. Brad and Brendon were past masters at keeping poker faces but an exchange between Bessie Roberts and Amity indicated that his predecessor would never have dared to take up a managerial stand in an eleven o'clock meeting, or anywhere else for that matter. They eased their bodies from the support of the wall, standing straighter, as though they were all in for some more interesting times.

"And, as you can see," Pauline continued, "Amity is back from her break, looking fabulously tanned and ready to get into the Panto rehearsals. Amity?"

Amity's tan was *the elephant in the room.* It came, as tans can, with an apparent nonchalance, a degree of relaxation that was unknown within the hallowed corridors of Gramwell Glade for both the staff and by most of its residents. The snail's pace on some Mediterranean island that Amity visited frequently had obviously done wonders for her complexion and temper.

"Welcome to Kalu," Amity acknowledged with fluid grace. The aqua linen shift dress and pale blue cashmere cardigan she wore over her shoulders echoed the tones of the azure sea she had reluctantly left behind at the same time as the Family Matters meeting had been soldiering on at Gramwell.

"Yes, we begin today at three in Ye Old Tea Shoppe."

"But we'll be seen!" Brendon retorted.

"And the problem there is?" Amity asked laconically.

"The problem there is that the Panto won't be any surprise then to anyone, will it?"

"But the rehearsals will be just as entertaining to the residents as the final performance. And, don't forget, there won't be enough room for them all to see the two final performances, so this way they can see some of the fun while we rehearse."

This explanation appeared to make perfect sense to the majority of the assembly but Brendon's lack of sleep and complete disdain for the idea of opening rehearsals to their 'public' ran against every grain in his being. He wanted to bring his *A-game* when it came time to perform and not have any of his practice errors seen. Brad sensed that silencing his partner would be the better strategy. He pressed his thigh into Brendon's, giving a firm impression that he should now cease and desist. The closeness of his pressing leg, it turned out, was a perfect muzzle.

Pauline seized the moment to try to continue with the day's business when Bessie Roberts interrupted loudly. "I'm sorry, Pauline, I'm going to have to leave," she announced, looking at the small receiver hanging on her belt. "There's an alarm going off in the café. It's Elsie Lister's alarm, which is unusual. I'll be back in a jiffy." Bessie's stockings rasped as her short legs motored her round body under Frank Goninon's arm while he held open the door he'd been leaning on.

"Never a dull moment," Peggy Hewson noted, brushing her hair back and putting her cook's cap back on her head. "It's never this complicated in the Kitchen. I never know what to expect the moment I pop my head out."

"Madhouse is what to expect," lobbed Frank Goninon.

"Sorry, Frank?" Pauline shot him a silencing look. "Let's get back to business, shall we?"

The door then pushed Frank almost into the middle of the room as Bessie reappeared. "Excuse me, sorry all. Frank, do you have any white spirits or turps in the Cleaning Cupboard?" she rasped.

"You know the rules say we're not to clean with those strong chemicals anymore," he replied.

"What's the matter?" Pauline asked Bessie across the room.

"Elsie Lister was in a tizzy. Naomi took her off to the Café to join in with the group making Christmas lanterns and she apparently Super Glued her hands together."

"How come they've got Super Glue, then?" asked Frank who had always sworn by white spirits as the best cleaner before the rules meant that he'd had to give up his arsenal.

"Glued her hands together?" Pauline echoed in amazement.

"We don't know how the Super Glue got there in the stuff Naomi brought from the activities cupboard but I don't need to tell you that this is a pretty nasty situation." Bessie explained while trying to keep any anxiety under wraps. The idea of having to send Elsie Lister to the hospital to have her hands separated was not something any of them would want to entertain.

"We've got some turps in the shed, Bessie," Eric Spence piped up. "I'll get it now. It'd perhaps be an idea to take Elsie to a room on her own, away from the crowd anyway and we can see if the turps will do the trick."

"Thanks, Eric. I'll take her to the hair salon. There's no hairdresser today. Meet you there! Sorry Mrs Graves." Bessie's swishing thighs left the room with the hope that the emergency could be dealt with in-house.

"We'll have to *notify* on this, Pauline," Brad threw in. "This is a Serious Matter. We are duty-bound to provide notification and a summary of how we dealt with it."

"Thank you, Brad," Pauline's fingers gripped the silver pendant that hung on the front of her pink shirt. "This shouldn't have happened, of course, we all know that. Please will you all make sure that all staff are being extra-vigilant. Reports like this one make us look as though we aren't competent in what we're doing when we all know that we absolutely are."

She was clearly flustered, her hands reaching for a few pens which she tapped quickly on the notes in front of her. "I think that will be enough for this morning, under the circumstances. Perhaps you can let me know when Bessie has prepared the report, Brad? I'd like to see it before it's entered into the system."

Pauline had looked pale from the long day's efforts that had preceded. She now appeared to need a strong coffee, at the very least, to deal with the rest of the morning.

"I'm going back to the refuge of my Kitchen," Peggy told Frank by way of getting him to move out of the doorway.

"Madhouse," was his comment to her as he followed her down the corridor and through the security doors to the cleaners' and maintenance rooms, the laundry and kitchen precincts: those back-of-house machines that drove Gramwell Glade.

Chapter Ten

BRING ME MY ARROWS OF DESIRE

Kayleigh Longbottom had gone to set up Daffodil Dining for lunch when she'd finished seeing to Barney in his room. Barney had been making a habit of pressing his alarm button for the smallest of requests. Kayleigh had told him when she went at speed to answer the alarm to find him stabbing the air with his index finger, pointing to the rug on his armchair while shouting "Cold! Cold!", that, if he used the alarm for these little things that weren't urgent, they couldn't be sure he wasn't *calling 'Wolf'* when he might really need them one day.

Her worst fears were realised when, entering the Dining Room, she found that breakfast hadn't been cleared: the place was a wreck. There were no clean dishes to set up. She wanted to scream but she was well aware that Brendon had always told the Carers they were not to raise their voices in the Home at any time. No reason would be counted as valid. Besides, there was no audience. She was the lone worker in the area, which was entirely the problem and, since Barney wasn't the only one who was confining himself to his room now that the short days of December had arrived, none of the residents had turned up yet.

Kayleigh gathered up as many of the dirty dishes as she could fit on the trolley and pushed it with too much force towards the dishwasher. Some milky cereal painted the floor among the spoons that had been forced into a glass which now lay in shards on the floor. Kayleigh grabbed for the yellow *Caution Wet Floor* sign in the cupboard which she erected as a tent above the mess while she packed the dishwasher in record time and selected the Quick Wash option in the hope that they would have some clean crockery before the lunch arrived from the kitchen.

From the corner of her eye she saw Frank Goninon walking up the corridor from the end of Daffodil rooms. He had a mop in hand. She flew to the door to summon his help.

"Frank, can you help me please?" she called in her softest shouting voice. "Please?"

Frank swung a bucket and mop from his left arm as he sidled into the Dining Room to be met by the glass and cereal mess.

"What's this?" he asked redundantly. "You've been having a fine time, then."

"Oh stop it, Frank! I'm the only one here. No one cleared breakfast and I'm trying to do the jobs of three people here."

"Tell me about it!" Frank grimaced.

"Could you do the floor for me, please?" She was clearly under pressure and Frank had imagined why.

"Is this because little Brian has been asking Tayla out?" he blurted.

Kayleigh threw a cloth into the sink. "Where did you hear that rubbish?" she turned to ask him with her cheeks blazing.

"Not heard, Missie, seen. Now, don't shoot the messenger but I saw it with my own eyes when she came on duty early this morning. He was first out there in Reception and he was there a while. Before Mrs Graves came in to work. She was enjoying chatting with him too, I can tell you."

"He's dead meat!" Kayleigh vowed but she knew that there were things to be dealt with before she could deal with her man. "Please, Frank. Can you mop this mess otherwise I'll never be able to get the tables set proper?"

"With this bucket? I don't think you'd want me to put this all over your Dining Room floor. Not when I've been mopping up the mess in Barney Perry's room. You'd never get lunch served at all if I spread this on the floor." He looked to Kayleigh's defeated face as the description and the odour hit her at the same time. "All right, Miss. I'll get this lot cleaned up and come back to fix your floor for you. Got to *exceed everyone's expectations in this home away from home* now, don't we? I spend more time here with you lot than I spend at my home as it is. I'll be back."

"I was just with Barney and he didn't tell me that he wanted to use the toilet. If he'd've told me, you wouldn't have a mess to clear. I'm sorry."

Frank shrugged his shoulders and left the room giving her the benefit of his wisdom as he was fond of doing, "Shit happens. Lots of it around this joint." he pronounced. "Be back in two shakes."

Kayleigh continued to reset tables around the room laden with thoughts of what Frank might be shaking, wondering where her colleagues had got to, how it had befallen her to do this alone and how to deal with Brian. Her blood boiled.

When Henry brought the bain-maries to the Dining Room, neatly dodging the mess on the floor and the yellow sign, the table setting exercises had been completed but not without a mammoth effort from Kayleigh who was now at her wits' end.

"Thanks a million," she shot at Naomi Page as she came in the door behind Henry, ready to serve lunch.

"Who got out of the wrong side of the bed today, then?" Naomi asked with a smile.

"Shut up!" Kayleigh burst into tears and threw down a tea towel she'd been using to wipe down the serving bench.

"Oh I'm sorry, honey," Naomi reached out to hug her colleague who stood back from her advances.

"No," Kayleigh pushed her away, "I've got to stay strong to get through this lunch today. No point in going in to it here. I'll only cry. Just help me out, will you? I came here to set up half an hour ago and no one had cleared breakfast. I spilled this shit on the floor, had to stack the dishwasher and lay the tables with burning hot plates because there was no time. I'm waiting for Frank to come back to clean the floor and all on top of all that, I've got man troubles. Or should I say boy troubles? Because he's just a boy." Tears dripped from her chin as she tried to hold in all of her stewing grievances.

"Here," offered Naomi, taking the glasses from the bench to distribute around the room. "This doesn't sound like you. Come on, you take a ten-minute break while there's no one here. Come back when you've had a chance to take a few deep breaths. I'll hold the fort."

"Would you? That would be lovely." Kayleigh's eyes welled again with tears. "Anyway, it looks like there will only be a few in today for lunch. Some's on an outing and quite a few have been eating in their rooms so there mightn't be too many takers in here."

Kayleigh pulled her apron off and went to leave the room. Looking back at Naomi, she realised "That's where the Team are? On that shopping outing? That's why I was the only one to do the set-up? I wish they'd bloody warned me. I could've got here earlier."

On her way to the Staff Tea Room, Kayleigh diverted her path to head for Tayla's Reception Desk.

Tayla looked up from her computer with her ever-ready look of expectancy and willingness, as she did with all comers as a matter of required routine.

"Hi Kayleigh," she proffered, her voice wavering with fear. Kayleigh looked completely out of sorts and definitely not to be trifled with, but Tayla knew exactly what trifling had gone on.

"Hi Tayla. Can I see you in the Staff Lounge for just a minute?" Kayleigh asked in an unusual tone of voice.

"I'm not allowed to leave my desk," Tayla was pleased to trot out as if by rote.

Amity had been walking by on her way to Pauline's office and, hearing that Tayla wasn't able to leave her desk, was pleased to offer her just that opportunity. She had often been concerned that the Receptionists seldom had a chance to make a proper loo break or even time to grab a cup of tea.

"Off you go, Tayla," she offered with ease. "I'll sit here until you come back. It's no problem."

Tayla had no further reason not to head to the gallows that Kayleigh had prepared for her. She got up from her chair and thanked Amity for her consideration, following Kayleigh down the dark road that was to become her penance. All she had done was just talk to Brian Petty when he had greeted her earlier in the day. Her hands were shaking as her heart thumped.

Kayleigh led the way down the corridor towards the back-of-house precinct but stopped in her tracks midway when the two of them were out of earshot of any interlopers. She turned to find Tayla's dilated pupils immediately in her sights.

"Did Brian ask you out this morning?" came the volley from her determined mouth.

Tayla was frightened. She had never seen this side of Kayleigh. Her blinking eyes and pinched mouth gave away her reply before she bravely offered up her confession.

"Yes, he did, but –" Her knees were shaking. Kayleigh immediately interrupted her with a purpose that took on the joy of a major discovery.

"I thought so!"

"But I said, no and I said, 'You're with Kayleigh' and told him to go away." Tayla could feel the pulse beating in her temple: this felt to her just the same as being baled up by the school bully in the girls' toilets when she was in Grade Five.

"Thanks. You're a friend, Tayla. And he is dead meat!"

Tayla's heart skipped a beat. This was not what she had expected. Things were appearing to take a better turn from that Grade Five nightmare that was deeply etched in her memory.

"And we're going to face him together, like friends do!" Kayleigh continued with the crazy plan that was quite apparently giving her a great deal of pleasure. "He's got to learn that he can't mess people around like this." Tayla thought she could see the dampness of a tear in the corner of her captor's eye. "You in?" asked Kayleigh. Tayla nodded, fearing that there was no alternative given the passion and drive that had driven Kayleigh on.

"OK," she explained, "but I don't feel very good about facing him like this," her voice wavered again.

"But how would you like it if he had done this to you?" Kayleigh was determined to press on. "Maybe he'll learn if we let him know that he can't do things in secret or on the side even," she rallied as she punched in the code on the keypad and led her disciple through the doors towards the Staff Tea Room where she knew Brian would be finishing his own lunch before working with her in Daffodil Dining Room. Turning back to see Tayla in the wake of her determination, she added: "At least we'll still be friends when this thing is over with Brian?" She offered an encouraging smile which Tayla tried to match.

Brian was sitting at the far corner table, facing the wall as he tried to eat the contents of his lunchbox in ignominious peace but Frank Goninon had joined him. Brian had his back to the interlopers when Frank announced in a loud voice, "Oh my boy, you're in big trouble now!"

Brian turned to see Kayleigh and Tayla: this was worse than his very worst fear.

"You should know better, son, than to do the dirty on Kayleigh." Frank lectured at the top of his voice. "Don't forget, you can't fart in Gramwell Glade without someone knowing about it." He smiled at Kayleigh and Tayla as he stood up carrying his mop and bucket.

"I'm off to deal with your mess now," he proclaimed as he swept past Kayleigh.

"What's this about?" asked Brian in a style that was more timid than his usual banter.

"What do you think it's about, bitch?" Kayleigh spat. Tayla tried to stand in her shadow so as not to be regarded as a player in the drama that was now spinning out of control.

"Kayleigh," he tried to reason, "it's not like –"

"Not like that?" Kayleigh quickly stood to the side to reveal Tayla, "Not like that?"

Tayla felt both ashamed and infuriated. There was nowhere to hide. She looked at the floor.

"Yeah, but –"

"But you're dead meat, Brian Perry! It's over. I'm not hanging around anymore to see you treat me like this again. It's just that you've been stupid enough to hit on my friend this time."

"I didn't know you was friends," he protested, his face pale.

"And does that make any difference?" Kayleigh posed the non sequitur as much to her own confusion as her rage flew. "Get lost, Brian. And I'll make sure that everyone stays away from you from now on."

"Kayleigh," he pleaded as he watched her nod to Tayla to signify that their business had been completed. Tayla followed, her feet gliding across the room towards the door, grateful to be leaving the scene which was causing her both confusion and embarrassment.

"Don't you even try to ask me to stay!" she shouted over her shoulder. "Come on Tayla. We'll leave this drop-kick to find out what it's like to mess with us," she yelled in the corridor as they left him empty in the corner vowing never to have anything to do with girls ever again.

Brad smiled at Grace Garrett who was making her way down the corridor as he headed towards the Foyer. She was apparently making her daily pilgrimage to the Guest Toilet.

"Lovely hand lotion," she told Brad as she tried to open the door of her favourite room.

"Enjoy!" he saluted blithely, holding the door open as she pushed the Zimmer frame into her nirvana.

Brad pushed with a flat hand at the door to the office which was now shared by Kalu and Amity. When Barbara had been ensconced in that office, there may as well have been a revolving door, he thought. Somehow she'd had staff in and out on a constant basis. Nowadays it seemed a perfect retreat. Work seemed to be less of a burden or at least less of a stress; so much so that he wondered if Kalu could actually be doing the same work that had caused Barbara her constant stress. These days the atmosphere was always pleasant. They sometimes played music. Brad could always find an ear and a trusted second opinion. He realised that the quality of his Gramwell days had been improved no end by Kalu's inclusion in their Senior Team.

"Ah, Brad, my man," Kalu spoke out as he looked over the top of his notebook, keying in some figures as he did so. It appeared that he could have worked blindfolded and still get things done, unlike Barbara who had spent her days and many evenings her head in her hands, swearing at the machine.

A hint of Portuguese jazz rifted from Amity's desk.

"This is what I like to see," Brad greeted him, "calm and happy campers. It's a joy to visit your room, guys. Somehow it's the most peaceful place in Gramwell Glade."

“And the most productive,” boasted Amity. “I bring them in: Kalu takes the fees. It all happens here, my friend!”

“Well, if I’m not needed,” Brad feigned an exit, “there won’t be any nursing and caring for any of our residents then or any need for this Special Matters report on Elsie or the next one I have to do for Dot Baker.”

“What’s up with Dot?” Amity asked as Kalu continued to press away at his keyboard while watching the discussion.

“You know that Mobo took a group to the Chelmsford shopping centre for the Christmas presents outing?”

“I thought that was a bit of a risk, actually,” Amity admitted.

“What, they went to that huge shopping centre?” Kalu stopped what he was doing. His face showed concern. “And so did Dot get lost?” he asked.

“Worse than that. No, perhaps not worse but at least as bad.” Brad pulled at his shirt cuffs and looked over to check what he thought he’d noticed at the eleven o’clock meeting. Kalu did indeed have his initials embroidered on the cuffs of his immaculately white shirt, just above the jet cufflinks.

“Dot had a panic attack in the middle of the shopping centre.”

“Oh no! Poor Dot. Have you phoned her niece?” she asked, moving immediately to *next steps* in the protocol manual for reporting Special Matters.

“Not yet. I need to get more information. I spoke to Mobo before he left. I need to hear from the staff who were there to get the full picture. It seems that she went into the centre court place to see Santa. There was a large crowd and she lost the plot, poor Dot.”

“That’s all she needs.” Amity was crestfallen. “You know, she’s been really down since last week. Not her usual self at all.”

“Really?” Brad’s face gave away some knowing. His lips narrowed as he chewed over the news. “I think I have an idea about that. I spoke with David last week. He wanted to take Dot out to dinner.”

“Oh sweet!” chimed Amity. “That’s the sweetest thing.” She looked to Kalu. “Don’t you think? It’s wonderful when that happens. *You’re never too old for love,* they say. And when it happens, it really is just the sweetest thing.”

“But I told David that it wasn’t a wise idea,” Brad rejoined.

“You meanie!” Amity charged. “You didn’t, seriously?”

“And I’ve just been proved right, sadly. Dot’s dementia manifests mainly as panic attacks. And David doesn’t even recognise his own dementia. There’s his heart, too.”

“Which is exactly what you’ve broken. No wonder they say he won’t come out of his room. He’s heartbroken.”

“Oh, do go on!” Brad remonstrated. “Shall I put that in a report for you? David Jack has had an accident. His heart is broken.”

“I believe we can all fall in love. No matter what age,” Kalu kicked in. “But I do see his point,” he directed at Amity. “What if she had had a panic attack when she and David were out at a restaurant somewhere? At least today there were trained staff with her. Is she fine now?” He looked up from the desk to Brad who was leaning against the filing cabinets and cogitating while he examined his fingernails.

“Yes, thankfully. She’s in her room resting and there is no damage, other perhaps than the scare that she caused all the others. And annoyance. They had to come home before any of them had bought anything. The trip was aborted. Now just imagine what an aborted romantic dinner might look like?” he directed at Amity.

“Romance is alive and well then?” she sneered. “Same root cause for Elsie’s incident, actually.”

“That’s what I was coming to ask you about. If you’d read over my draft report.”

“Of course I will, dear heart.” She reached for the notes he held in his hand and handed him some of her own.

“But, Ms Cryptic, what do you mean about romance hurting Elsie?” he asked as he handed them over.

“Oh, this one is special,” added Kalu with a warm smile. “There must be something in the water here,” he chuckled as Brad’s eyes flicked from left to right across the notes that Amity had handed him.

“That’s fine, Brad,” Amity said as she finished reading the page. “That captures what happened as such.” She looked across the desk to her co-lodger. “Elsie’s been at the root cause of many a hoo-hah here. Her family thinks that we’re trying to show her up. Believe me, she does that all by herself.”

“They say that *there’s always one*. Sounds like Elsie is Gramwell’s *one*, then?” Kalu surmised.

“You’re kidding!” Brad steamed when he’d finished reading the three-page letter that Amity had handed over. “I s’pose that explains her skittishness of late. I hadn’t realised that she’d been so invested in John Nicholls.”

“Or that she would have told her family about it. It’s not the sort of thing you’d usually discuss with your children is it? Falling in love. Or infatuation, which is more like it.”

“But don’t children become like parents once theirs have reached a certain age?” Kalu asked. “In Nigeria we always listen to our elders but the *rules* of the family, if you like, are sort of the premise of the working generation, the ones who have to find the money to fund the family." He laughed as his own words triggered a realisation for him. "In fact, that's the way it is already for my old dad, bless him. He really has to do what I suggest to him these days because I'm the one who pays."

"But you don't let him feel as though you're the one in charge?" Amity queried.

"Never! He wouldn't be letting me take the lead now. Or probably ever. It's a fine line, that's for sure."

"So," Brad flipped back to the first page of the letter, "Her son-in-law says that John had been showing her a lot of interest?"

"We think that was mostly in Elsie's imagination. What she wanted. She's a looker, our Elsie. She seems to think she's still in the prime of her life and that all the men will fall for her."

"And good for her!" Brad chimed. "I keep having to tell Brendon that there's no point in going through life as a pessimist, expecting the worst. It's exactly that lively spirit that keeps a twinkle in old Elsie's eye."

"I would have said that *you* were the pessimist in your relationship," Amity teased.

"Really?" Brad did a double take as his mind briefly took him to the argument they'd had that very morning. It was true that Brendon had been singing and prancing around the bathroom and he was the one objecting. He brought his attention back to the matter at hand so as not to give anything away. "I'll have to ask the Team who was doing the moving and shaking then between Elsie and John I mean."

"Clearly it was Elsie. I've heard from Evelyn Dunwoody that Elsie was following John around like a lost dog during choir rehearsals."

"So he's told her it's a *no go*?"

"That's about the shape of it, according to all that I've heard too. And they've seen her knocking on the door of his room. He's *just not that into her*!" joked Kalu.

"Poor Elsie," lamented Amity.

"Like you were ever thwarted by any of your suitors!" Brad teased. "But we can't do as the daughter wants. We can't *make* John like Elsie."

"Apparently it all came tumbling down when John started to sit with Hilda in the Dining Room," Amity continued.

"Hilda! Oh come off it! She's a head taller than John and she has a beard!" Brad tried to imagine John squiring Hilda to the Scrabble.

"That's not what matters is it?" Kalu asked, "especially not when they're this old. It's more about who you can talk to, be comfortable with."

"And Elsie wanted to get comfortable with John. The Hilda thing was annoying her for days but, when she came to make the Christmas decorations this morning, no doubt to track him down and spend time with him, she saw John chatting to Hilda over a cup of tea, she flipped and then, somehow, she found the Super Glue." Amity outlined the sequence of events.

"So you think she did it deliberately?" Brad was trying to put two and two together in detective mode.

"That's possible," Amity warned, "but how would that read in a report? I like what you've done here. It's enough as it stands. It all makes sense to say it's just a confused old lady who got mixed up while making Christmas decorations."

"You'll still need to think about how to explain the Super Glue being there," Kalu spelled out.

"For sure," Brad agreed. "How do we explain that? Perhaps we make reference to the locks we keep on the Activities Cupboard?"

"How does that explain the Super Glue being in the cupboard, though?" Kalu leant back in his office chair.

"It's our fault. There's no getting away from it," Amity reasoned.

"You're right. We're just going to have to *'fess up*." Brad agreed. "there's nothing harder to explain than the truth. So they say."

"Who do you think put it there?" Kalu asked.

"Let's not go there!" Amity opened her compact and traced the outline of her lips in coral pink lipstick. "Let's just thank our lucky stars she didn't try anything more dramatic."

"No, you're right." Brad took his draft report back and handed Amity the letter in return. "I guess you just tell Elsie's daughter that we can't interfere in the relationships of our residents and I will have to point out the safeguards we're going to put in place so that this can't happen again."

"How do you plan to do that?" Kalu asked, his eyes wide.

"Ban Super Glue. Simple. It's banned from the premises!"

"I guess that will do it," Kalu chuckled. "I'll check my drawers right now."

"It was *YOU*?" Brad gasped.

"Just kidding you, buddy."

Brad took a deep breath before heading back into the breach. He turned back for one last whiff of the apparent serenity that Amity and Kalu had created in their room. "You don't really think I'm a pessimist, do you?" he asked thoughtfully.

"Get out, silly," Amity teased. "You are the best ever Nursing Team Leader – conscientious, capable," she reached for another adjective having fed his ego back to functional levels, "and pessimistic."

"A low blow, Madame! I know when I'm not loved. I'm going home. You can deal with it all by yourselves." Brad let the door slam behind him as a gesture to his high dudgeon. He headed to the Nurses' Station to lodge the report about Elsie and start work on explaining Dot's unfortunate episode in the shopping centre.

The curtains were drawn against the early sunset in Daffodil Lounge by Marigold who smiled at each of the residents gathered. Marjorie and Albert had parked their wheelchairs side by side in the television area which was being shared by Hilda since she had noticed the Foreign Secretary speaking on a news brief and lumbered over to berate him, blocking everyone else's view.

"Haven't changed a bit, have you? Thirty years later and you're still a pompous ass!"

"You know him?" Bert asked, astounded.

"Could you move a bit to the side, Hilda?" Marjorie suggested.

"Know him? He was the bane of my life for a few years when he thought he was *cock a hoop* when I was trying to teach him Geography." She railed again at the television, "And you thought that you knew it all, didn't you?"

"Quiet, Hilda! I can't hear him and he can't hear you anyway." Marjorie remonstrated as she grasped Bert's hand to summon him to shut Hilda down. However, it appeared that Bert was more interested in the brush with fame that had tickled his interest.

"So what was he like?" he asked as Marjorie now slapped the hand she'd taken for support.

"Well, you can see, can't you? He thinks he's just *it*! Don't you?" Hilda shouted at the television.

"But, well, he is, isn't he?" Bert argued. "He's done very well for himself."

"You don't know what goes on behind those scenes, Albert," Hilda explained. "It's all about *who you know* and, I'm almost ashamed to say, where you went to school."

"Shut up, Hilda!" Marjorie insisted as she wheeled closer to the television.

"Marjorie, that's not a very nice way to speak to Hilda," Marigold came over to them in an effort to referee.

"We're allowed to fight!" she insisted, "Because we're friends."

"And Hilda knows this chap," Bert added with enthusiasm. "She used to teach him, didn't you Hilda?"

“Not that it did him much good,” Hilda sighed before turning back to give him one last roar, “Did it? It didn’t do you much good, do you hear?”

“No, Hilda. He can’t hear you. I keep telling you. Will you please shut up!” Marjorie had lost any composure with Hilda and was contemplating giving up on the idea of being on Bert’s team too.

The news service flicked to an item about birdwatchers in Suffolk so Hilda’s rage against the Secretary of State was quickly forgotten, but Bert now twigged that he’d been birdwatching somewhere one summer long ago and began to bang his feet on the rests of his wheelchair. “Look Marjorie! I’ve been there!”

Marjorie decided to give up on any possibility of watching the programme uninterrupted and wheeled her chair back to park it beside Bert as she shook her head in submission.

Darragh came bowling through the double doors into the Lounge carrying a large box. This was labelled for adult continence pads but actually contained all of the lantern decorations that had been put together in the café that morning.

“Got ’ em, Marigold. We’ve been told to put them up in here so I’ll go back and get a ladder and maybe you can find us some helpers to sort out where we’re going to hang them.” He plopped the box down near the table where David Jack was quietly on a jigsaw puzzle of a Norfolk stately home.

“OK, Marjorie and Elizabeth, it’s nice to see you here today and Hilda, would you like to help me decide where best these lovely decorations should be hung?”

Hilda was quick to turn down the offer. “Leave it to them,” she grumped as she left the room, muttering about the Foreign Secretary having put her off doing anything else this afternoon.

Marjorie and Elizabeth were thrilled to be asked to take on an important task and dragooned Maisie as she came in with her doll to let her know.

“We’re in charge here!” Elizabeth explained. “When Darragh comes back with the ladder we’re going to tell him where to hang the lanterns.”

Marjorie wheeled over to Maisie and tried to whisper but managed to catch the attention of most of the room to explain, “They were fighting over there,” as she indicated the group watching television.

“We weren’t fighting,” Bert retorted. “But anyway we’re allowed to if someone’s being annoying.”

Bert patted her hand to calm her down as he tuned into the game show that had followed the news break

“No point in fighting, is there?” Maisie asked her friends. “We’re here to be enjoying ourselves.” She reiterated what had been told to her over the past few months. “And aren’t we lucky to have such a lovely home?”

“I think things are jollier now than they ever were in the past.” Elizabeth romanced.

“I’m not sure about that?” Maisie asked her doll.

“There’s no two bones about it,” Maisie concurred. “I’m very happy here with all of you.” They bumped shoulders as they giggled together.

Darragh appeared with the stepladders and a tool belt decorated with silver tinsel. “Right, ladies,” he summoned in a booming voice, “let’s see where we can hang these. Marigold,” he directed, “can you take charge of the drawing pins here and the sticky tape?” He handed some small boxes past the assembled helpers directly to Marigold.

Maisie, Millie and Elizabeth looked somewhat disappointed as, as yet, they had nothing to be in charge of.

Seeing this, Darragh immediately put out the fire that was about to spark with his usual good nature. “No, ladies, none of the hard work for you. We need your expertise to let us know where to hang them all up.” The ladies looked to each other with a sense of importance as he continued with his suggestions. “What about over the fireplace? Do you think they would look good there?”

“I’m not sure that nailing those to the fireplace will look all that good. Don’t you think so, Maisie? Surely it should be stockings not pants?” Elizabeth, who had seen the writing on the box, asked in dismay.

Ronnie Chan was despatched from the Nurses’ Station by Amadia Stokes to check on Dot Baker in Daffodil 6 since she hadn’t been seen since returning from the shopping centre debacle at lunchtime. Ronnie knocked quietly on the door. She and Rosie Rowson exchanged smiles as Rosie headed up the corridor with her cleaning trolley. Ronnie knocked again. She hadn’t heard a reply but, since the corridor was seeping extraneous noises from all the rooms with open doors, a quiet reply may not have been heard. Ronnie opened the door to the darkened room. The curtains had been pulled. No light had been turned on.

“Dot?” Ronnie asked tentatively. “Are you awake?”

Dot’s tiny body straightened from the foetal position as she turned to face the intruder.

“I’m fine. Who’s that? Oh, Ronnie. How are you?” Dot asked in a small voice.

“Good, darling. Just a bit concerned about you. Can I get you a cup of tea? Milk no sugar?”

"That would be lovely," Dot tried to smile, relying on good manners to mask her sadness.

"I'll be back in a tick then," Ronnie assured her, closing the door behind her.

In Daffodil Dining Room, while pouring water from the boiler over a tea bag Ronnie found Rosie mopping the floor.

"How's Dot?" Rosie asked.

"I'm not really sure yet," Ronnie shut off the tap and dipped the bag a few times in the hot water.

"She had an attack when they was out at the shops." Rosie had obviously heard the story.

"That's what I heard too," Ronnie tried to dampen any wilder stories that might be doing the rounds."She'll be OK."

"Now that she's home. There's no place like home," Rosie added while sweeping the mop into the corners by the dishwasher. "Home sweet home."

Ronnie put some milk into the teacup and twisted her hand into the large glass jar to snaffle a couple of biscuits to put on the saucer. "That's right," she added absentmindedly as she left the room and headed back to Dot's where the table and standard lamps had been turned on. Dot had put her dressing gown on over her clothes and was sitting in her armchair.

"Here we are!" Ronnie put the cup and saucer beside Dot on the table. "Are you feeling cold, sweetie? Shall I turn up the heat?"

"No, it's fine." Dot assured her. "It's just because I've been lying still. I'll be right as rain when I have some hot tea inside me."

"A stressful day, was it?" Ronnie led in an effort to ascertain just how deeply Dot had been affected by the panic attack earlier."

"It was silly really. I just got really worried when there was a big crowd around me. I couldn't work out where I was but it was all over and done with in a flash. I was fine by the time we got back on the bus with Mobo. It's just about how much I've let the others down that worries me. They were going to go shopping for their grandchildren's Christmas presents and because it was decided that we should come straight home when I got in a tizzy, they didn't get a chance."

With the cup near her mouth, Dot's tears prevented her taking a sip.

"Come on, sweetheart," Ronnie sat on the edge of the bed with an arm around Dot's shoulder. "It could have happened to anyone. No one was hurt and the others won't mind – just as long as you're alright. That's the main thing. And isn't it good to know that there's always someone around to help you out if anything happens?"

"I suppose so. I just feel silly. And they might be cross with me." She burst into tears, out the cup and saucer on the table and snuggled into Ronnie's arm.

"No one is cross with you, darling," Ronnie soothed. "Now, come on. Drink up and have one of those Rich Teas. You didn't have any lunch. We can't have you fading away."

Dot wriggled herself straighter in the chair and took several sips of tea before looking Ronnie in the eye.

"Thank you for looking after me."

"That's what I'm here for," Ronnie assured her. "And there's another reason for my visit," she added. "Dr Dunwoody has asked me to see you."

"Oh no! They're going to change my medicine because of what happened this morning?"

Ronnie laughed. "No, nothing like that, Dot. Dr Dunwoody is running the choir for the Panto."

"I know, I'm in the choir." Dot retorted, afraid that she was now going to be treated as some kind of idiot or, worse, lose her place for the singing.

"And Dr Dunwoody has noticed that you have a wonderful voice!"

"Well, that's a surprise. How can she hear one above the rest? But I do love singing. Somehow all my worries go away when I'm singing."

"Well that's good to hear because, even though I'm not sure this is quite the right moment to ask you about this, Dr Dunwoody would like you to do the duet since, basically, Nan Sweetman has not taken well to it all and has now decided to bow out."

"The duet? With David?"

"Yes, the duet with David, who is fine about it I should add. I think he's been missing you. Dr Dunwoody checked with him before asking me to come to you. They would both be very happy for you to do it."

Dot looked at Ronnie and smiled. "I think I probably could do it. Funny but I don't get nervous about the singing the way I do about being in the crowded shops." She thought for a moment, checking with herself that she could manage an audience, if not crowds. "Do you think I could do it?"

"Absolutely I do!" Ronnie hugged Dot.

"Can anyone join in?" japed Brendon as he and Brad appeared in the doorway.

"You're wearing your nurse's uniform," Ronnie pointed at Brad. "What's this all about?"

"Nwaoma's sick and I can't get anyone else to fill in so I'm just back from a power nap at home, ready to do the night shift as Lead Nurse."

"And not even Agency?" Ronnie asked.

Brendon was quick to jump in. “I know. That’s what I said. ‘Take the night off.’ But you know what he’s like.”

“What am I like then, Mr Smarty Pants? You know the residents don’t enjoy having Agency staff here, and neither do the staff for that matter. And we couldn’t put one on as Lead Nurse anyway, so it’s best to keep it in-house and then everyone’s happy.”

“I’m not,” Brendon moaned.“I will be very unhappy and very lonely.” His exaggerated facial expression made Dot laugh.

“You can come and stay with me, Brendon,” she offered with uncharacteristic aplomb.

“You’re on Dot!”Brendon lifted her hand and kissed it. “What’s brought on all this *bonhomie*?”

“Let’s not get ahead of ourselves,” Ronnie chipped in. “Dot’s feeling much better though, aren’t you, Dot?”

“And has she agreed?” Brad asked impatiently.

“Again, let’s not get ahead of ourselves,” Ronnie remonstrated.

“How did he know?” Dot turned in surprise to Ronnie who was distracted by the buzzer on her belt. “How come everyone knows everything here? It’s like Barney says in his very special way.”

Squinting to read the room number that was calling, Ronnie looked to Brad and Brendon who were waiting to hear who was currently pressing their alarm.

“Speak of the devil,” Ronnie announced to them. “It’s only Barney. Again. I’ve answered his buzzer a dozen times today if I’ve answered it once.”

“What’s the problem?” Brendon asked.

“He’s been waxing philosophical. Every time I go in he talks about something different. He’s been reminiscing and *putting his affairs in order*, I suppose is the best way to sum it up. I’ll go back to him in a minute.” Turning to Dot, she asked perfunctorily, “So you’ll be fine then? I’ll let Dr Dunwoody know that you’re up for it and she can arrange some rehearsals for you and David.” Ronnie scooped up the emptied cup and saucer from the table.

“What *was* the thing that Barney says?” she asked Dot.

“You know. One of his special sayings.” Dot appeared to be slightly uncomfortable on the topic.

“I know, he says *Never trust a fart!*” Brendon guessed.

“No, not that one. He says that’s the thing you can’t do in Gramwell Glade without everyone knowing,” Dot was amused herself. Quite miraculously she seemed to be a woman transformed from the shell that had been brought home from the morning's excursion – which was an observation that Brad was delighted to able to include in the Report he completed and submitted later that evening.

"So what's it all about this time, Barney?" Ronnie asked as she pulled his curtains against the night sky. "This must be the umpteenth time I've had the pleasure of your company today."

"Was it you before?" he mumbled from his bed. Barney's prone body was covered with a duvet and any number of blankets.

"Yes, it was me. Who did you think it was?" she asked, straightening his blankets. "And don't tell me that you're feeling cold again because you've got four blankets on here on top of your duvet. You'll melt under all of this bedding!"

Ronnie turned on the table lamp. The room took life when faces appeared at every corner. Framed photos of his daughters and their children were scattered around the walls. A large picture of a military troop was fading to sepia tones above the chest of drawers. Barney appeared to have all of his people around him. One single frame on the side table showed a big-boned woman with a serene face. Barney could see that Ronnie's gaze had alighted on the portrait.

"That's my Olive. I'll be seeing her soon," he announced clearly.

"Seeing her?" Ronnie thought that Barney had been a widower and by a margin of some years.

"We always said we'd be seeing each other again on *the other side*," he continued.

"You'll be with us on this side for a long time yet, Barney, you'll see," Ronnie encouraged.

"You may be mistaken there, my girl. You just wait. And don't think that I'm frightened to go there. I want to stop feeling sore and cold. I want to see my Olive. It's what I have to look forward to."

Ronnie was writing some notes on her tablet. "Did you have a cup of tea this afternoon?" she asked.

"I don't know. I have a cup of tea most afternoons, don't I?" His impatience was growing as he felt that almost everyone failed to listen to what he had to say these days. "It's those stupid things. Tea in, wee out. And you write it all down! Who's the silly one here, then?"

"Too true, my love. It happens like clockwork but we have to write it all down and, if it didn't happen like clockwork," she lifted his head forward into her chest as she punched his pillow into submission, "then we would have something to worry about."

Ronnie lay his head back on the fluffed pillow. His rheumy eyes were watery.

"Are you OK, Barney?" she asked tenderly.

"About as OK as I'll ever be anymore," he sighed.

"Are you worried about something in particular?" she asked.

"Not worried at all. By the time you realise that all you need to do is let it wash over you, you're too old to worry. Although I do have to fix those girls of mine. Will you just listen to me and take a note of one thing for me?" he asked with new purpose.

"What would that be, then?" Ronnie asked as she removed the thermometer from his ear and recorded that his temperature was normal.

"For my funeral, I want them to sing 'Jerusalem'. That's a good song for a soldier."

"Isn't this something to talk about with your daughters?"

"I've tried. They won't hear about it. And I want to be certain that it will be sung and not 'Onward Christian Soldiers' or any of those stupid new hymns or pop songs that go on at funerals nowadays."

"Well I can certainly let them know when the time comes," Ronnie assured him.

"The time is sooner than they think. I want to know that this one thing I ask for *will* happen so write it down on that computer of yours so that everyone knows. I want to hear 'England's green and pleasant land' as I canter off to see Olive."

"If you insist. There isn't really a spot in the records to put something like that." She was puzzled both by the request and what to do with it.

"If it comes to all those notes having nothing to do what we want, what's the bloomin' purpose of writing down all those wees and teas?"

"Good point," she conceded.

Barney's eyes were closing. He seemed to be exhausted after expressing such a strong opinion.

"And I'll tell Joan when I see her."

"Tell them both. Not that they'll listen. That's why I want *you* to hear me. Put it on the ruddy record!"

"I hear you, Barney. Now, is there anything else that you need before I leave you this time? Supper should be here before long." She packed her tablet into the front pocket of her apron and collected his cup which was full of cold tea. He hadn't drunk it. The notes had already gone in to the record. She thought twice briefly about making the change before deciding to leave things as they were. Missing one cup of tea wasn't going to kill him.

"Thank you for making sure of that. 'And did those feet in ancient times'!" Barney bellowed before falling silent when she left the room.

Lavinia Marin answered the phone in the Nurses' Station and turned to Ronnie Chan while holding her hand over the receiver. "Did someone order pizza?"

"Brad did. But he's in Tulip. There was something going on there but he's been a long while now. Has he paid for it?"

Lavinia shouted into the telephone, "Has it been paid for?" Happy to proceed, she said, " I'll be just a minute, meet you at the front door," and she headed out of the room while Ronnie continued entering data into the desk top computer with the background accompaniment of a couple of room alarms beeping in the background.

Lavinia came back some time later. "It's in the Staff Tearoom if he's asking. I couldn't find him anywhere." She was short of breath after having tried to unite the pizzas with their rightful owner and, having disposed of them, was now concerned that others might devour the lot before Brad even got sight of them. "Who's ringing?" she asked Ronnie who was able to answer without looking up from the keyboard. "It's Barney again, and Elsie. But I'm pretty sure that all that she needs is someone to talk to. Barney, on the other hand, has been talking of dying all day. It's been worrying me because he's not spoken like this before."

"Does he want euthanasia?" Lavinia asked bluntly.

"No," Ronnie answered, looking over the top of her reading glasses, "but there are a few who might want it for him." They laughed together as Lavinia gathered her keys while swigging the last of her cold tea. "I called both his daughters because he'd summoned them this afternoon."

"I let Freda in when the pizza guy was here," Lavinia explained. "And I think Joan had been waiting in the café on her own for her sister to arrive. I'll go see Elsie first," she offered, "since Barney's daughters are both here now. We don't often see them here together, do we?"

"Which is what Barney had been on about yesterday. He's put his foot down and insisted that they both turn up together. I'm not sure that's such a good idea but no doubt he's regaling them with instructions for his funeral." Ronnie sighed.

Brad suddenly appeared in the doorway. "What funeral? You two have got multiple buzzers going?" he queried.

"Lavinia's going to check. It's Elsie and it's Barney again." Ronnie explained.

"I thought his daughters were here?" Brad asked.

"They are. Or they were. And the pizzas you ordered are in the tearoom. I took them from the driver about ten minutes ago and looked for you but I couldn't find you."

"I've been with Daphne Shaw. She's very poorly tonight. Lowest BP she's ever recorded. I'm glad I stayed tonight so I can keep an eye on her. The pizzas are for us to share," Brad emphasised with a sing-song intonation. "You didn't think I was going to eat four large pizzas on my own, did you?"

Ronnie looked up from her work. Her eyes were tired; smudged mascara heightened the appearance of exhaustion.

"You're looking rough," Brad observed as he looked more closely at her.

"On that note," Lavinia observed, squeezing past Brad in the doorway " I think I'll go and check on our squeaky wheels."

"Well thanks, you don't look too clever yourself," Ronnie threw back at him. "Will Daphne be OK, do you think?"

Freda and Joan sat on either side of their father's bed in the room now lit only by the table lamp. It was a vigil. Each held one of their father's hands. They tried not to look at one another in the eye but this was proving difficult as the only other person in the room was lying with his eyes shut, the central focus and yet apparently not a part of the company.

Joan's eyes welled with tears as Freda tried to comfort herself with reminiscences of their childhood years. "Do you remember when we'd go down to the horse paddock to find Dad and then we'd fight over who wanted to come home on his shoulders?"

"We thought he was big enough to carry us both, like a carthorse!" Joan gulped back a laugh in her tears.

"And if he asked whose turn it was, we'd both say *'Mine'* and he'd have to try to remember who he'd taken on the last trip."

"And you usually won because you were the baby." Joan had tried all of her life not to show her dismay when her father's attention was side-swiped by her baby sister.

"But he always liked you the best because you were cleverer." Freda acknowledged.

"Rubbish!" Joan swatted her down as was their usual patter. "Perhaps it's best not to argue. This isn't a time for it, really, is it?"

"No, you're right." Freda conceded.

"Of course she's right!" Barney stormed, shaking both women to their core. "You're not getting rid of the old buzzard quite yet. But I do need you to be able to spend time in the same room. It's never going to be a good time to argue. Get used to that!" he demanded. "You need to be together. Your mother would expect better of you both."

Joan and Freda looked at one another, both joined by the shock of seeing their father spring to life as well as by the ignominy of being addressed as youngsters, a feeling now most unfamiliar.

"I expect to see you here together from now on until my days are over. I'm not much use for anything anymore. I'm not a soldier, not a farmer nor a husband but, by Jove, I am still your father! And it's still my job to make sure you two behave. Now, it's time we had some tea. Sit me up and press the buzzer again. I called them before you came in and I'm still waiting!"

Joan shuffled some of the bedding. "We thought that this was the *end*!" She burst in to tears.

"What it is, is that it's time to stop arguing and to look after your little sister." Barney's voice was full-blooded and stern. Their father had spoken. Joan went to the other side of the bed and put a stiff arm around Freda's shoulder. Both women stood, weeping profusely while Barney asked himself if this is really what he had wanted.

Lavinia's head appeared around the door after a cursory knock. She looked across at Joan and Freda and then questioningly to Barney whose expression conveyed some annoyance.

"No pleasing my girls," he told Lavinia. "Looks as though I've made them both cry. And not for the first time, mind."

"It's not your fault, Dad." Freda sobbed into Joan's shoulder.

"I think it's our fault, really," Joan admitted to Lavinia.

"What can I do to help?" Lavinia's instinct discounted the possibility of a family reunion as such.

"Dad wanted some tea. How about we go to the café and bring him some back?" Freda offered."Because you must be so busy."

"If you're sure," Lavinia immediately saw wisdom in the suggestions, knowing quite how many rooms she and Brad were going to have to check between them tonight, especially given that Daphne Shaw was going to take up so much of his time. "I tell you what," she offered, "Why don't we put Barney in his wheelchair and you all go there for an outing?"

"But he's in his pyjamas," Joan was fussing, as ever, about his appearance.

"Wouldn't we be disturbing people if we go there at night?" Freda asked.

"He'll be just fine like that, with his dressing gown on," Lavinia counselled. "There are a few others there this evening. Well, there were about ten minutes ago when I let you in, Joan. And I think there is a small rehearsal for part of the Panto because Dr Dunwoody was going to set up after seeing one of our Tulip ladies. So there might even be some entertainment." Looking at Barney, she was delighted to see that he would agree to venturing out of his room for the first time in a week or so. "The change will do you good, my friend."

"Sluice the slurry," Barney winked at Lavinia as she took his dressing gown from the peg on the back of his bathroom door and handed it to Joan.

"He'll be fine," she smiled at Barney's daughters who were looking at each other quizzically. "The change will do him the world of good!" she reiterated.

In the café they found Dr Dunwoody setting up her husband's electric keyboard. She was chatting with Millie and Albert who had come for an evening rendezvous.

"No Harold today?" Millie asked the Doctor.

"Just me," she replied happily as she plugged a lead in to the keyboard. "Harold has a Trivia night at his Golf Club. And it's only a small rehearsal for the duet. Just a bit of practice."

"Do you mind, then, if we stay and watch?" Albert asked.

"It would be good if you would. A small audience would be appreciated, I think, give them some idea of what to expect when the dress rehearsal happens tomorrow."

"It's hard to believe that we're almost ready for Christmas," Marjorie observed. "I used to think that time moved slowly but, since Bert and I have been keeping company, time has just flown by!"

"That's because I make you happy, old girl!" Bert observed.

Evelyn Dunwoody laughed. "Not so much of the *old*, Albert. But you're probably right about the happy part."

"I am!" he boasted. "You'll know yourself, Doctor, when you're unhappy, life just drags its tail. But, when things are going your way, it races past."

Marjorie laughed out loud. "So, am I the *going your way* factor, Father Time? Anything else you're good at?" she winked.

"You should know the answer to that question by now," he joked.

Evelyn Dunwoody felt that she had heard a confidence out of turn but did not want to seem prudish.

"Well, all I can say is that you two, in particular, will enjoy this evening's rehearsal, then."

She switched on the keyboard and keyed a short rendition of 'Wish Me Luck As You Wave Me Goodbye' which Albert attempted to follow in raucous voice a full two bars behind the melody.

"Oh Bert, for Pete's sake, stop it!" Marjorie laughed "You sound dreadful tonight!"

"And there was I, thinking that you fancied me," Albert lamented.

Evelyn Dunwoody looked up from the flourish she'd used to bring Albert's song to closure to see David Jack and Dot Baker come into the café, arm in arm. Waving one hand above her head she summoned their attention, "Over here, you two."

Having taken in the gathering, David and Dot headed to join her.

"Lovely to see you both," Dr Dunwoody greeted them. "Are you ready for our little rehearsal?" She knew the question held a number of nuanced enquiries about the state of play between them so was relieved to hear Dot answer, "As ready as I'll ever be, I expect." She looked around the room again, aware that Barney Perry was there with his daughters, the Dunstable family as well as another man with his wife. She'd seen both of them previously but couldn't place them.

"Actually," David admitted, "we've had a cheeky practice in the Daffodil dining room when there was nobody about. Didn't we, Dot?" They sat down at the table with Marjorie and Albert while Dr Dunwoody leafed through her music and told them all, "I think you'll all find out that you're in for a bit of a treat."

"So you're pretty good, are you?" Albert asked David and Dot.

David shook his head apologetically. "I wouldn't say that exactly."

Marjorie punched Albert's arm while assuring David "Well don't be listening to him. He can't sing for nuts!"

"But Dot's in a different boat," David enthused. "She has a beautiful tone, and," he added with aplomb, "she's *pitch perfect*!" So you're both in for a treat indeed."

Dot sat with David enjoying a modest smile.

"Well, that's more than could be said for the last one," Albert attempted a whisper across them both which came out at such a volume that could be heard on the other side of the room had the coffee machine not been gurgling out hot water for the Dunstable family sitting behind Charles Worrell and his wife, who was wife *number three*, according to popular wisdom.

"Enough said," Dr Dunwoody shut down that strain of conversation perfunctorily. "I'm really looking forward to this," she encouraged, shuffling on her seat. "Don't mind Albert and Marjorie. They will be nothing but encouragement itself. Besides, it's time you had an audience when we're *on* in just a couple of days.

"Will we stand?" David asked.

"I think that'd be best," Evelyn Dunwoody advised.

"I'd like to stand facing you, then," Dot told the Doctor. "Just so I can't see anyone else's face. That might put me off just yet."

"Whatever suits best." Evelyn Dunwoody played an E as the signal to take a nice, deep breath before both hands launched onto the keyboard to mark the introduction to the refrain that reminded all in the café of the rapturous tune of 'True Love'. Charles Worrell turned his neck quickly to take in exactly what was going on.

David and Dot stood in front of the keyboard, sending their harmonies back to the Doctor. Other heads turned as the blend of their voices captivated the room. The Doctor finished with another flourish as applause was heard from all directions.

David put his arm around Dot's waist to give a congratulatory squeeze.

"I must say," Evelyn Dunwoody exploded, "my expectations have been totally exceeded! That's the expression around these parts, isn't it? Who would have guessed?" she confessed, shaking her head as though surprised. "No, that was absolutely marvellous!"

In the far corner, near the bar area, Charles Worrell had maintained a fixed gaze but now conspicuously stalked through the seating area out to the foyer and on to Pauline Graves' office door where he knocked only once before barging through. Kayleigh in Reception sat open-mouthed at his audacity. She had managed to swing off her seat but had been too late in crashing through the office to intercept the interloper who was now in the Manager's office having closed the door behind himself.

Chapter Eleven

SLEEPING BEAUTY

"Thank you all, as usual, for coming," Pauline's courtesy was welcoming but mechanical as the Team assembled at the eleven o'clock meeting to *take the temperature*, as she explained, of Gramwell in all its endeavours. Amity looked sideways at Pauline's outfit and thought that it may not have seen the light of day for quite some years. Instead of wearing one of her duller coloured business suits, Pauline was decked out in a red woollen jersey dress that came just above her knee. She didn't look a lot like herself today.

"And, as we know, it's going to be a challenge because you and Eric are unveiling your Empire building, I believe, Peter?" Her intonation was uncharacteristically high as she put the question to which, she had to believe, the answer would be in the affirmative. Few understood the reference. So much of what Pauline had to say seemed far-fetched to the majority of the staff that they had developed well-worn looks of impassive absorption to get themselves through the daily meetings. It was a time for inner reflection for many, just letting the waves wash over them.

"Just about done, Mrs Graves," Peter dutifully acknowledged. "Eric's painting the last touches. We've modelled it on our own castle wall. Shame it wasn't summer, like you said. We could have done it outside with the real castle wall and saved ourselves a shed-load of trouble."

Peter they did listen to. The gathering laughed in support of the mammoth effort that Peter and Eric had mounted. In their own break times they had all ventured out to the shed to see the two large pieces of interlocking scenery that the Spences had created, mostly in their own time on weekends. It was a fair depiction of the Gramwell Glade castle wall indeed. And the ingenious design, that could move from dead-thorn wall to one of blooming rose trellis, had to be seen to be believed.

"We've done it in two pieces and measured those. They will fit in through the front doors – just – but they will need some manoeuvring when we get them to the café," he explained. "So we was wondering what was the best time to bring 'em in, so as not to mess up any plans youse all might have?"

He looked around the room at his colleagues who were in awe of the work that he'd done for the Panto, while managing to keep up the regular maintenance over the past couple of weeks when he and Eric had been working away in the shed with only an old paraffin heater to keep them from freezing.

"Any problems there with activities in the café?" Pauline looked up over the top of her reading glasses as she sat at her desk, apparently following her own script.

"Just the usual dominoes and Thursday afternoon craft with some of the Tulip ladies, I s'pose," Marigold offered up.

"And so they can be relocated, I expect?" Pauline smiled. "Tulip Dining Room should work if you all club together to do the table cleaning after lunch, then?"

No opposition appeared to be raised. It was palpable that everyone wanted to do all that they could to work with Peter on this and to support the Panto in general.

"Now, we seem to have a problem in terms of casting," Pauline continued. "Does anyone know why Nan Sweetman has been replaced by Dorothy Baker in the duet?" She looked up again and around the room to see Phoenix and Marigold exchanging a giggle.

"Do you know what's happened?" she shot at them.

Amity stepped in from the corner of the room where she stood holding her hands behind her in case someone were to suddenly try to come into the meeting and smash the door into her back.

"I think you'll find, Pauline, that Nan absented herself," she explained.

Marigold and Phoenix laughed again, holding their hands over their mouths like naughty school girls

"What's so funny?" Pauline accused. "You wouldn't have been laughing if you'd been working late, as I was last night, to find Charles Worrell barging in to my room in high dudgeon because his mother's been replaced in the duet."

Amity's eyebrows rose. "Was there a problem?" she asked innocently.

"He was furious because he and his wife were sitting in the Olde Tea Shoppe, trying to calm down after a fraught visit with Nan when suddenly the duet music was played and Dorothy Baker was singing her part!"

“Ah.” As the situation dawned on Amity, she spelled it out for Pauline. “What had happened, as far as I know, was that Nan had tried singing the duet and failed. Failed herself. So, she herself realised that she wasn’t hitting the notes and she clearly had no idea about the harmonies which of course are the whole point of ‘True Love’.”

In support, Marigold offered, “You should’ve heard her, Mrs Graves, she was terrible!”

Phoenix laughed, crossing her legs as though she were about to wet herself. “It was a ‘True Mess’, I’m not going to lie.”

“That’s enough.” Pauline countered. “Apparently Nan was in a dreadful state when Charles and his wife came to see her in the evening. She hadn’t eaten and she was distraught.”

“She *had* eaten, Mrs Graves!” Phoenix exploded. “I wrote up her notes after yesterday’s tea. She wanted it in her room and she had two helpings of chicken goujons. I had to go back and get her a second plate of them.”

“We can deal with the record later. The concern of the family member was that his mother had been unfairly dealt with by our lack of consideration.”

“Pauline,” Amity’s voice took on an uncharacteristic authority. “I can assure you that Evelyn Dunwoody has dealt with this. Nan told her that she couldn’t perform properly with an electric keyboard by way of bowing out. She said she needed a proper piano accompaniment and she flounced off. She even had a dig at David’s singing and he was really very good and patient with her too.”

“He *was* really good,” Phoenix chipped in. “I heard him when I was signing out last night. And Dot is dope! They sounded so lovely together.”

“Evelyn checked with Nan later that she didn’t want to continue and then went to speak with David to see if he’d mind trying it with Dot,” Amity explained.

“We all know that David wouldn’t mind trying it with Dot!” Stan laughed until Pauline gave him a halting stare.

“So you’re staying in today, Stan, for the first dress rehearsal?” she asked in changing the subject.

“Ready, willing and able, Mrs Graves,” Stan reported, clicking his heels together.

“All right. Well, it looks as though we’re on target with the plans for the rehearsal. Make sure you all bring as many residents as you can to watch, particularly those who won’t be seeing it the performances on Saturday. We have quite a few takers for seats at the matinee and the seven o’clock show. And we’ll have some VIPs to seat so let’s get as many residents there today as we can.”

"But we're not really ready yet," Stan protested.

"They won't know that. What I mean is," Pauline corrected herself, "they will be interested to see whatever you do, even if some parts have to be redone while you work with the staging and props. Right," she turned a page of her notes,"any residents unwell today?" She looked around the room.

"Dear Daphne passed away last night. Well, this morning," Brendon spoke slowly. "Brad was with her. She passed at around three-thirty." Heads were bowed in a second's reflection before Pauline interrupted.

"So he won't be in today?" she asked.

"Well, he shouldn't be. He was coming home in a taxi when I was leaving home this morning, poor love. He was very close with Daphne so he was really upset. But he will be in, Pauline, don't worry." Brendon was fidgeting, almost cross. "He's coming in after a sleep, to do his bit in the rehearsal."

"Yes, of course, he's your King, isn't he?" Pauline asked Amity. "He's a good man not to let us down – looking after Daphne and making the dress rehearsal. Hopefully he's catching up on his sleep as we speak. And we'll have to speak with Daphne's family to see what help they might want with funeral arrangements."

Peggy Hewson lips tightened as she realised that, along with all the usual efforts for Christmas, there was likely to be a large buffet coming up for the Shaws in the not too distant future. She remained silent on the matter, biting her tongue while checking her fingernails.

"And we've been reminded again about using the pool. There are instructions again to make sure that we are using it. Apparently Akin has arranged for some corporate visitors to see Gramwell Glade next week and he's insisted that the pool is in use during their visit."

Pauline held up her hands against an imaginary tide. "I know. You don't want to make residents cold. Especially at this time of year. I'll speak with Brad about it and see which ones could usefully brave it. And Peter, we can turn up the heating there? Both the water and air temperatures, just to make it can be that little bit more inviting but we're certainly running some aqua exercises next week. End of." They watched Pauline tick off the list. "Catering for Saturday, Peggy?" Pauline's statement, or question as it seemed to Peggy, came as a bolt out of the blue.

"Catering?" she asked numbly.

"Yes, we'll need to think about afternoon tea to follow the matinee and then a finger food supper for the evening performance."

"This is my weekend off!" Peggy was almost in tears as she immediately brought to mind the efforts her son had gone to in organising the family for her birthday tea at the Dog and Gun. Her brother was coming from Suffolk. It had been arranged for weeks now.

"That's fine. You're allowed a weekend off!" Pauline assured her. "If you give Henry instructions, I'm sure he'll come through for you with flying colours, and some help from Janette."

"I don't think as Henry has got it in him." Peggy began to explain while she muttered under her breath "Flying by the seat of his pants, more like."

"*Oh Ye of Little Faith*," Pauline countered. "I'm sure you've taught Henry well. And can't you prepare some of the items before you leave on Friday for your weekend?"

Peggy was flummoxed as finger food menus flashed through her brain. Poor Henry wasn't able to come up with much more than a sandwich, she thought. And, even then, it wouldn't be a pretty sandwich.

"We'll have to do our best, Mrs Graves."

"And you will no doubt succeed beautifully, as you always do, Oh, and some gluten-free options please for Charles Worrell's wife and, no doubt, a few others."

Peggy wrung her hands in her apron as the spectre of two catered Pantomime events loomed over her own birthday plans.

"That looks like *IT* then," Pauline noted, closing her large diary over the handwritten notes that had guided her through the meeting. "Any other business?" she asked, looking around the room.

Carers were eager to get on with their tasks. The eleven o'clock meeting always got in the way of their busy mornings. Peter Spence asked Stan if he might be able to help him and Eric since he was now no longer on shift. He had thought of imposing on Henry for his strength but now realised that Henry was going to be tied up for the next few days by the time Peggy had got back to him in the kitchen with a long list of things to be produced for the Saturday hospitality extravaganzas. The kitchen was going to be a good place to steer clear of for a while, he knew from experience.

He left the office, deep in thought, and immediately bumped into Maisie Dunstable who was carrying her doll as usual but today was wearing a huge grin and a flounced party dress.

I'm so sorry, Maisie," Peter acknowledged, stepping back whereupon he bumped into the Visitors' Signing In table. "I wasn't looking where I was going," he explained.

"I've got a new grandson," Maisie couldn't contain herself. "And his name is John!"

"That's lovely news for you, dear," Peter patted her on the shoulder. "Congratulations to you."

"And to John. *This* John," Maisie corrected, pushing her doll into view.

"Absolutely," Peter agreed as he marched his steel-capped boots out the front doors to the car park. He resized the doors in his mind, going over the moving exercise that was to come later in the day while Maisie headed over to Tayla at the Reception Desk to relay her news.

Stan and Gosia had been a while in the Change Room beside the Staff Tea Room. This came as little surprise but quite a deal of annoyance to Tayla, Bessie and Marigold who had been delivered of their costumes: respectively swathed as a cow, a pig and a chicken. Little was going to amuse them about the upcoming charade.

"How very dare they make me a pig!" snorted Bessie as she pushed her face mask high onto her brow to enable an attack on her cup of soup and packet of crisps.

"Everyone's going to laugh at me," rued Phoenix.

"And isn't that the freaking point," spluttered Tayla. "It's not often we get a chance to make them all laugh." She picked out the lettuce from her burger piece by piece. "Anyway, I don't know why youse are moaning. I'm a freaking cow"

"A cannibal cow!" Bessie pointed and laughed, spraying crisp crumbs over the table. "You're eating cow!"

"Check this out," Marigold's chicken tail sprang out as she leapt to the window. "Look here!" she screamed as Brad walked up the driveway with a huge swathe of scarlet velvet draped over his arm.

"No, not him," she chided as the others showed little surprise. Bessie had already told them that Brad could be expected to be seen wearing almost anything these days. He'd become a great deal braver with his wardrobe since he and Brendon had set up home together. It was not entirely out of the question that he might arrive with this bright red bedspread. But their gaze was immediately diverted to the sight of Eric holding his weight against the side of a painted castle wall that was precariously perched on the trailer behind his father's car and now making its way up to the front door with only Eric, walking beside it, between it and a crashing fate.

"It's bootiful!" Tayla exclaimed. "Look at all the roses painted on it! Oh it's gawjus!"

"How on earth do they expect to get that into the café? It's huge?"

Phoenix arrived in the Tea Room to find her friends crowded around the window. "Has anyone seen Gosia?"

"She's in next door. Bonking Stan, no doubt." Marigold turned briefly from the spectre of Peter and Eric now manoeuvring the painted wall from the trailer onto a board they'd made up with castors on the corners.

"They've thought of everything," Tayla applauded. "I reckon Eric's probably as clever as Peter."

"You're basically in love with Eric now, aren't you?" accused Bessie.

"Shut up! I am not!" Tayla protested.

In Ye Olde Tea Shoppe, Amity had taken it upon herself to direct traffic in clearing a space for the impending invasion of the Panto sets. Amity's idea of effecting the impossible was to casually praise any of the carers who were in a fifty-foot radius into doing her bidding.

"Darragh, sweetheart, would you mind moving those chairs and tables nearest to the French doors out of the café so we can free up room for the stage?"

Darragh swung around in surprise. "But there's people sitting there. And where are we going to put all the spare tables and chairs?"

"Peter and Eric have planned all of that," she reassured him, pressing on with the need for some pretty instant action. "They're going to load some of them to store in their shed and we'll put some of the chairs in rows for the audience."

"We?" he asked sceptically.

"Well, *you* actually. Thank you, Darragh, you're a darling. Oh, look!" she indicated the pulling and puffing of the Spence men as they negotiated the scenery through the double doors into the foyer. The boards they'd used to wheel it in had been measured within an inch of success. It was all possible; it just took a great deal of pushing backwards and forwards to find the proper angles to allow its passing.

The commotion had enticed Pauline from her office. She watched while Eric and his father worked away at their carefully planned exercise. Pauline walked slowly towards Amity in the café, greeting various residents on the way.

"Good afternoon, Hilda, what do you think of this, then?" she asked as Hilda's elbow was brushed by Darragh's shifting of a neighbouring table.

"Not much, to tell the truth," Hilda reprimanded. "So this is Birnam Wood coming to Dunsinane then, is it?

"Sorry?" Pauline had always expected lucid conversations with Hilda but today things seemed to be taking an inevitable turn.

"*Inane* is more like it," Hilda scolded. "*Macbeth*, don't you know? I'd have expected our General Manager might know that much." Hilda hoisted her weight on to her hands as she lumped up from her chair and leant on the table ."Looks as though there's no peace to be had here this afternoon, then."

"Thanks, Hilda," Darragh immediately dragged Hilda's chair over to the side wall where he was lining up others. "Why don't you come back later on to see the rehearsal?" he offered by way of compensation before it dawned on him: "You're in the choir anyway, aren't you?"

"Can't be bothered with that. I'll be happier on my own, thank you." Hilda pushed past Pauline who skirted to the other side of the room to speak with Amity as Darragh took advantage of a freed table and cleared yet more floor space.

"You're doing a good job here," she smiled at Amity.

"It's not as easy as it looks, is it?" Amity returned. "But Peter and Eric have done such a super job. Have you seen the scenery?"

"Just now, as they were pushing to get it inside."

"It's well above and beyond the call of duty. We should probably think of a way to thank them when this is all over?" she suggested.

"No, I've already thought of that. Don't worry. And there's a lot of you who have already put in a good effort."

Their eyes were immediately drawn to the vision that was Stan and Gosia dressed as Sleeping Beauty and her Prince as they headed into the Café. Gosia's long blonde hair was free from its usual up-style. No one had known that it fell all the way down to her waist. She'd threaded it with fabric flowers from her Polish dancing costume. A long silver gown sparkled with sequins. Some of the ladies who had yet to be evicted by Darragh's superhuman furniture-clearing exercise gasped and clapped their approval. Beside her, Stan's gym work was on show through the silhouette offered by his tights which where tucked into knee boots. The ruffled sleeves of his *whiter-than-white* shirt emphasized his strong and capable arms.

Hilda pushed past them to show her annoyance at the nonsense, whereas most of her fellow residents couldn't keep their eyes off them.

"Excuse me, your Majesty," Eric backed the home-made trolley past the fish tank into the cleared space. "Any chance of lending us a hand, Stan?"

"Just in front of the French doors please, Eric." Amity directed. "The stage is roughly the area of the curtains there so you can rest the scenery against them."

"We'll be blocking out the light," Peter acknowledged, wiping sweat from his brow.

"That won't really matter for the next three days. Your scenery's beautiful. Everyone will want to look at it. Besides," she added, looking at Maisie Dunstable, "there's almost no daylight to be had at this time of year, nothing worth bothering about, is there, Maisie?"

"Not now I've got a grandson and his name is John!" Maisie replied.

"That's wonderful news, Maisie, big congratulations!" Amity trilled.

"You've got a new great-grandson, Maisie," Pauline pointed out. "And his name is Henry John. Your family told you that this morning, don't you remember?"

"Yes, of course." Maisie bowed out of the conversation, wondering if she'd been on the right track with her news and whose baby it was if it wasn't her son's. It didn't make sense.

"I'll leave it all in your capable hands, then," Pauline regaled them as she headed back to her office to record the minutes of the morning's meeting and the information required about the death that had taken place in the early hours.

Dr Dunwoody appeared in the doorway and looked across to Amity. "Can I bring the choir up now? We've been rehearsing in Daffodil Lounge and we're ready if you are."

"Come on down!" Amity swung her arms to indicate the space that was available. "Darragh's done a tremendous job clearing the space. You can sit them here for the time being. This is where the audience will sit. We've actually got to work out where the choir will be."

"And they will need chairs," Dr Dunwoody warned. "We can't expect them to stand the whole time."

"Darragh, did you hear that? Can you move those chairs back in? We won't need them to go to the shed after all, Peter."

Peter looked up from the corner where he was fixing his sets into place. "That's good news for us because we haven't really got any room for them."

"Problem solved, then!" Amity declared as she turned to face Brad who was swathed in red velvet and ermine. "OMG! Did you ever look more handsome?" she teased.

"Your King at your service, Milady," Brad swished his cape aside revealing white stockings, black patent shoes and a large sword on a gilt buckled belt.

"You should wear that more often," Evelyn Dunwoody teased.

"And give them all coronaries?" Brad was clearly delighted with the attention that now included Marjorie who was stroking the back of his cape from her wheelchair.

"Don't move backwards," Evelyn Dunwoody held on to his elbow to insure that they didn't land on Marjorie's knee.

"Are you turning the head of my girl?" Albert wheeled his chair up beside Marjorie who was now giggling as Brad turned around to bow to him."Nearly scared the pants off me!" Albert chided. "This is going to be something. Look at them roses on the castle wall, Marge," he pointed out. "This is going to be some do alright."

With the choir seated, Harold's stool behind the electric keyboard was wedged at the end of the bar where the lighting was far from optimum. Fortunately, there had been a few practices by now so Harold hoped that he could maintain the melodies without letting the team down, even though he couldn't see the score very well.

Mollie Tipple was squashed at the other end of the keyboard making it look as though they might both be sharing in the playing.

"So if you get stuck, Harold," Mollie explained, " I'll just take over from here" and she leaned over to press out a one-fingered version of 'Chopsticks' while Harold tried a polite nod. The Storricks were next in line with Marie Taylor and John Nicholls. Despite the proximity to John Nicholls that the choir experience would have afforded, Hilda was not in good temper on this occasion as Dr Dunwoody had found when she had tried to round her up for the 'all-important' dress rehearsal and spied Hilda walking away. Maisie Dunstable had been dragooned into the front row with Delphine Thomas who was pleased to be associated with the stars of the choir, David and Dot. Their seats were just a little way away as though to underscore their importance in the ensemble.

Cows, pigs and chickens had caused a major disruption when they appeared into the room. Most of the residents were pleased to see them, whereas the farmyard cast were still puzzled as to their part in the proceedings. Bessie found a seat but Marigold's chicken and Tayla's cow propped themselves against the wall quite comfortably either side of the aquarium.

Amity then swanned into the room in her Queen's cloak and crown to the delight of the entire assembly, but she had made it clear by her demeanour while shouting orders that she was still in charge of the staging for this first coming together of all parts of their 'all-singing, all dancing' production. Those who did not have parts settled back to enjoy what was going to be the biggest entertainment they'd seen since coming to Gramwell Glade. What was more, they were told that it was going to be their privilege to be the first to witness the upcoming extravaganza.

"Listen up, everyone!" Amity commanded. "Can you hear me?" She called more loudly above the chatter. "Thank you for coming to our dress rehearsal. We've all been practising our parts when we can, I know, but this is the first time that we've all come together so it may not be perfect quite yet but hopefully you'll have an enjoyable time while we try our best now to finally put it all together."

By this time all eyes were on the regal director as she swept her long sleeve across the room to indicate Kalu standing in the doorway. "For those of you who don't know him, I'd like to introduce Kalu who has kindly agreed to be our Narrator for this performance and I'm sure you'll all enjoy hearing his wonderful voice as he explains to you, and perhaps the rest of us," the cast tittered nervously with their worst fears on show, "what will be going on in the story of *Sleeping Beauty*."

Kalu took a half-bow. He was dressed, as usual, in an immaculate dark suit and dazzling white shirt that matched the wide smile he now offered up. Many of the residents had never met Kalu, let alone heard his supposedly wonderful voice, but the gathering was shifting into gear to suspend their disbelief, as they did on every other day at Gramwell Glade, and languish in a melee of odd performances which promised to be a worthy distraction from the daily schedule.

The applause drowned out any possibility of adequately managing phone calls at Reception and Rosie danced down the corridor with her mop as the choir's introductory medley struggled to keep time with Dr Dunwoody's large gestures that might have doubled as swimming lessons. It took a few attempts for the choir to manage a recognisable version of 'There's a Place for Us'. By the end of the passable third attempt, the choir was permitted to sit down to watch Kalu, resting his arm casually on the lectern that usually displayed the daily menus in the Foyer, as he explained that there was once a castle on a hill. Peter interrupted at this point. "Can I just explain that there are three scenes here." He lifted a polythene overlay from the side of the left wall. "There's the castle on an ordinary day, so to speak, for the start." As he repeated the exercise on the other side of the set, the painted cover showed the castle covered with moss, occasional blue tits and fields of corn at the entrance to the moat.

"Then," he said, rushing back to the left side, "this overlay has the thorns for when the spell has been cast." The grizzly tangle of brambles covered the trellis of the castle wall. "And the same on the other side," Peter explained. A low rumble in the audience warmed his heart. All the painting that he and Eric had put in seemed now to hit the mark. "And, then for the last part, the sun comes out, and the roses," he repeated the exercise, pulling out the third overlay on both sides, "and you will see that the spell has been broken."

Kalu had been watching with great interest and led the audience in a round of applause.

"It's a dream, Peter. Yes, let's thank Peter and Eric for all their beautiful work," Amity enthused.

"It might be best to have someone posted at either side," Peter suggested, "so they can move the overlays at the right time. They'll need to be pretty sprightly to get it done quickly and properly," he suggested.

"And perhaps quite little to get into those corners?" Amity mused. "OK. Can the chickens go either side of the set, Marigold and Ronnie? Can you give it a try? It starts off with the first overlay and then you move the second and so on. That's right, isn't it, Peter?"

Marigold had managed to tangle herself in the second overlay so that all the assembly could see was a chicken tangled in a mess of barbed thorns. Peter explained quietly to her how best to hold the edges to bring the plastic sheeting to cover the set. Ronnie, working alone on the other side, appeared to be up to the pretty picture with no trouble and was in the business of taking each layer back carefully to be ready for the start.

"Lovely. Let's get going now with the action. And no overlay to start, girls. I'll give you the nod for the changes as they arrive. Thank you, Kalu. Can we get cracking with the story now or we'll run out of rehearsal time?"

Lavinia put her fingers in her ears as she headed from the Daffodil corridor to Donna at Reception and asked her to make a phone call. Bessie came up behind her and made more requests. Donna quite sensibly decided to use the phone in the Manager's office so as to make clear the request for an ambulance and for Joan and Freda to come in as quickly as they could manage.

"And the farm animals were happy because the King and Queen announced that they had a baby girl," Kalu announced.

"This is the time for you animals to move around the front here," Amity coaxed. "Chickens, you can come too because you don't need to change the set just yet. Lovely," she decreed, holding a doll swathed in a pink blanket as she and Brad gazed lovingly at each other and the baby.

"Each of the special guests that had come to her christening when she was a baby had bestowed a generous wish," Kalu's mellifluous voice had everyone enthralled. "They had granted her the gifts of beauty, of virtue and of riches. But the thirteenth fairy –" Kalu nodded to Brendon who had just appeared around the corner of the entrance to Ye Olde Tea Shoppe. Brendon jumped into the aisle between Marjorie's wheelchair and Elsie who had joined the audience at the last minute. He pulled what he hoped was a scary face from under his black cape and made his way to the castle, gesticulating at the Royal couple. "The thirteenth fairy told them all that the Princess would prick her finger on her fifteenth birthday and would fall down dead."

The audience booed Brendon who whooped it up for them as the most exaggerated panto baddie he could muster before flashing his cape and making away through the audience and out of the room.

"But the twelfth fairy had not yet spoken and she was able to undo at least part of that bad spell even though the finger-pricking part was set in stone."

"Amadia, that's you!" Amity called through the café to summon the Good Fairy to rectify the spell.

"And so, on her fifteenth birthday the beautiful Princess was picking flowers in the meadows." Kalu continued.

Gosia sailed into the room to the delight of the crowd. She pretended to pick flowers which she placed in her basket. The audience couldn't detect the collapsible flowers being produced from the basket and were happily tricked into believing that Gosia was producing them from thin air in the gardens around the palace. Tayla's cow lifted up its haunches pretending to eat one of the flowers and was given the laugh she'd hoped for.

Gosia gasped as she made out that one of the roses she had picked had just caused her the most terrible of injuries and, moving quickly to the bed at centre stage, she lay down and closed her eyes.

"The magical twelfth fairy had said that she would not die but that she, and the whole castle, would sleep for a hundred years," Kalu explained while Amity nodded at Marigold and Ronnie to bring the overlay of thorns over the castle walls. Amity and Brad sat on their thrones with their heads slumped on their shoulders. The farmyard animals fell to sleep where they were. The audience feigned despair.

Dr Dunwoody summoned the choir to attention while Harold played the introduction to 'Once upon a Dream', which appeared to go really smoothly for the first time, as was evidenced on the Doctor's face when the choir fell still.

"And they did indeed sleep for a hundred years."

The phone rang at the Reception desk, causing a few of the sleepers and many in the audience to giggle in the moment of stillness. They could hear Alex Durwyn trying to keep her voice down as she gave the required greeting and answered that, yes, they had called for an ambulance. Obviously further information was required. Brad, the King, looked sideways at Bessie, the pig, who shrugged her forequarters. He could see that Freda was waiting outside the front door.

"But, the Bad Fairy –" Brendon again appeared around the side of the cafe's entrance. Brad's eyes asked him the question about what was up and Brad returned a *wait and see* expression with a shake of his head. "The Bad Fairy's wish had been altered. A handsome knight came riding by. He had seen the castle in the distance and wondered who lived behind the wall of thorns. He also needed to feed and water his horse because they were miles from home and needed a rest."

Stan appeared in the doorway to the delight of the old ladies and some of the younger ones. He swash-buckled his sword as he pretended to cut through the growth that had covered the castle. "And he made his way into the Palace where he found the King and Queen asleep on their thrones."

Marjorie pretended to fall into a deep sleep in her wheelchair beside Albert who immediately dug her in the ribs to try to wake her.

"And there he saw the most beautiful woman he had ever seen in his life. She was fast asleep on her bed. The Prince went quietly over the Princess, amazed by her beauty. He knelt down beside the bed and touched her golden hair before, being unable to resist her any longer, he kissed her lips."

Albert kissed Marjorie on the cheek at which point she pretended to wake and kissed him back before punching him on his upper arm.

Amity nodded at the chickens to change the scenery at this point.

"Suddenly the whole castle came to life!" Kalu announced. "The animals went about their business in the farmyard and fields." Bessie got up with slow, arthritic stiffness which fortunately suited her role as a pig and started rooting for truffles with Nwaoma around the knees of the seated choir. Marigold and Ronnie left their stage management duties as the final scene was now in place and pecked at the front of the stage.

"The Princess woke up and saw the handsome Prince. They fell in love at first sight and were overjoyed to have found one another."

Stan's passionate embrace was admired by all. It had not previously been possible for him to legitimately kiss Gosia at work so he made the most of his opportunity.

Harold gave the first bars of the introduction to 'True Love' as Dot and David stood together by the keyboard. Their blended voices brought the harmonies to life, delighting the audience who hung on their every word. On the other side of the room, Stan and Gosia gazed lovingly into each other's eyes while, in the audience, Marjorie and Albert held hands. Everyone was spellbound for the duration of the song and burst into happy applause as it came to its conclusion.

Brad could see Freda and Joan heading down the Daffodil corridor, no doubt to visit their father together. That had been some kind of magic, he reflected, that Barney had somehow mended the bridge between his warring daughters.

"And they all lived..." Kalu looked around the room, inviting the gathering to join in the forgone conclusion, to which they all rejoined, "Happily ever after" as the actors took bows and curtsies. Kalu clapped his big hands together in the direction of the choir while Dr Dunwoody and Harold nodded their appreciation. David stood, reaching his hand for Dot to stand beside him so they could bow together.

Amity looked at her watch. "Twent-two minutes," she announced to Kalu. "Not bad. That's just about the right length so the audience won't get too bored with us," she smiled. "Well done everyone," her volume increased to penetrate the many excited conversations that filled the room. "That was it, then! Our one and only dress rehearsal and if it's half as good on Saturday, they'll all be pleased with us. Good show, everybody!"

Amity went over to check with Evelyn Dunwoody and her husband that they had been satisfied with the performances as David and Dot were also chatting to their choirmistress.

"Wonderful job, both of you," Amity cooed. "I had no idea that you could sing like that."

"I'm not sure we did either," David couldn't contain himself. He reached for Dot's hand. "But I'm sure that we'll fill many hours singing to each other."

"With each other," Dot corrected.

"Both," David conceded.

"You have a real gift," Kalu looked over Amity's shoulder to congratulate the happy couple. "You should go on the stage."

"Here will be fine," Dot calmed his enthusiasm. "We don't need an audience any bigger than this."

"But you had fun?" Kalu asked.

"Absolutely!" David agreed.

"Then that's all that matters," Kalu pronounced.

The Staff Tea Room filled with fancy dress as people queued at the boiler to make their cups of soup for a late lunch or grabbed their sandwiches from the fridge. Brendon appeared at the door still in his costume and was booed.

"I know. I'm used to it – usually behind my back, of course," he teased, "but now I've got my cossie on, you can do it to my face, can't you? Has anyone seen Brad?"

"I think he's gone down to see Barney. Lavinia had to call an ambulance for him: his vitals were way down. She's called his daughters, too," Nwaoma answered, still dressed in her cow costume.

"Thanks Oma. I'd better get out of this, then," Brendon replied, twirling in the doorway. "Last thing Barney needs is to see a Bad Fairy fly into his room."

Fully reinstated in his three-piece suit, Brad stood at the end of Barney's bed. The curtains had been drawn against the white light of the day. Joan and Freda sat at either side of their father's bed, each holding one of his hands. One of the paramedics sat at the table in the window, using what little light there was to write up some notes. She looked up at Lavinia beside her. It could be a few days more. Looking over to Freda and Joan, but you want him to stay here? You're sure?"

The girls looked at one another before nodding solemnly to the ambulance lady. "It's what he said he wants," Joan ventured.

"He won't want to be in hospital. Mum died in hospital. He always says that hospitals give him the creeps." Freda explained.

"Just the smell of them," Joan added.

Lavinia and the paramedic exchanged glances. "Well, if you're sure. We can leave you to it." She looked over at Brad. "You're the one signing off, is that right?"

"Yes." He went to authorise the paperwork with his signature. "We have to abide by our residents' wishes. And their families'," he added, bringing Joan and Freda into the conversation. "We'll call you if there looks to be any complications, but he will be fine with us. That's what we're here for."

"You're the one who was with the lady last night?" the male paramedic recalled.

"That's right," Brad frowned slightly to indicate that the least that was said at this point, the better the situation would be managed.

"You must be tired then?" the man in uniform suggested. "Like me. These rotten twelve-hour shifts. And back to back."

Brad was not going to add complaints to muddy the waters for Barney's family. He nodded. He wasn't going to brook any competition with the ambulance service although, in his heart of hearts, Brad firmly believed that no staff were as dedicated as those in care homes who had to take residents into their thinking in the same ways as they would their own families. In his view, they didn't really understand the half of it.

Some mumblings came from Barney's lips. They were almost indecipherable.

"What did he say?" Joan looked at Lavinia. "Did he say he's in a hurry?" She shuddered at the thought of it. Freda took Joan's other hand and squeezed it.

"There! He said it again." Joan looked to her father's craggy face now resting, slacker and longer than it usually looked and dominated by his nostrils.

"He said *Sluice the slurry*," Lavinia quietly told them before Barney repeated it again.

"What's that mean?" Freda was puzzled.

"Something they used to say on the farm when he was little," Lavinia explained patiently while not wanting to look as though she had the inside running on Barney these days. "It means something like *get rid of the rubbish.*"

Joan burst into tears. Brad came over to put his arm around her.

The paramedics packed up their kit and packed away the paperwork.

"Call us if you need us. Oh – which way?" the male asked with his head halfway out the door, looking up and down the corridor of single rooms.

"To the right and then right again will find you back in the foyer," Lavinia explained.

"Come on, you two," Brad tried to quietly comfort Joan and Freda. "Let's go and find a cup of tea for us all." Turning to Lavinia, he asked "You'll be all right?"

"We'll be fine. Won't we, Barney?" she assured them so that they wouldn't feel that their father had been left alone while they tried to gather themselves together for what looked like becoming the *home run.*

Lavinia took Barney's hand as she looked at his tired face, sitting beside him in the otherwise lonely room. His breathing was becoming louder which was to be expected. Barney tried to speak but his mouth no longer seemed to work for him.

"I know," she patted his hand. "They're friends again now. You managed that, Barney. Even when things have become hard work, you managed that."

A loud gurgle caught in Barney's throat. There was very little that Lavinia and Barney hadn't had to deal with together over the past months. They were as comfortable in one another's company as it is possible for a man and a woman to be. She patted his hand softly again as a throttling sound came, a breath missed, a sound he'd not made before. She recognised that rattle. At home in Romania, she'd sat by while both her grandparents had passed away: none of this frightened her. Why Barney was choosing to leave when his girls were comfortably out of the way was only for him to know. But they were together now, as they would find each other from now on: in their sixties but feeling that they were orphans for the first time in their lives.

Lavinia sat quietly with him as the last gasping breath left his body. She held on to his hand.

"Sluice the slurry, Barney. Go with our love."

Chapter Twelve

DAYS OF CHRISTMAS

The guitar notes sounded the final chord of 'The Little Drummer Boy' under Gerry's hand as the audience began to clap with enthusiasm.

"Thank you all again," Harry announced. "And now, because it's Christmas Eve, we want to wish you and your families all the joy of Christmas."

"We sure do," Gerry added as he turned to unplug his guitar from the portable amplifier that they took to so many of the care homes in Essex on a regular basis.

They'd been packed in to the café for the show this week, those who weren't confined to their rooms. Finding diversions during the shortest of days presented great challenges to the Gramwell staff. Gerry and Harry were a *'get out of jail free'* card.

The aqua aerobics that had been tried with the hardiest residents had been a resounding belly-flop, with many refusing to go in at the last minute and only two bobbing, rubber-capped heads in the pool when Kalu had brought a squadron of suited men to take in the sight of blue-veined legs on knobbly feet shivering in their towels as the brave Marie and Ron Storrick tried in vain to follow the instructions that Amadia had been shouting from the far end of the pool.

The Storricks had been duly missing from today's activity, not because of the diarrhoea and vomiting that was sweeping Tulip community but because they were nursing their chesty colds in the rarefied quarters that was their home at Daffodil Ten and Eleven.

Brendon lobbed up behind Kayleigh on his way to Tulip where he was taking a large box of adult incontinence pants.

"Oh my gawd!" she shrieked. "You scared the living daylights out of me!"

"I brought you a Christmas present thinking that they would be on your list and this is all the thanks I get?" he proffered the cardboard box.

"Don't be disgusting," she moaned. "They're for you, more like."

"And while you're in such a good mood, could you please email the photos from this camera stick, lovely?"

"And while you're at it, there's the medicine man." Kayleigh indicated the chemist's van pulling up in the emergency spot near the front door though the afternoon gloom.

Brendon started to walk away towards Tulip where Betty Harrison's supplies had suddenly dwindled during this period of exceptional demand. It had been touch and go as to whether they might have to close the Home to the public temporarily while the outbreak played itself out.

"Come on!" Kayleigh shouted at Brendon. "Fair's fair. I need a nurse to sign for the medicine and the others are busy."

"I'm here. Just joshing you. Calm down," he urged.

"Well, you try carrying on with your work while those two old dudes carry on with their naff songs," she countered.

"You know the residents love them and they love hearing the same songs."

"Over and freaking over," she laboured.

"Exactly," he assured her. "And tonight it's going to be piped carols and Crosby songs, so get used to it."

"I'm out of here at seven and I'm not on again until Wednesday so get used to *that*," she hissed at him.

The courier came through the double automatic doors and smiled at Kayleigh and Brendon while greeting them as he checked the packages, placing them on the Reception Desk. "Two for Storrick. One for Dunstable." He continued lining up the white paper packages until they completely covered Kayleigh's work space. "And I think that's your lot!" he concluded.

Brendon checked the list on the clipboard and signed his name with a flourish at the bottom of the page.

"Thank you, Sir." The courier doffed an imaginary cap. "See you after Christmas. All the best," he said over his shoulder as he disappeared into the murky afternoon.

"I should have shares in Imodium," Brendon lamented. "I'll have to leave this here for a minute." He placed the cardboard box beside Kayleigh's chair and juggled the packages up his arms, finally picking up the last of them in his fingertips.

"Back shortly," he warned. "Can you please email those prints for me now? I need to attach them to the clinical notes before I leave this afternoon.

Thank you," he called behind as he headed to the Tulip nurses' station to distribute the bulk of the drugs against the current malaise.

Pauline and Kalu sat quietly in her office.

"But what I don't understand is, if you knew, why you didn't have the decency to tell me?" she put to him, her sallow eyes betraying her.

"I was asked not to make any comment so I did as I was asked," he explained calmly.

"Even though I'm your boss?" She hadn't wanted to pull rank but it had to be noted.

"And I was asked by *your* boss." Kalu laid his cards on the table. "So you see, my reasons are the same as yours."

His calm logic infuriated her but she tried to hold a poker face.

"So who has given over all these figures about our performance?" She slapped at the bound file on her desk.

"This is the property of Empire Homes, not of Gramwell Glade, not of Pauline Graves. Perhaps something you should take up with Akin," he answered impassively.

Pauline noticed the angle of his jawline and the authority in his stare were so reminiscent of Akin, his cousin. It was an uneasy fact that she could so despise Kalu at this moment while holding such a longing for his double. Her stomach lurched with the hatred that was growing as more of Kalu's purpose was becoming evident. A thought licked in her brain: she had wondered, when a letter had come to her from Empire Homes as the Power of Attorney for her mother, what might actually have been meant about the proposed changes to contracts that, the letter claimed, posed no substantial changes to the excellent care that could be expected for their loved ones at Jesmond Lodge.

"Do you know anything about letters to families that spell out some 'changes to contracts'?" she asked, trying to hold her face from betraying the myriad of ideas that were now circling her mind.

"That's something you should perhaps take up with Akin if you're not sure about it," Kalu answered impassively.

"I would take it up with Akin if I could," she turned from the window to face her opponent. "Unfortunately, it seems that he is in touch with only one of us and, clearly, while that person is you, I have had limited or *no* access to my boss for the past few weeks." She was fighting back tears while desperately trying not to let that show.

"I think you'll find that he's coming here later this afternoon," Kalu offered up something to preserve whatever working relationship they might need to sustain them through the next few days.

"Here today?" she looked as though all the blood had left her face. "He's been in touch with you? Again?"

"We're family above all, Pauline. But we're business partners too. He needed a business manager to make the necessary due diligence and provide accurate reports."

Pauline's jaw dropped as she continued to stare at the person whom she had thought had been her Office Manager.

"Damn you, Kalu. You've been duplicitous," she was reaching for some understanding, some way of framing what she intended to report to Head Office. "Treacherous, even."

"It's business, Pauline, straight up business. It goes on every day." His face broke into a gentle smile.

"Not here it doesn't!" Pauline heard herself. She sounded naïve, ridiculous.

Kalu stood opposite her, a head taller and streets ahead in his comprehension of what had happened to Gramwell Glade. "There's nothing more that I can tell you, really. Akin will answer any questions you might have." He went to leave.

"What will happen to all our ladies and gentlemen?" she asked in a childish tone.

"Take it up with Akin." Kalu's demeanour was hardening. He was losing patience, she thought.

"There will be no discernible change as far as they will know,' he continued. 'The word *Empire* will no longer appear on their menus or on the invoices their families are sent but, overall, it won't make the slightest bit of difference. Most of the staff will stay on. They will be offered new contracts when the sale takes place." He reached for the door handle and looked back at Pauline who was biting her lip to contain her anger.

"Unlike you then, Kalu. You came here under false pretences and have made an astonishing, destructive difference."

"I am really surprised, Pauline, that you appear to understand so little about business. And about Akin, for that matter."

He left the room, closing the door quietly behind him as tears pushed grey lines of mascara down Pauline Graves' face.

In the Tulip dining room an early Saturday night tea consisted of finger food – sandwiches, baby quiches, scones, mince pies and fresh fruit – which was largely ignored. Very few takers had shown up as so many were indisposed and remained in their rooms on a limited diet.

Millie, Maisie and Elizabeth sat together. If they were given their druthers, this was the sort of supper that much preferred and would gladly eat every day. There were even some bowls of crisps and fizzy water on the benches.

"Anything I can get you, ladies?" Darragh asked as he offered them a plate of finger sandwiches.

"Can we have a bowl of crisps, please?" Maisie whistled through her dentures. "They are always John's favourites."

Darragh played hard to get. He had a never-ending repertoire of ways to jolly his *old dears* along. "If you don't tell anyone. They're supposed to be there for everyone but, since there aren't many here and youse are my favourites anyway, sure, what's the harm at Christmas?"

As he pretended to be a stealth burglar on the other side of the room, the ladies gazed appreciatively at him.

"Have you seen all the tattoos he has on his arms?" Elizabeth asked, as though a scandal had been uncovered.

"And on his neck!" Millie added aghast. "Imagine having that!"

"But the Carers have to have them," Maisie informed them quietly, hoping that Darragh wouldn't be offended should he hear her. "They aren't allowed to be Carers if they don't have tattoos. Isn't that right, John? A little birdie told us," she confided.

"Well, I never knew that!" Millie was surprised that she'd been here all this time and had no idea about Carers' initiation rites.

"What didn't you know, Millie? I'm sure you know everything there is to be known," Darragh placed the crisps on their table as though he had just brought gold, frankincense and myrrh for them.

"That you were our favourite boy," Millie had cottoned on. "We don't want you to know, though. It might go to your head!"

Darragh smiled. Their appreciation was what made it for him. He smacked the side of his head when the others noticed for the first time the tattoo that they had actually seen a thousand times before.

"It's a big enough head as it is," Darragh deferred. "Don't be doing it any more damage now, will youse? And quiet about where you got those crisps. Now, are you all ready for Father Christmas? He's coming here tonight!"

The ladies looked at each other with excitement.

"If you're good, he'll be leaving a present for you. But, mark my words," Darragh bent down to confide to them, "if you leave your teeth in a glass near your bed, the Tooth Fairy might come instead!"

Maisie looked as though her world might end, until she saw the Elizabeth and Millie were laughing along with Darragh and gesturing for him to go away.

Maisie asked timidly, "She won't be there though? The Tooth Fairy? Will she?"

"Not at all. I'm only pulling your leg, Maisie!" Darragh replied before he walked off, leaving Millie, Maisie and Elizabeth to pick one crisp each from the bowl in turn so as not to be unfair to their best friends.

Pauline had been rereading the letter that had arrived a couple of days ago. She'd been too busy to really take it in. There had been the Panto with all the visitors and complications that entailed. The D and V outbreak had taken its toll on both residents and staff. It was hard enough to make the rota as fair as it could be around the days of Christmas without staff calling in sick. And, it seemed, some of them took quite some pleasure in knowing that they had to be clear of all symptoms for a full three days before they were allowed to return. This meant that only the hardiest and most dedicated staff were on duty over this Christmas weekend. Brad and Brendon had taken a few days' holiday to go up to Brendon's family home in Birmingham and see Brad's mother in Lincoln on the way back. Their relationship had reached the *meet the parents* stage already, she reflected.

Two blinding circular lights bored a tunnel through the white fog of the early evening as she stood to close the curtains. As the lights became blinding, she could make out the shape of a sleek car. It was Akin! Kalu was right, he was making a Christmas Eve visit after all. Pauline pulled the curtains very slowly while watching to see who the other head in the car might belong to. Akin's visits were always solo but there was a distinct shadow of a person sitting beside him.

The car reversed into the emergency spot outside the front door. Akin stepped out and went to the passenger door which he opened with a sweep. Amity Leighton stepped out elegantly, holding his hand as she smoothed down her coat behind her. Pauline was in shock. Why on earth would he be driving Amity anywhere, to work and on Christmas Eve?

She quickly grappled for the lipstick case in her bag and, in the sliver of mirror the case offered also patted her hair. There would be no time for a full make-over. She recalled the ghastly feeling of having been discovered in the hair salon on the occasion of his last visit and immediately checked the feelings of annoyance with herself that had followed.

There was a knock at her door which was immediately followed by Akin appearing. He was on his own. She was grateful for that mercy at least.

"Happy Christmas, Pauline," he smiled widely.

"And to you, Akin." She moved from behind her desk to take his outstretched, large handshake. "I'm surprised to see you. There's so much

I've wanted to say but haven't been able to catch you at Head Office for a while now."

"It's been a very busy time, Pauline. That's one of the reasons that I thought it best to come to see you."

Her stomach immediately tightened.

"First of all, I want to apologise that you found me in the hairdresser's last time. That hadn't been my intention but –"

"No need, Pauline. That's water under the bridge, as they say."

"And then there's a personal matter." She saw a shift in his demeanour for a second. "About my mother. About Jesmond. There was a letter that mentioned changes to the contracts?"

"Ah, yes, that is the matter I wanted to speak to you about," he nodded in recognition. "Please," he asked, "let's sit down?"

Pauline was a little irked. It was usually she who would ask people to sit when in her territory. It appeared that Akin was pulling rank. She sat, nevertheless, at the other end of the pink sofa as he rested himself at the other, his long legs spreading out diagonally in front of her.

"We've been working on assigning Empire Homes," Akin began, "for some time now. And the deal has been done so that, on the first of January, the contracts will belong to Oakwood Retirement Villages."

Pauline found herself unable to frame any of the questions that were swirling in her brain.

"Don't worry," he assured, "this will be transparent to residents. Their contracts will be taken over by Oakwood and the care will go on smoothly, just as they're used to."

"But what about the staff?" Pauline had meant herself as much as anyone else.

"There's a letter going to staff on Monday offering them a rise in their hourly rate when they sign their new contracts," he explained. "And even the smallest raise makes a good difference to them on an hourly rate, you'll know that."

"And when was this decided?" she demanded to know.

"The deal was settled in Capri, of all places," Akin gave a smile.

"Capri?" It dawned on her. "I know someone else who was in Capri recently!" she spat.

"You don't say?" Akin replied calmly. "It's a popular holiday spot, you know."

Cogs were turning for Pauline. Her eyes looking from Akin and back to her desktop. It couldn't be so. While she'd been working away day after day, running Gramwell Grange, he and Amity had been swanning about in Capri. Surely not?

"So you are here to tell me that I am supposed to be working for Oakwood Homes as from next week? Oakwood Homes? I don't want to work for Oakwood!" Her voice was becoming louder. "They're cowboys. They couldn't take on where we leave off"

"That's interesting," Akin explained. "Because that's what I came to talk to you about. You see, Oakwood have their own team, as you know. And it so happens that they already have a General Manager in Essex."

"What? Someone to manage two homes simultaneously?" Pauline didn't think that things could get any more ludicrous.

"Indeed. And, if you have made the decision that you don't want to work for Oakwood, and they do have a manager for Gramwell, then," his deep voice announced, "it behoves me to offer you a *get out of jail free card,* so to speak."

Pauline rose from the sofa and retreated slowly to the relative comfort of her desk.

"You can leave with dignity and the thanks of Empire on Boxing Day. We thought that you would want to share Christmas Day saying goodbye to people here."

"*People*? These are my staff and my residents!" she protested.

"As I said, leave with dignity and a *golden handshake*, of course, since your position has been made redundant while the Oakwood manager will oversee both their Essex homes."

"Did you go away to Capri with Amity?" Pauline couldn't keep it in any longer.

"I'm not sure that this is pertinent to our discussion, is it?" Akin asked solemnly. He stood up to face her square on, his eyes burning into her very being.

"Did you?" Pauline asked again with determination. Her tone was very much stronger and louder all of a sudden.

"You'd be well advised to take the offer that's on the table," Akin explained calmly.

"You did!" she shouted at him. "How could you do that to me?"

"I'm not in the business of doing anything to you, Pauline, that much is clear.'

"But you did with Amity!" she exploded. "What about poor Giles?"

"Amity's personal circumstances need be of no concern to either of us," he continued.

"You beast!" she railed. "I had you all wrong!"

"Apparently so," he acknowledged, the thought didn't appear to unnerve him in any way.

"You're not the man I thought you were, Akin. What about all the residents who rely on us? And their families?" She was mustering enforcements, her anger flushing her cheeks and fuelling a confrontation that Akin definitely had not expected: nor did he intend to countenance it.

The door knocked. Amity came in. Behind his back, Akin presented a pink palm to signal that her interruption should immediately interrupt itself.

"You!" Pauline screamed at Amity. "You've been a traitor!"

Amity looked again at Akin's hand as she remained near the door and she took heed.

"I'm sorry, Pauline," she pretended not to understand but to continue with her purpose, " I just came to tell you that Santa is ready to start going around the residents' rooms so –" she looked at Akin and back to Pauline, "I won't interrupt."

"Because *that* would be inappropriate?" Pauline shrieked. Looking at them both in the same room, she was overcome by the whirlpool of betrayal, the loss, grief and shame that the past year had suddenly come to represent. "I tell you what. I'm out! Why don't you both deal with that?" She ripped the name tag from her jacket and threw it across the desk. "Keep your wretched *handshake*. Golden or not, there's nothing I want from either of you. You sold me out! Deal with it!"

She frantically pulled open the drawers of her desk. Her frenzy was unlikely to render a sensible reckoning of what actually belonged to her and what was Empire property but she seemed to be making a selection of sorts by throwing things across the room while stuffing others in her briefcase.

Amity left the room while Akin continued to observe her unexpected fury.

"It's up to you, Pauline, but you would be advised to take the offer. Leave with dignity, some friends to tide you over, a reference, a chance to start again without losing ground."

"You can't begin to imagine what I've lost. Granted, the residents probably won't notice that a new company has taken over. Things will look to them much the same on the ground, I have no doubt. They often don't know who I am anyway. Probably the staff will take the meagre pay rise. Oakwood can buy their commitment. But you had mine. I had thought that you were a far better man. I can see how wrong I was."

She tried to hold back tears as she poked notebooks, her pens and a small Waterford vase that had been her mother's into her bag after throwing the orchid and water across the desk.

"There! You mop up the mess you've left, Akin. I resign. Why don't you say goodbye to everyone for me since you've seen to it that I have nothing to offer Gramwell Glade or you, for that matter!"

Akin had always refused to lean into the idea that Pauline had a crush on him, even when Amity had teased him about it from time to time. It was something that he had regarded as a far-fetched, ridiculous notion; however, the volume of her behaviour now seemed to indicate her apparent instability which was wholly inappropriate to the role she'd been struggling to maintain. His decision to let her go, as Amity had explained to him, had been vindicated. It would be a better proposition for Oakwood Care Homes to take over Gramwell Grange with a manager they were happy with.

"No need to see me out," Pauline tripped her foot on a leg of the coffee table as she lumped her over-stuffed briefcase across the room on her hip. "No need for you to be hypocritical towards me anyway, even though that's your nature, because I'm out of here!"

"I really don't understand this level of –" Akin threw his arms in the air as he searched for the words to describe the maelstrom he had just witnessed, "this storm in a tea cup."

"There you go, Akin. You're right. You don't understand – the care sector, the needs of these individuals," she held her tongue for only a brief second before she blurted, "ME!"

Akin stood tall and silent as she pushed past him.

"And I won't say that 'it's been nice' knowing you, Akin, because it's been a nightmare." She flounced out of the door and into the foyer.

Ye Olde Tea Shoppe was lit up with Christmas decorations. A Bing Crosby Christmas tape was piped through to remind the residents of the fireside cosiness of the season.

Pauline looked across to the Reception desk where Tayla was singing aloud to the tape. She looked absurd to Pauline whose eyes were full of tears although her anger was preventing them from falling quite yet. Tayla wore a red crepe paper crown from a Christmas cracker. She looked relaxed and happy to have a day less busy than usual. The phone had barely rung. Families had come and gone. Some had taken their loved ones home to have a meal in the comfort of their homes. Most had been returned by this hour. Gramwell Glade was glowing in the expectation of all that was sentimental and giving about celebrating Christmas.

In the café a few couples sat with their arms around one another. Pauline was tempted momentarily to put down all the belongings she'd assembled and go in, to tell everyone she was being replaced and then hear their heartfelt sadness about the news and wish her well.

But it wasn't what she was able or permitted to do in the circumstances. If she had been convinced that she could manage it without breaking into floods of tears, she might have given it a try.

Akin stood behind her in the doorway of the Manager's office that used to be hers.

"Do you need some help in carrying all that to your car?" he asked.

Tayla looked over at them. So often, after a meeting, she would be approached with a pile of typing or photocopying together with its unrealistic deadline for completion, but she seemed to recognise that wasn't going to happen on this occasion. Maybe because it was Christmas, the season of goodwill. And because Peter Spence was coming down the corridor dressed up as Father Christmas. Some of the carers skipped behind him in their elf costumes.

Gramwell Glade Residents, Staff And Visitors

Note: D = Daffodil Community; T = Tulip Community

Residents

Name	*Age*	*Room*	*Details*
Albert Watts	85	D2	Retired engineer from Manchester.
Barney Perry	91	D7	Father of Joan and Freda.
David Jack	83	D5	Widower. Father of Sarah.
Delphine Thomas	89	T3	
Dorothy (Dot) Baker	74	D6	Never married.
Dorotka Gryzyna	78	T13	Daughter lives in London.
Elizabeth Hollick	81	D3; T14	D3 before moving to T14
Elsie Lister	86	D9	
Grace Garrett	93	T4	
Harold Sherry	92	T18	Requires assisted eating.
Hilda Matters	89	D8	Retired teacher.
Joan Fairs	78	T7	
John Nicholls	79	D3	Retired dentist from London.
Marie Storrick	78	D10 & 11	Lives in D10 & 11 with husband Ron.
Marie Taylor	87	D12	Widowed mother of Andy.
Maisie Dunstable	88	T2	Mother of Don, mother-in-law to Maureen.
Marjorie Simmonds	84	D1	Widow of Capt. Godfrey Simmonds.
Meg Hardy	RIP		Previously resident of T14.
Mildred (aka Millie) Absolom	83	D4	Previously from Coventry. Moved to Tulip.

Millie (Millicent) Cloudsdale	82	T5	Mother of Arabella Merton-Jones.
Molly Tipple	83	T8	
Nan Sweetman	82	D4	Mother of Charles Worrell.
Ronald Storrick	79	D10 & 11	Lives in D10 & 11 with wife Marie.

Staff

Name	***Age***	***Position***
Akin Akindele	42	Nigerian MD and Business Development Manager, Empire Homes PLC.
Alex Durwyn	31	Receptionist.
Amadia Stokes	48	Nurse. Originally from Nigeria.
Amity Leighton	46	Sales and Events Manager. Married to Giles.
Barbara Fenway	62	Office Manager.
Bessie Roberts	65	Assistant Care Manager.
Brad Fletchley	38	Care Manager since inception of Gramwell Glade.
Brendon Longacre	32	Senior Carer (aka Brenda).
Brian Petty	22	Carer.
Darragh Noonan	37	Carer originally from County Galway.
Donna (Herbie) Herbert	46	Receptionist. Mother to Sam (16) James (18).
Eric Spence	28	Maintenance Assistant to father Peter.
Frank Goninon	48	Cleaner.
Gosia (Malgosia) Matkowska	28	Carer. Originally from Poland.
Henry Platt	20	Apprentice cook.
Janette Gosling	31	Kitchen hand.
Kayleigh Longbottom	18	Apprentice carer.
Lavinia Marin	37	Nurse. Originally from Romania.
Marigold Pratt	24	Carer. Friends with Phoenix.

Mobo Tarfa		Bus driver for Empire Homes. Originally from Nigeria.
Naomi Page	31	Carer originally from South Africa.
Nwaoma (Oma) Katsina		Nurse. Came to England from Nigeria as a child.
Olga Dean	55	Administration Manager. Empire Head Office.
Pauline Graves	45	General Manager for past year. Hotel management background.
Peggy Hewson	52	Head Cook
Phoenix Kennedy	24	Carer. Friends with Marigold.
Peter Spence	52	Maintenance Operative. Father to Eric.
Ronnie (Veronica) Chan	36	Carer. Originally from Hong Kong.
Rosie Rowson	58	Lead Cleaner/ Laundry worker.
Stan (Stanislaw) Novak	35	Carer. Originally from Poland.
Tanya Chester	23	Cleaner/Laundry worker.
Tayla Miles	23	Receptionist.

Visitors

Name	***Age***	***Details***
Andrea Wallace	52	Daughter of Mildred Absolom, grandmother to Archie.
Arabella Jones-Merton	54	Daughter of Millie Cloudsdale.
Archie Garner	8	Grandson of Andrea Wallace.
Ben Thompson	35	Presenter for Channel Four TV news.
Don Dunstable	48	Son of Maisie Dunstable.
Dr Evelyn Dunwoody	58	Visiting GP and choir leader.
Freda Thorpe	47	Younger daughter of Barney Perry.
Harold Dunwoody	64	Retired chemist. Husband of Dr Evelyn Dunwoody.

Joan Payne	49	Elder daughter of Barney Perry.
Maureen Dunstable	45	Wife of Don, owner of People Dolls Ltd.
Rebecca Grant	25	Channel Four Production Assistant.